HOT, BLUE & RIGHTEOUS

Concho Book Two

A.W. Hart

Special thanks to Charles Gramlich for his contribution to this novel.

Published by Wolfpack Publishing
5130 S. Fort Apache Road, 215-380
Las Vegas, NV 89148

Paperback IBSN 978-1-64734-653-9
eBook ISBN 978-1-64734-652-2

CHAPTER 1

It was a quiet day. Until it wasn't.

Concho Ten-Wolves, a Texas Ranger stationed out of Maverick County, Texas, on the US/Mexican border, was cruising along US Highway 277 outside the town of Eagle Pass when his radio squawked for attention.

"Ten-Wolves here," he said into the mic.

The dispatcher's voice came through loud, clear, and urgent. "Bank robbery at IBC. 3165 Del Rio Boulevard. Red convertible. Please respond!"

Concho keyed the mic. "On my way. Three minutes out."

The street in front of Concho was clear. His gaze darted to his rearview mirrors, saw only empty asphalt. He rehung his mic and slammed the brakes on his big Ford F-150 Crew Cab. Black smoke whipped into the air as his tires squealed. He rode the skid and brought the truck's nose around in a U-turn in the middle of the street.

Barely out of the turn, he punched the gas. The heavy-duty engine growled as the truck launched itself along the highway in the opposite direction from the way he'd been traveling. Hitting his lights and siren, he listened to them wail as he raced past Gutierrez Tire Center on his left and headed back into Eagle Pass.

US 277 and Del Rio Blvd were two names for the same highway here. IBC bank had several branches along this stretch, but he knew the one at 3165 Del Rio. He'd used its ATM.

Traffic began to appear as he approached town. Drivers heard the siren and tried to get out of the way. They moved slower than Concho liked. He wove in and out. The Wagon Wheel restaurant and the Dollar General whipped past. The bank materialized on his left.

A fire-engine red convertible—a late 1960s GTO—came squealing out of the IBC parking lot. Four people occupied it. At least two carried guns he could see. Concho twisted his steering wheel, tried to cut the car off. The driver had talent. He whipped his vehicle to the right, took the GTO through the shallow ditch bordering the parking lot and up onto the blacktop.

Concho hit his brakes; the truck's rear end slid into the ditch but the Ranger kept control and stomped the gas. Dirt spun up under the tires as the Ford plunged back onto the highway. The GTO had gained a few seconds on him, though, and it was fast. Concho floored the gas pedal, trying to gain back what he'd lost.

As a getaway vehicle, the GTO had the speed but the bright red paint job made it hard to miss and, if they wrecked in a convertible, the chances were good someone in the car would be killed or badly hurt. Concho considered letting the robbers run and backing off to protect any civilians who might be in the way of this chase. He'd gotten the convertible's license plate as it roared past him, had committed it to memory. Then his radio crackled with a general bulletin update:

"Be advised. One guard shot at the bank. Perps armed and dangerous!"

Concho pressed down harder on the gas pedal. If the robbers had already shot one person, they wouldn't care about killing or injuring bystanders. He needed to stop them. Cutting in and out of traffic with the shrieking of brakes and tires, the bright red GTO whipped back and forth across the road in front of Concho like a flag waving before a bull. He hung on their tail, staying close, using every ounce of his driving skill.

The right-side passenger in the back seat of the getaway car turned to look back at Concho. He'd already seen the long brown hair. Now he saw the face. A shock punched him; it was a woman. In her early twenties. She pursed her lips, blew him a kiss.

The robber on the left side of the back seat turned too. Another woman, a redhead. She was older than her companion, but not by much. Her hair was shorter; she didn't bother with a kiss. Her left hand lifted into view holding a pistol the size of a small cannon. She unleashed a barrage of bullets.

Concho tapped his brakes, cut the wheel left to dodge lead. Even over the roar of his engine, he heard shots boom. But it wasn't easy to hit a weaving object with a handgun, especially when you're weaving too. If anything punched into the Ford, Concho didn't hear it.

The GTO's driver, who, Concho suspected, would be another woman, must not have been expecting the shots from her colleague. She instinctively let up on the gas. The convertible slowed. For the moment, the road ahead lay empty of other traffic. Concho straightened his steering wheel and stomped his own gas pedal.

The Ford pickup lunged forward like an ambush predator; its bumper slammed into the rear of the GTO with a screech of rending metal. The convertible's passengers were thrown violently forward against their seatbelts. The redhead with the gun banged hard into the driver's seat in front of her. The big pistol went flying.

The getaway driver fought her car for control. Its tail whipped back and forth, tires squealing. Concho swung into the left lane, accelerated, then jerked the wheel back to the right. The right side of his bumper struck the left rear side of the convertible in a pit maneuver.

The GTO's driver was skilled, with fast reflexes, but she wasn't trained in defensive driving. She tried to steer against the push from Concho's truck but overcorrected as Concho tapped his brakes and dropped back. The convertible's rear end slewed wildly back to the left. The car leaped toward the ditch which was sharp and deep.

The getaway vehicle hit the edge of the ditch and went airborne. With mouths wide, its passengers screamed, though Concho couldn't hear them. The car came down on a speed-limit sign and ripped it out of the ground. The vehicle hit dirt and bounced before slewing sideways into an electric pole with a crunch of metal that the lawman could hear, even inside his Ford.

Concho slammed on his brakes, rode the Ford to a screeching stop on the wide shoulder of the road. He slammed the truck into park and leaped out. The sun hammered bright in a clear sky. Automobile exhaust and burnt rubber stabbed his nostrils. He ignored the heat and scents as he ran toward the wrecked convertible.

The Ranger always carried two standard-issue Colt Double Eagle .45s, one on each hip. He drew the right-hand gun. The factory grips on the Colt Double Eagles were large. Some called them awkward and ugly. They fit Concho's big hands perfectly.

Prepared for anything, Concho reached the wrecked automobile and scanned it for trouble. Late 1960s GTOs didn't have airbags. The driver, a slender brunette, was unconscious from where she'd slammed against the steering wheel. Blood clotted under her nose. The woman from the passenger seat, also dark-haired but much heavier, had managed to get out of the car but had fallen to hands and knees as she gasped for breath. She wasn't going anywhere fast.

The two women in the back seat had bailed, though. Concho saw the redhead who'd shot at him running one way and the brown-haired woman running the other. Sirens wailed down 277 toward the scene. Police officers would be here inside two minutes but the fleeing robbers would have a good head start.

Concho couldn't chase both fugitives. The redhead gripped a duffle bag in one hand—money from the bank robbery, he figured. He took off after her, shouting at her to

"Freeze."

She only ran harder and Concho saw another gun holstered at the small of her back. Scattered houses lay along this stretch of 277, mostly with dirt yards and a few oaks and mesquite trees for shade. Cicadas droned in the branches, oblivious to the excitement on the ground beneath them.

The woman ran between two houses, toward Clavel Street and Dahlia Street beyond, into a community called Elm Creek. She was headed roughly east, toward Elm Creek itself. Beyond lay Pete Gallego Elementary School.

School was in session.

CHAPTER 2

The woman Concho chased was tall, athletic, fast. But Concho stood 6'4", with a stride to match. By the time she crossed Dahlia Street, he was closing quickly. She must have heard his footsteps. She ran harder into the scrublands beyond the last house on Dahlia. Still, the Ranger gained on her.

Almost at the bank of Elm Creek, the redhead turned at bay, grabbing for the pistol holstered behind her back. Before she could swing the weapon to bear, Concho took a shooting stance with his Colt and shouted:

"Freeze or I'll kill you!"

The woman froze, holding the pistol at waist height. Her gaze met his, her eyes green and intense. She wore tennis shoes, black jeans, and a black T-shirt that clung to her with sweat in the heat of the day. Her almost-orange hair hung damply to her shoulders. Her lips curled into a snarl.

"I bet you won't shoot a woman," she growled.

"You'd be betting your life," Concho replied. "And keep in mind, you already shot at me. So I'm a might irritated. Besides, you're headed for an elementary school, and there's no way I'll let you reach those kids with a gun in your hand."

The woman's gaze blazed, dimmed, darted away from his. Her

shoulders slumped. "All right," she said, "maybe you will shoot me. You look the type."

She tossed the pistol to the side and behind. It splashed in the creek. She dropped the duffle bag at her feet.

"Get flat on the ground. Hands behind you."

"You know, tits get in the way of that, don't you?"

"Lie on your side if you need to."

The bank robber smirked as she knelt. "Aren't you sweet?"

She lay down on her right side and brought her arms behind her. Concho circled her, squatted and put a knee on her shoulder while he holstered his pistol. Drawing handcuffs from his belt, he snapped them closed on the woman's wrists and pulled her to her feet. Scooping up the duffle bag, he unzipped it far enough to see wads of greenbacks winking back at him, then zipped it closed again.

"How much did we get?" the woman asked. "Have you heard?"

"You got nothing," Concho replied. "I just got it back."

"Let me go and I'll split it with you."

"Reckon not."

"What are you anyway? You ain't black. Even with that dark skin. Not completely anyway."

"Kickapoo," Concho said as he gave her a little shove to get her moving back toward US 277.

"Indian! You should be helping us rob banks. What do you owe the powers that be? Nothing!"

"In case you don't realize," Concho said, "you have the right to remain silent."

The woman smirked again. "Maybe I don't have the ability."

"Yeah, I've heard that bit," Concho said. "So now you've asked about money and about me. What of your friends? Don't you care whether they're OK or not?"

"Who said they were friends?"

"Good to hear. They won't have any reason not to rat you out."

"Unless they know what's good for them," she snapped.

"Just walk."

They reached a quiet Dahlia Street, moved to cross it. A black Cadillac Escalade parked a block down started up. Concho glanced at it suspiciously. The windows were tinted too dark to see through as it pulled away from the curb. The expensive vehicle seemed out of place in this neighborhood, but, hey, lawyers and drug dealers are everywhere.

A roar erupted from beneath the SUV's hood as it accelerated directly toward Concho and his prisoner. The Ranger and the woman had time to leap to safety, but the prisoner spun toward the vehicle and turned suddenly into a mannequin.

Concho had to make a choice. He dropped the duffle bag full of stolen cash and grabbed the woman with both arms, then flung himself forward across the street. At the last instant, he twisted his body so he didn't come down fully on top of the woman but still shielded her in case someone opened fire from the Cadillac.

The heavy SUV squealed to a stop in the middle of the roadway; a door snapped open and shut again on the opposite side of the Escalade. Concho snagged his right-hand Colt and drew it. Keeping the woman hidden behind him, he sat up and took aim as the Cadillac peeled away, leaving behind smoking rubber.

Concho held his fire. More than a dozen onlookers stood on the porches or in the yards of the nearby houses. They'd already been drawn outside by the sounds of police sirens. Now they gaped with mouths wide at the scene right in front of them. Concho suspected the Cadillac of being armor-plated and a ricocheting bullet could kill one of the locals. He couldn't take that risk.

Concho sighed. The duffle bag full of loot he'd dropped no longer rested in the street. What had been stolen once had been stolen again. The robber who'd taken it first laughed and laughed.

***

"What's your name?" Concho asked as he offered the laughing bank robber a hand and pulled her to her feet.

"Anne," the woman said, during a break in her chuckles.

"You know who was in the Escalade, Anne?"

The woman's humor finally subsided. "Would you believe me if I told you, 'no'?"

Concho let go of the woman's hand and grasped her elbow instead as he started off again toward US 277 and the sound of police sirens. People watched curiously as he walked past them with his prisoner in tow. He tried to give them all a smile and not the shark smile of which he was capable. He'd likely need to interview many of them later and wanted them in a receptive mood.

Finally, he answered Anne's question. "I might. Given that it would be hard for anyone to know just where the getaway car would wreck, and which direction you'd be running in, and that I'd catch you and bring the duffle bag full of money back across any one particular street."

"Yeah, that does pose a quandary, doesn't it? Maybe I was in psychic contact with them. Real woo-woo stuff."

Concho didn't respond. They crossed Clavel Street and reached the highway. Half a dozen police vehicles and two ambulances crowded the scene. Paramedics loaded one ambulance with a stretcher. Concho figured it for the convertible's driver. He hoped she'd be OK.

The heavy-set woman from the passenger seat of the getaway car had a splint on her left arm. She was being questioned by a Texas Highway Patrol officer with blond hair whom the Ranger didn't recognize. Concho pulled Anne in that direction but Terrill Hoight intercepted him.

Hoight was a deputy in the Maverick County Sheriff's office which called Eagle Pass, Texas, home. He worked for Sheriff Isaac Parkland, whom Concho considered a friend. Today, Hoight wore brown uniform pants and a matching shirt. The shirt was far too tight, emphasizing Hoight's gym-built physique. Despite that touch of vanity, Hoight was a good officer.

"Concho," Hoight said.

"Terrill."

"Glad to see you lookin' good."

Concho knew Hoight was referring to the events of barely a month gone when the big Ranger had been stabbed in the back and came within a hair's breadth of being left paralyzed—or dead.

"A twinge once in a while," Concho said. "Otherwise, I'm good." He jerked his chin toward the loaded ambulance which was just pulling out for the hospital. "How's the driver of the getaway car?"

Hoight turned his head toward the ambulance, then looked back at Concho. "A mild concussion and some bruised ribs. They say she'll be OK."

"Good."

Hoight gestured at Anne. "This another of the desperados?"

"Yep. There's a fourth one too," Concho said. He pointed in the direction where the brown-haired robber had disappeared. "She and this one split up. This one had a duffle full of money so I followed her."

Hoight looked around for said bag. He frowned. "Where is it?"

Anne started laughing again and Concho gave her elbow a squeeze. She shut up.

"Therein lies a tale," Concho said. He explained to Hoight what had happened with the Cadillac Escalade. "Couldn't read the license plate," he added. "Obscured with dirt. Deliberately, I imagine."

"Wow!" Hoight said, reaching up and scratching his head. "How did they know about the money? And the place?"

Concho shook his head. "No idea, but get an APB out on the vehicle right away." He pushed his prisoner toward the deputy. "Take Outlaw Anne with you and I'll go back and ask the witnesses what they know. Be sure to read her her rights. She threw her gun in Elm Creek. I'll fetch that too. Better pat her down to see if she's got anything else to use as a weapon."

"Gotcha," Hoight said.

"Thanks for your hospitality, Ranger," Anne said to Concho as Hoight grasped her elbow. "I'll remember you in my prayers."

"Probably better to leave me out of your prayers," Concho said. He turned without waiting for a response and headed back into the Elm Creek community.

Many of the witnesses Concho wanted to question still loitered around outside their houses along Dahlia Street, but he passed them by for the moment. He headed straight for Elm Creek to pick up the gun Anne had ditched.

As Concho approached the creek, the dryland plants of the scrublands gave way to greenery. The creek ran sluggishly between banks covered with native grasses and wildflowers. Shrubs and a few bigger trees, oaks and Texas willows, grew right up to the water. At this spot, the stream itself was shallow and mostly clear.

Concho tried to spot the gun from the bank and couldn't. He took off his boots and socks, rolled up his jeans and waded in. The water was surprisingly cool for a Texas August. He still couldn't find the gun.

Concho had a good memory and could see the grass tromped down where Anne had been standing when she tossed the pistol. He could visualize the arc the weapon made as it flew from Anne's hand into the water. It wasn't there now, and the flow wasn't fast enough to have moved it. Someone had taken it. Just like someone had taken the money. Were the two events connected?

With frustration riding him, Concho returned to the creek bank and pulled on his socks and boots. He walked back to Dahlia Street and began to interview everyone he could find. The community was overwhelmingly Hispanic. Not everyone spoke English but Concho had been a language major in college and spoke fluent Spanish.

Every person Concho talked to was friendly and sincere. Everyone expressed a wish to be helpful. None of them knew anything about a black Cadillac Escalade in the neighborhood or anything about a gun taken from the creek. At least, so they said. Concho didn't believe it. Not from them all. Someone was lying. But he couldn't prove it.

He'd reached a dead end.

CHAPTER 3

By the time Concho finished interviewing potential wit-nesses along Dahlia Street, the day was growing late. He radioed in a report to Texas Ranger headquarters and got an official assignment to investigate the bank robbery.

Afterward, he called Terrill Hoight on his cell phone and gave him an update. Hoight offered him a little information back. The getaway driver was still at the hospital but appeared to be out of danger. The injured guard at the bank had been wounded in the shoulder but would also live and likely make a full recovery. The prisoners weren't talking.

Trying to fight off his frustration by filling his empty belly, Concho stopped by the Wagon Wheel restaurant to drown his sorrows in chicken fried steak with white gravy and half a dozen glasses of sweet, iced tea. Afterward, in the last light of day, he turned toward home.

Home for Concho Ten-Wolves was the Kickapoo Traditional Tribe of Texas reservation, which lay about eight miles southeast of the town of Eagle Pass. It consisted of one hundred and twenty-five acres of land with a population of less than a thousand.

The biggest structure on the reservation was the Kickapoo Lucky Eagle Casino and Hotel, which had brought both good and bad to the tribe. As part of the good, the casino had provided a steady income and employment for many. As part of the bad? Well, some bad always goes along with gambling.

Concho often felt conflicted about the casino. He'd been glad to see a decrease in the poverty in which many of the tribal members once lived but money didn't always make things better. More money sometimes meant more addictions, to drugs or to anything that might distract people from their struggles, but often it did nothing to improve their lives. The casino existed, though, and Ten-Wolves always played the cards as they were dealt.

The Ranger lived outside the main cluster of reservation homes, sometimes called Kickapoo Village. He lived in a double-wide trailer off a dirt road, with a dry arroyo just outside his back door and low, shrub-dotted hills as a backdrop. He pulled into his driveway and parked. He didn't get out.

The last cicadas of the day sang at him through the open windows of the Ford; he generally drove the Rez with his windows down. With the sun almost gone, but the sky still holding light, he studied the gray trailer sitting between clusters of prickly pear cactus. The trailer wasn't new but it was new to him. He'd had it barely a month.

Just before the knife attack that had nearly paralyzed him, his old trailer had burned down. Arson. He'd laid in the hospital for several days after the attack, and when the woman he was dating, Maria Morales, picked him up, he thought she was taking him home with her. She'd brought him here instead, to what he expected to be a site containing only ashes.

In the three days while he languished in bed, however, someone—someones—had cleaned up the site and replaced his trailer with another. He didn't know who those someones were and no one would tell him. It made him smile and grimace. He never liked being indebted to anyone, but he had such debts now and couldn't directly repay them without the names of those he owed.

Insurance on his burned trailer had ultimately paid the cost of the replacement house but not of the furniture and other items to fill it and make it a home. And the work, the effort many people had put in to clear away the ruins of the old trailer and get the new one up so quickly…

Concho knew folk on the reservation who didn't like him, who accused him of serving the white man as one of their police enforcers. But nothing had proven to him better than the new trailer that others in the world of the Rez cared about him. Maybe even loved him. It was a powerful feeling and one he'd seldom experienced since his grandmother had been murdered right here on the reservation when he was fifteen.

Wiping his mouth on the back of his hand and taking a calming breath, Concho rolled up his windows and slipped out of the truck. Opening the door of his new trailer, he stepped inside and flipped on the lights. A little bit of melancholy returned.

He had his furniture. People had donated a couch, chairs, a table, a bed, dishes, utensils, a TV and refrigerator. But things were missing he could never replace—the chess set one of his professors at Haskell Indian Nations University had given him, the old stereo his grandmother had owned, the king-sized bed he'd purchased with his first check from the Texas Rangers, and the medicine shield he'd been given at his naming ceremony. The last, most of all, he would miss.

Other things he'd lost could be replaced but only with time and expense. He'd owned several thousand books, from textbooks to history works to novels and poetry. Some, like his collection of Ray Bradbury's poetry, had been first editions. Others, such as the books of N. Scott Momaday, Joy Harjo, and Ernest Gaines, had been signed by the authors.

And there'd been the nostalgia factor. Though he'd gotten most of his reading material as a kid from the library, he often spent any birthday money he got on books. He'd still owned copies of a few favorite tomes he'd read when he was eleven and twelve—A Princess of Mars by Edgar Rice Burroughs, Desert Dog by Jim

Kjelgaard, The Incredible Journey by Sheila Burnford. The connections he'd felt to such books were broken, even if he rebought the same editions.

Moving from his living room into his den, he unbuckled his gun belt and hung it up on a rack he'd installed for the purpose. Opening the fridge revealed a couple of cold bottles of Shiner Bock. He typically avoided hard liquor but after this day he figured he could use a beer.

Taking a Shiner out of the door rack, he twisted off the cap and took a sip. His cell phone rang. He pulled it out, checked the caller ID. An unknown number showed on the screen. Most of his civilian friends didn't answer unknown numbers in an effort to evade spam callers but Concho never felt he could follow that habit. He was a public servant. What if someone called who really needed a Ranger and he didn't answer because he didn't recognize the number?

He swiped to take the call. "Ten-Wolves here!"

"I didn't expect to get you," a woman's voice said. "Thought I'd have to leave a message." The voice sounded young with the inflection on the words "off" in a way Concho couldn't quite describe. Maybe the woman was scared but trying to mask it with bravado.

"A Texas Ranger always answers," Concho replied. "If he can. Who is this?"

"We've met. In a way. But this is the first time we've spoken."

"Cryptic of you."

"It was today actually. I blew you a kiss. You didn't bother to catch it. Then you ran me and my friends off the road."

A flashbulb memory of a woman in her early twenties with long brown hair sitting in the back seat of a getaway car snapped into Concho's awareness. So, he had the last free member of the bank robbery team on the line. He had to handle this carefully.

"I remember," he said. "That was around the time one of your friends tried to shoot me. And I believe there was a bank robbery a little before. Or is this one of the many other women who blew me a kiss today?"

The woman chuckled. Concho rather liked the sound.

"No," she said. "You're on the right track. I apologize for a… for my friend trying to shoot you. That was uncalled for."

"You're talking about Anne. She told me her name. She the one who shot the bank guard too?"

A little hesitation came before the voice answered. "Yes, unfortunately. But it was only a…a warning shot. No one was supposed to get hurt."

"But they did."

"How…how is the guard? Anne said she only grazed him."

"It was more than a graze. He'll live. Though whether he'll regain full use of his arm remains to be seen."

The woman sighed. "What about my friends?"

"The driver and front seat passenger had some injuries but will be OK. Anne's fine but in jail. What about you?"

Another low laugh came, full of more stress than humor. "Alive. Who knows if I'll stay that way? I know who took the money and the gun."

CHAPTER 4

Concho considered the woman's statement. It might not be true. It might be partially true. But it was the best lead he had and she certainly sounded scared enough to convince him that she believed someone would be willing to kill her for what she knew.

"I'd like to know who you're talking about," he said. "And if you're afraid of them, I can make sure you're protected."

"I doubt it," the woman said. "But I'm not unwilling to share. I need some guarantees first."

"Like what?"

"That I won't go to jail."

"I can't guarantee that, but I can put in a good word for you with the prosecutor. And they're often willing to make deals in such cases."

The woman did not respond. To keep her talking, Concho asked a different question.

"What should I call you by the way? I'm not fond of Jane Doe."

"I guess…call me…Catniss."

"All right. Catniss. How did you get my number?"

"Information is gold," Catniss said. "And it's all I've got to negotiate with. I already gave you Anne as the shooter in the robbery."

"And I gave you information about your friends and the guard from the bank."

The woman's tone intensified, became urgent. "Look, I'll have to call you back."

"Wait!"

"Another time!" She hung up.

Concho stared at the silent phone in his hand. Although he imagined the woman had used a burner phone and wouldn't call him from this number again, he pressed save on his cell. When prompted for a name, he stored "Catniss."

***

Though Concho had plenty of paperwork to catch up on, he went to his laptop computer instead and loaded Google. He typed in "Catniss" got back "Did you mean: 'Katniss?'" Clicking on that took him to "Katniss Everdeen" and a Wikipedia page.

He knew right away that he had the source of the brown-haired woman's alias. Katniss Everdeen was the protagonist of a young adult, dystopian trilogy written by a woman named Suzanne Collins. The first book, called The Hunger Games, had been published in 2008, with a book a year after. A movie based on the first book had come out in 2012. The others had also been filmed.

The dates were right too. Concho figured "Katniss" to be in her early twenties. She would have been ten or so when the book was published, fourteen when the movie came out. Just the age to be influenced by fiction as he himself had been.

The internet had plenty of information about Katniss Everdeen but Concho wanted the source material and clicked over to Amazon to buy the first volume of the trilogy as an e-book. His laptop had a kindle app so he immediately started reading. The story got off to a quick start and was enjoyable although not something Concho would have likely picked up on his own.

Katniss was a tough young woman. Her father died when she was eleven. Her mother fell into a deep depression, leaving Katniss to keep the family together and provide much of the care for her younger sister, Primrose.

Katniss and Primrose lived in a harsh world. The United States had fallen and much of the country had been divided up into thirteen districts surrounding an administrative area called the "Capitol." Katniss's district, number 12, ranked as the poorest. Food was hard to come by and Katniss, who'd learned to hunt from her father, had to scratch and scrounge to keep her family alive.

At sixteen, Katniss volunteered to join a competition called "The Hunger Games," a kind of futuristic Olympics in which contestants had to battle each other and the losers died. She did so to save her younger sister from having to take part. As was usual in most young adult fiction, and in a lot of other fiction as well, Katniss discovered hidden strengths in herself through her ordeals. Concho found her easy to root for.

As he finished the book, Concho considered the woman who'd appropriated the name of this fictional character. She'd left him a clue. Whether intentionally or accidentally, he couldn't be sure. But what did it mean? Had the pseudo-Katniss lost her father too? Did she have a younger sister who she felt she had to save? Or did the connection represent only a general feeling of kinship in the young woman's mind?

He needed to find out. But how?

Glancing at the clock revealed the time: 11:00 PM. Maria Morales would still be awake. Maybe it would help to get a woman's perspective. Besides, he wanted to talk to her anyway. He punched in Maria's contact number on the phone. It rang.

Maria answered. "Hello, big guy. I thought maybe you'd forgotten me today."

Maria managed the Mall de las Aguilas, the Mall of the Eagles in Eagle Pass. She and Concho had dated a while before breaking up. They'd gotten back together about a month ago after Concho rescued Maria and a bunch of other hostages from the band of neo-Nazis who'd seized the mall. Her voice never failed to send exciting shivers running through him.

"Such forgetting will never happen," he said. "Sorry to call so late, though. I got caught up thinking about a case."

"Do tell."

"Bank robbery. You hear about it?"

"Saw it on the news. An all-female bank robbery team. Not something you see every day. And Concho Ten-Wolves took them down! Any of them cute?"

"One of them blew me a kiss while they tried to outrun me."

"Ohhh," Maria said. "And so my death list expands. What's her name?"

Concho chuckled. "Nice segue into why I called. You ever read The Hunger Games books?"

"No, but I saw the movies with my niece, Angelina. She was a big fan. What's the connection?"

"One of the robbers got away. She called me earlier tonight. Don't know how she got my number. She wouldn't give me her real name but told me to call her "Katniss."

"I see," Maria said. "Katniss Everdeen. And you're trying to figure out why she made that choice?"

"Exactly. Not expecting answers, of course. Just…any insights you might have."

The line hummed quietly on its own for a moment. Finally, "One thing might interest you. Suzanne Collins, the author, had a signing here once. At the Mall. I wasn't manager but took Angelina to see her."

"When was that?"

Maria hmmed. "Let's see. Angelina was about twelve, I think. So sometime around 2012."

"Right when the film came out."

"Yep," Maria said, snapping her fingers. "It was a couple of months after I took her to the movie."

"From the look I got at this Katniss, I'd say she would have been a few years older than Angelina then. But if she was a fan, maybe she went to that signing too."

"Could be. You know, they have pictures of the signing in the office. In fact, there's one up on my wall of Suzanne Collins and the manager at the time. No kids in it, though."

"Any other pictures of the event? Maybe with the audience included?"

"Maybe. I'll check in the morning." Maria's voice dropped an octave and dripped with sudden honey as she added, "Does this make me an honorary Texas Ranger? Working close beside another gallant officer to solve a dastardly crime?"

"No, but that voice you're using makes me a horny Texas Ranger." As soon as he'd said it, Concho felt horribly embarrassed but the words were spilled and Maria ran with them.

"Concho Ten-Wolves! You perve! Hitting on a fellow investigator. You need some sensitivity training, Mister!"

Concho felt his face flush even more. Maria was the only woman who could ever do that to him. And the only women he'd ever felt comfortable enough with to joke around in such a way.

"I'm thinking that 'taking things slowly' isn't working so well," he said. "How about us moving a little faster?"

Maria laughed. "I'll call you tomorrow. If I can find some information for you, maybe we'll need to…'get together.'"

"It'll be tomorrow in another forty-five minutes," Concho said.

Maria laughed again. "You sleep well now." He heard her blowing him a kiss through the phone line but she disconnected before he could say anything. Concho put the phone down with a grin.

CHAPTER 5

Concho habitually rose at 6:00 AM. This morning, he felt the need for a run and dressed appropriately in shorts and a T-shirt. Taking the trail he often used—which started behind his house, reached to the nearest hill, circled around it and back—he let himself work up a good sweat, enjoying the feel of his muscles moving and his lungs drawing in air.

The world he passed through lay drenched with the sights, sounds, and scents of a Texas dawn. Juniper and mesquite perfumed the air. A rabbit startled from almost beneath his moving feet. Grackles and cardinals and meadowlarks whistled for attention. Gnats swirled in shafts of early sunlight like animated particles of gold.

Since the doctors wanted him to continue rehabbing after his recent knife wound to the back, he followed the run with some weight repetitions, a shower, a shave, and a hearty breakfast of eggs and sausage. He planned to wait to hear from Maria before leaving the house and so he decided to get in a little reading. By 7:30, he'd seated himself with a book of poetry in a lawn chair under the shade of a big mesquite tree in his front yard.

The book was called Night's Pardons, by a writer named James Sallis, who he'd recently discovered. He read a poem or two each day. This morning, he found:

Yourself
and light, being both mortal, have much
in common.

He was musing on that thought when a white SUV with the emblem of the Kickapoo Tribal Police on the side pulled into his driveway. Roberto Echabarri, who'd been made chief of the tribal police less than a month before, climbed out of the vehicle and walked over to Concho.

Concho rose from his chair, shook the man's hand. Echabarri was barely twenty-six but looked older. Seeing half a dozen dead bodies and getting shot by a hired assassin will do that to a person. Echabarri had been the only one out of three tribal policemen to survive last month's insanity. He still complained of pain in his shoulder where a hitman had put a bullet in him while trying to kill Ten-Wolves.

Echabarri stood just under six feet. He'd lost a few pounds since Concho first met him and probably weighed no more than one-eighty. He wore his dark hair cut short. Echabarri had gotten a degree in political science from the University of Texas at Austin before returning to the reservation to take a deputy job.

Rumor had it he'd meant the position to be temporary, that he was saving money for graduate school. If so, those plans had been put on hold. Echabarri had always been a serious type, but that trait had gotten stronger. He took his job as chief of the tribal police very seriously indeed.

The old chief, Benjamin Deer-Run, had been murdered. Ben had been a fine man but not a modern one. Echabarri had already completely revamped the police force, hiring more and diverse deputies, including two female officers. He had drive, common sense, and commitment. Concho liked him.

"Ten-Wolves," Roberto said by way of greeting.

"Good to see you, man," Concho replied. "How you feeling?"

Echabarri rolled his left shoulder, most likely an unconscious gesture. "Shoulder's a little tight. It coulda been worse. How about you?"

"Getting better each day. What brings you out this way so early?"

"Got something I'd like your input on."

"OK."

"I'd rather show than tell."

Concho scratched his cheek with the edge of his book. "No problem. Let me throw on my gear and I'll ride along."

"Appreciate it!"

Ten minutes later, after radioing Texas Ranger headquarters with his morning plans, Concho joined Echabarri at the SUV, dressed in boots, jeans, a work shirt, and his pistols. The two men rode in silence for a while. Only when they turned onto a dirt road that Concho recognized did he speak.

"George Night-Run's farm?"

"Yeah. What I want to show you is in his barn."

"You've got my curiosity fired."

"Good," Echabarri replied.

Less than four minutes later, Echabarri pulled up in front of a big slat-sided wooden structure squatting in a field surrounded by brittle brown grass, dryland scrub and prickly pear. The barn, once painted red, had long since faded to gray.

To one side of the barn stood a small grove of cedars. Behind it rose a creaking windmill with a water tank beneath. On the other side stood a new metal pole corral, while off in the distance Concho spotted a few shabby cows standing around their breakfast, a big bale of hay.

As soon as Concho stepped out of the SUV, he smelled it. Something in the barn was dead and rotting. He was surprised to see no buzzards around. His gaze found Echabarri.

"Tell me that's not a person in there."

Echabarri shook his head. He went to the wooden door of the barn and slid it back in a rattle of hinges. Concho stepped inside. Echabarri followed. Dim light bled through holes in the slatted sides of the barn but the interior was still shadowy. Echabarri pulled a flashlight off his belt, flicked it on. The barn lay empty of hay but there was something else here. Echabarri pointed his light up toward the ceiling.

Concho's face wrinkled in disgust. A pig had been hauled up by its rear feet on an old nylon rope and hung suspended from the barn's central rafter. The rope had been tied off to one side. The hog, a feral sow, had been about three-quarters skinned, with the hide hanging down around its head like a shroud.

Someone had gutted the animal. Ropes of intestines and a pile of glistening organs lay just beneath the pig's head. Blood had dripped everywhere and clotted to black. The scene swarmed with flies and squirmed with maggots. A smell other than death lived here too, a biological odor that was acrid and musty at the same time, like something long unwashed.

Concho spat, then glanced over at Echabarri, whose face was twisted as if he were about to throw up. Stepping toward the tribal police chief, Concho took the flashlight out of the man's hand and walked a circle around the slaughtered animal, examining it from every angle.

A pitchfork for tossing hay leaned against one wall. Concho picked it up and squatted beside the pile of viscera. He used the tines of the fork to move things around until, satisfied with his study, he straightened and put the pitchfork back. Motioning to the police chief, he led the way outside into the clean air. Only then did he take a deep breath.

"Guess you don't know who did this?" Concho asked.

Echabarri shook his head. "No. George says it was a Chupacabra."

"Hmmm! He the one found the pig?"

"He and his oldest boy, Manuel. He'd been looking for a missing cow for a couple of days. They found this last evening and called it in to me. I didn't have a chance to check it out until this morning."

"Looks like a sharp knife was used to slit the sow's belly," Concho said. "What made George say it was a Chupacabra?"

Echabarri hesitated. "He claims he saw it. Manuel, too."

"Saw it?"

"It was late. Getting dark. When George came out of the barn, he said a shape as tall as a man was standing in the cedars over there with purple eyes. Manuel said the same thing. Though, of course, they'd discussed it between them before they told me so the agreement might be artificial."

"Any tracks?"

"I didn't notice any but I only had a quick look before I came over to get you."

Concho nodded. He handed the flashlight back to Echabarri, then began a systematic sweep of the area, starting in front of the barn and spreading out from there. He found plenty of tracks by the barn—cows and calves, and the marks of several booted feet, which he was pretty sure were left by himself, Echabarri, and George Night-Run.

He found a few individual pig tracks farther away from the barn and, as he reached the cedars, he could see a whole swath of torn-up ground. Individual tracks were indiscernible, but he didn't need to see any to know what had caused the damage. He returned to the young police chief.

"Feral hogs been all over here," he said. "Mostly rooting around by the cedars. The dead one's probably from that sounder."

"What about what George saw?" Echabarri asked. "There's no pig out here as tall as a man."

"I'd buy that before I'd believe it was a Chupacabra," Concho said. "And George could have been mistaken about the thing's height. Or maybe it was standing on a rock or fallen log."

"With glowing purple eyes?"

"When a person or an animal is dark-adapted, the whites of its eyes will be a shade of purple from the buildup of a photopigment called rhodopsin. Depending on the angle and refraction of light hitting them, they might look purplish at night."

Echabarri blinked. "I remember rhodopsin from my intro to psych class."

"What's more interesting is that whoever killed the pig took pieces of it with him."

"Oh!" Echabarri said.

"When I checked the pile of organs, the heart was missing, the sweetbreads, the liver, the kidneys."

"What? What for?"

"Food, I'm guessing," Concho said.

"I could have gone without hearing that."

Concho grinned. "Sweetbreads are good eatin'."

"You can have 'em. How was the thing killed?"

"Don't know. I didn't see any wound other than the one made by the knife in the belly. But with the hide peeled down, I could have missed a small bullet hole. From a .22 or something. The shot might have been in the head which was hidden by the hide."

"You think something like this happened to George's missing cow?"

"Hard to say, but possible."

"George is going to want me to arrest someone."

"For what? The best you'd get them for would be trespassing. The pig didn't belong to anyone, and the government encourages people to kill them for all their destruction of local habitats."

"If they got the cow though."

"Yes, if they got the cow."

"Something else," Echabarri said. "George's cow isn't the first missing animal I've had reports on lately."

"Oh?"

"A couple of missing cats have been reported. Selina Garcia had an Irish Setter up and disappear. Juanita Ramos says something took or killed a bunch of her chickens. And left no sign behind but feathers."

"Coyotes most likely."

"What I figured. Until now. This was no coyote. And maybe some of the others weren't either. You remember when Joseph Big-Pine and Tall Horse killed a deer and left its head outside your trailer?"

"I remember. But Tall Horse is dead and Big-Pine's in jail. I doubt we've got some animal serial killer on our hands."

Echabarri nodded, then added. "Those two were trying to work dark…magic. Sorcery. Could this be some kind of ritual like that?"

Concho hadn't considered the possibility. He did now. His brow furrowed as he worked it over. Finally, he said, "Can't rule it out. The heart, in particular, is often used in medicine rituals. Of course, there aren't many people today who believe such things have true power."

"But there are some?"

"You know there are. You should talk to one of the elders. Maybe Meskwaa. If you really think this is ritualistic."

Echabarri nodded again. "Maybe I will." The officer motioned for them to return to the SUV. Only as they drove away from the scene, did he add, "Something's happening on the Rez that I don't understand and don't like."

Concho had nothing further to add but his thoughts were troubled.

CHAPTER 6

Silence lingered in the SUV until Echabarri asked anoth-er question. "What's happening with Joseph Big-Pine, by the way?"

Big-Pine was a young Kickapoo from the Oklahoma tribe who'd been flirting with joining the NATV Bloods, an Indian gang. He'd come to Texas with a few others about a month before and quickly gotten in over his head with a gun-running, drug-dealing criminal businessman named Jacob Drake. Half a dozen people lay dead before Ten-Wolves brought Drake down. Concho had almost been one of them. And the scar on his back from the knife that had come close to severing his spine wouldn't let him forget it.

"Big-Pine is still in jail awaiting trial," Concho answered. "But he's given enough to the prosecution to convict Drake of ordering the murders of Ben Deer-Run and Donnell Blackthorne." He didn't bring up the fact that Blackthorne had been his biological father. It wasn't something he cared to think about most days.

"How much time you reckon Big-Pine will serve?" Echabarri asked.

Concho shrugged. "I'm not privy to the deal the prosecution made with him but, since he didn't do any of the killings, I imagine he'll get five to ten and be out in five. If he behaves himself. Why?"

Echabarri glanced over at the Ranger. "I think he's salvageable. Don't you?"

Concho considered: After he'd gotten out of the hospital and returned to the reservation, Big-Pine had come out of hiding to turn himself in to the Ranger. Concho knew why, though he'd kept that secret. Another Oklahoman Kickapoo named Bull Knife had persuaded Big-Pine to do so.

Bull Knife himself was an enigma that Concho had yet to solve. The man had first put the Ranger's life in danger and, later, saved it. Concho had no idea why and Bull Knife had completely disappeared by the time he'd recovered enough from his wound to look for him. But Echabarri hadn't asked about Bull Knife.

"I agree," Concho said. "Big-Pine is salvageable. You planning to take on the job?"

"Considering it," Echabarri said.

Concho's cell phone chirped. He pulled it out, checked his messages. He had one text from Maria Morales.

"Found some photos that might interest u. Be over your place around 6:30. U owe me a steak dinner."

Concho smiled and texted back. "I always pay my debts."

Concho was putting away his phone as they pulled up to the turn that would take them toward his house. The radio in the SUV crackled and the voice of the dispatcher for the Kickapoo Tribal Police, KTTT, spilled across the airwaves.

"All units. Fight at the Lucky Eagle. Please respond."

Echabarri reached for the mic but glanced over at Concho before he keyed it.

"Let's go!" the Ranger said. "I'll be your backup."

Echabarri nodded, spoke into the mic. "Unit 1. On my way. Two to three minutes."

"Acknowledged Unit 1," the dispatcher said. "Unit 4 is ten minutes out."

"Good!" Echabarri said as he rehung the mic and flipped on his sirens and lights.

Turning away from Concho's place, they sped along a dirt road until they hit Lucky Eagle Drive. They whipped past the reservation's head start center and, in two minutes, barreled into the parking lot of the Lucky Eagle which was six stories of mostly red brick hotel with a casino filling part of the bottom floor.

The site of the disturbance was unmistakable. A crowd had spilled out of the casino's front door and milled about beneath the entrance pavilion. Concho had his window down; he could hear the shouts of agitated patrons.

Echabarri squealed his SUV to a stop and bailed out, leaving his lights and sirens blaring. Concho followed. The arrival of the police didn't have any effect on the crowd. People whooped and hollered.

Echabarri pushed through the outside ring of onlookers. Concho added his considerable weight to the effort. They broke through, saw the source of the conflict in the center of the excited gathering.

Two women—girls really—writhed around on the ground, punching, kicking, and clawing at each other. Both had long black hair; both were Kickapoo. Both were shouting. Concho heard one phrase repeated: "He's mine! He's mine!" The Ranger had no idea who "he" might be.

"Here, here now!" Echabarri shouted.

The crowd jostled. Concho pushed people back as Echabarri leaned down to grab the struggling women.

"Let 'em fight!" a group of young men shouted.

Echabarri got hold of an arm from each of the women, started tugging. Concho realized he was going to have to help. He stepped forward, and one of the men shouting for the fight to continue shoved Echabarri from behind. The new chief of the tribal police stumbled, tripped and went sprawling across the fighters.

The same man tried to kick the downed officer. Concho intervened. He grabbed the fellow's shirt collar, jerked him close. "Nope!" he said.

The man had probably just turned twenty-one, a college kid on break. His face was red and flushed with sweat. His breath stank of alcohol.

"Screw you!" the fellow shouted.

He took a wild swing at Concho. The Ranger caught the fist, twisted both fist and arm around behind the young man's back, and forced him to his knees.

"Calm down!" Concho snapped.

"Hey, leave Steve alone!" someone in the crowd shouted.

Several men, apparently friends of "Steve," pushed forward. One was a good size, standing over six feet and weighing over two hundred pounds. He held a Tecate beer bottle which he swung suddenly at Concho's head. Concho blocked with a forearm. Beer and bottle went flying, spraying warm amber liquid over a dozen people.

Concho let go of Steve and straightened. He sent a short jab into the bottle-slinger's chin with his right fist. The blow had little of Concho's power behind it. He didn't want to break the kid's jaw. The fellow's eyes crossed. He sagged and would have fallen if Concho hadn't caught him.

But now, two more of Steve's friends rushed the Ranger. Concho shoved the man he was holding into them. All three crashed drunkenly to the ground. A blow into his back startled Concho. His head jerked around.

Steve had gotten up and punched the Ranger right in the spot where, a month before, he'd been stabbed. It hurt and brought back emotions Concho thought he'd freed himself of. Before he could even think, he snapped an elbow back into Steve's chin, sending the young man stumbling away to fall in a heap.

From the corner of an eye, Concho saw Echabarri regain his feet and drag the two young women apart, though they continued to shriek insults and slash at each other with their nails. Concho wanted to help but the three young men he'd just knocked to the ground were getting up.

The three didn't look like they wanted to continue the fight though. Concho thought it was over until yet another man pushed the three aside and stepped up to face him. This one was bigger than them all, 6'2" or better and maybe weighing 240. He was older too, and revealed his identity with his first words.

"You mess with my son, you mess with me."

"Not sure which one your son is," Concho said, "but you saw him attack me. I could have hurt him badly and didn't. You need to back off, or I will hurt you."

The man had been drinking but wasn't drunk. His skin was flushed, his eyes small and piggish. He pulled his right fist out of his pocket and a set of brass knuckledusters caught a gleam from the sun.

"Don't push it!" Concho warned softly.

The man uttered a racial slur. He snapped a jab toward the Ranger's face. Concho swayed aside, sent a jab of his own back. He missed as the man wove his head back and forth. The fellow had both fists up. He was on his toes, hands and upper body moving. Clearly, he'd had boxing training. Maybe quite a bit.

"Kill him, Dad!" the biggest of the younger men shouted.

The man responded to his son's words. He sent a left hand snapping forward, then swung a hard right across. Concho dodged both punches. His hands were up too, but open rather than closed into fists.

Now that a law officer was involved in the fighting, the crowd had sobered and quieted. But they weren't walking away. Concho could see that Echabarri had an arm solidly around each of the young ladies and was forcibly holding them apart. There wasn't much the tribal policeman could do to help Concho. He didn't need it anyway.

The boxer swung two more haymakers. Concho dodged the first, merely swayed aside for the other. The man was quick on his feet and had heat in his punches. If they'd connected…

After the second missed swing, Concho threw a jab of his

own. This one did connect, snapping the fellow's head backward. But the man could take a punch as well as sling them. He stumbled back a step but got his hands up as Concho lunged in for the finish.

Two of Concho's punches were blocked. A third exploded with little effect against the man's shoulder. The fellow riposted with jabs. One grazed Concho's cheek. Fists smacked against arms. Mouths grunted with effort and impacts. The boxer had almost as long of a reach as Concho. The Ranger had to get through it, somehow.

Keeping his hands high, Concho crowded the other fighter, forcing him to back away through the gathered onlookers. He needed open space to work. With his hands up, Concho's sides and belly were vulnerable. The man turned his focus to them.

A fist thudded into Concho's ribs, only partially blocked by his elbow. Another punch snapped into his side up high near the shoulder. This came from the fist with the brass knuckles on it. It hurt, but it gave Concho the opening he needed.

Too fast for the man to block, the Ranger sent left and right jabs into the fellow's face. The first blow cut the lip and spattered blood; the second widened the cut and let the crimson flow.

The man shook his head, tried to get his hands back up to protect his face. Concho slung a fist into the man's belly below the sternum. The boxer lurched forward, bent over with pain. He tried to roar as he swung a roundhouse right but the sound hardly whiffed the air, and the swing didn't do much better. Concho blocked with his left arm before sending another right jab searing into the fellow's mouth.

The man cried out as more blood and what looked like a fragment of tooth went flying. Concho jabbed with his left now, again into the mouth. The man swayed, his eyes dazed. Concho measured the man with a right but pulled back without letting it go. The fellow groaned and sank slowly to the ground. He was finished.

Concho glared around at the watchers. The smile that coiled on his lips must have been terrifying. The crowd split like a school of minnows charged by a barracuda. In moments the open area in front of the casino was largely empty.

The boxer's son rushed to his father, knelt beside him. "Dad! Dad!"

"He might need stitches for the lip," Concho said calmly. "And better have the tooth examined."

The young man looked up at Concho, his eyes frightened now and very, very sober. "What… Are we…under arrest?"

"What you're under," Concho said, "is an order to get out of here and not come back until you can all behave yourself."

The boy nodded. He stood up and pulled at his father's arm. A couple of the other boys gathered around. One had Steve's arm draped over his shoulder. The other helped the son with his father. The crew of them stumbled toward the parking lot.

"Take a cab home!" Concho called after them. He saw several nods, then turned toward Echabarri.

The two young Kickapoo ladies had finally ceased their feud. Concho recognized them both—Tamara Redvine, sixteen, and Selena Garcia, fifteen. He was surprised at Tamara, a sweet and shy young girl interested more in poetry than boys.

Selena, on the other hand, was the niece of Daniel Alvarado and shared some of her uncle's bullying tendencies. Concho had had many run-ins with Daniel over the years, especially when Alvarado had served as a deputy in the tribal police. Of course, Alvarado was dead, murdered to keep him quiet by the same man—Cole Chase—who'd nearly killed Concho with a knife in the back.

The two young women looked chastened as Echabarri gave them a stern warning to stop fighting and stay away from the casino since they were underage. Just then, another police car screeched up with its siren blaring. Officer Nila Willow emerged, the first woman to serve as a deputy in the Kickapoo Texas tribal police.

Echabarri had appointed Willow to the force. He handed the girls over to her with instructions to get them home safely and to tell their parents what they'd been doing.

Finally, Echabarri turned to Concho. "Glad to have you for backup!"

"Owed it to you," Concho replied. He grinned. "Just don't call me Tonto!"

CHAPTER 7

"You smell like beer," Echabarri said as he drove Concho away from the Lucky Eagle and toward home.

Concho glanced down at his spattered shirt where the young man's brew had sprayed when he tried to brain the Ranger with the bottle.

"And I didn't even get to enjoy any of it," he said.

Before Echabarri could respond, Concho's cell phone rang. He pulled it out of his pocket. The number showed up as "unknown," but Concho had a feeling.

"Hello, Katniss," he said.

A silence was followed by, "Wow, I guess you're some detective. How'd you know it was me?"

"Information is gold, remember?"

The woman chuckled. "OK," she said. "I'll tell you how I got your number. Though not from who."

"I'm listening."

"People in the community. They know about Concho Ten-Wolves. Mostly, they say he's someone you can trust. They keep the number. In case of emergencies."

"Glad to hear it. As for how I knew it was you, it was an educated guess. I've been expecting you to call again."

"Shoulda figured."

"So, if people are saying you can trust me, why aren't you? Tell me where you are."

"I'm not ready for that yet."

Concho glanced over at Echabarri who was clearly listening but trying to look like he wasn't.

"From what you've told me, you're in danger," Concho continued into the phone. "Let me make sure you don't face the danger alone."

"You can't watch me 24-7."

"At least tell me who's threatening you. Maybe I can clear the way for you."

The woman sighed. "I don't understand it all. But Anne does. She's the one who planned the robbery. She's got…connections. Just don't tell her I said so."

"All right," Concho said. "I won't. How do I get in touch with you after I talk to Anne?"

"You won't. But I'll get in touch with you. I'll call in a couple of days."

"A long time."

The woman who called herself Katniss sounded scared again as she said, "I know. Maybe a lifetime."

"OK—" Concho started and stopped as he realized the woman had disconnected.

Concho drew a deep breath and put up his phone. Echabarri's gaze shifted back and forth between the road and the Ranger. His face showed both curiosity and concern.

"You heard about the bank robbery yesterday?" Concho asked Echabarri.

The chief nodded. "Yeah. An all-female gang from what I was told."

"Yep. We caught three. One got away. That was her on the phone."

"Really? What does she want?"

"I think she's scared for her life but doesn't completely trust me. My guess is, there's more to the robbery than what we see."

"Sounds like it."

"Or," Concho continued, grinning "she just thinks I'm cute."

Echabarri laughed. "So, a blind bank robber is what you're saying. She shouldn't be that hard to catch."

"Ouch!" Concho said. "And here I thought we were friends."

***

After Echabarri dropped Concho off at his trailer, the Ranger went inside and quickly took two T-bones out of his freezer to thaw for the evening. He then climbed into his Ford F-150 and headed into the town of Eagle Pass. After Maria Morales's text, he'd figured on driving over to the mall to pick up the photos she'd mentioned but the call from Katniss pointed him in a different direction.

Taking Highway 57 to Balboa-Jones Blvd, he stopped off at the Maverick County Sheriff's Department, the glass-fronted office home of Sheriff Isaac Parkland. Normally, the place was quiet. This morning it roiled with activity, with officers, civilians and vehicles of various types zipping in and out of the building and parking lot on unaccountable errands. Something had happened and Concho's instincts told him it had to do with the very reason he'd come here—to see the bank robber named Anne.

After making his way through the frenetic scene, Concho found Sheriff Parkland inside talking to someone wearing a lawyer's suit. Parkland noticed the Ranger enter. At his size, Concho was hard to miss. The Sheriff lifted a finger as a way of saying to give him a minute. Concho nodded and found an out-of-the-way corner where he could lean against the wall.

Parkland soon disengaged from the suit and walked over. They shook hands. At 5' 7", Parkland was almost a foot shorter than the Ranger, and with a considerable gut from spending too many hours behind a desk rather than on the street. He was a very competent officer though. He and Concho had worked together before and meshed well.

After the handshake, Parkland vented a long sigh and pushed back his white, ten-gallon hat to scratch a sweaty and nearly bald head. "How you'd hear?" he asked.

"Hear what?" Concho replied.

Parkland looked surprised. "I figured you were here because of Anne Reese."

"If you're talking about the red-haired bank robber from yesterday, then I am."

"Ah," Parkland said. "You don't know she's dead."

Concho frowned. "Nope, I didn't know. Was hoping to speak to her. What happened?"

"This morning. Over at the detention center somewhere around eight or nine. The jail is crowded. She was in with two other inmates. One or both of them killed her. We're not sure yet. We're trying to keep a lid on the news about it. Until we learn more."

"Interesting, considering I just found out this morning, from a little birdie, that Anne was the one who orchestrated the robbery. And that there was probably more to it than just grabbing some fast cash."

Parkland arched one eyebrow, something Concho had never been able to accomplish and of which he was slightly jealous.

"Oh?" the Sheriff asked. "What else did the birdie tell you?"

"Nothing. I was hoping to get more from Anne herself. You said her last name was Reese? That her real name?"

Parkland nodded. "Yeah. She was born right here in town. Went to Eagle Pass High. She was twenty-five. Looked older to me. Had a few priors that never went anywhere serious. A juvey charge for marijuana possession. Joy riding in a stolen car she didn't steal. Drunk and disorderly. Nothing to suggest an ability to mastermind a bank robbery."

"Wasn't masterminded too well," Concho said. "We got them

pretty quickly."

"True."

"And the suspects in her murder?"

"Jade Harmony. Her real name. And Marta Hernandez. Both are in on prostitution charges. They've got long histories of that. And various drug offenses. Jade served six months for assault a couple of years back.

"Both women claim Reese started the altercation by using racial slurs against them. Jade is African American. Both are denying doing anything more than punching her. But Reese had her head repeatedly rammed into a bunk, it looks like. The coroner hasn't completed his exam but he told me it was probably a brain hemorrhage that killed her."

The Ranger frowned. "How big are this Jade and Marta? Reese was a strong and athletic woman. It would take some muscle to whip her."

"Jade could probably bench press you," Parkland said. "She's a weightlifter. Muscles on muscles. We've had her as a guest before, and she's knocked the heck out of a couple of my deputies."

"Don't suppose I could talk to them? The women, not the deputies."

"You mean the robbers or the ones who killed Anne Reese?"

"Both actually."

Parkland shook his head. "Not a good time, I'm afraid. We've got Harmony and Hernandez on a round of interrogations and I don't want to break that rhythm. But as soon as they're clear, I'll give you a call."

Concho nodded his understanding. "What about the other bank robbers? Gotten anything from them?"

"The driver is still in the hospital," Parkland said. "We interviewed the other one. A woman named Tessa Mercadel. Her family's got money and she's lawyered up. So far she's given us nothing other than her name. You got any leads on the one that got away?"

"She's called me twice on the phone. Last night and this morning."

"Really?"

"Yep. Didn't give me much information though. She's scared of something. She used the name 'Katniss' with me. I think it's a reference to a trilogy of young adult novels. I'm looking into that."

"How did she get your number?"

"She said folks in the 'community' know it. Whatever that means."

"Hmm," Parkland mused. "Give me a heads up if you get anything else from her."

"Will do. Also, Reese was certainly no charmer and it might be true about the slurs, but I doubt it's the reason for her murder. I suspect someone wanted her shut up. Did either of the potential perps get a phone call before the murder?"

"Actually, yes. Jade did. We've already asked her about it and she claimed it was her lawyer. But…" Parkland shrugged.

"There's something about this robbery that doesn't scan," Concho said. "Might be some kind of organized crime thing."

"I'll let the interrogators know your thoughts," Parkland said. He sighed. "You ever get involved in anything simple, Ten-Wolves?"

"I'm a complex fellow," Concho replied. He slapped the Sheriff on the shoulder. "But I mean well."

"Right," Parkland agreed. "Glad to see you anyway. Looks like you're fully recovered from your bout with modern medicine."

"Pretty much."

"Oh, by the way," Parkland said. "Probably doesn't mean anything but I found out the same bank was robbed a few weeks back. In a different way."

"Oh?"

"Yeah. One of the clerks was embezzling. Making false notes on deposits and withdrawals and slipping a buck here and a buck there into her purse. They don't think she got more than a few hundred but they revamped their whole security system. That's why they had a guard in the bank on the day of the robbery. The one who got shot. They also put in scanners to check all the employees going in or out."

"Interesting," Concho said. "Not sure what it means but I don't like coincidences."

"Yeah, yeah," Parkland said. "Agreed."

Concho sighed. "Well, I'll leave you to it."

"I'll get back to you as soon as I can about talking to our female bandits."

"Appreciate it," Concho said. The two shook hands once more, and Concho worked his way back out to his truck. He sat thinking for a bit before starting the engine. Another dead end. Literally, this time. This case was full of them.

He only hoped "Katniss" would not be another one.

CHAPTER 8

She thanked the truck driver for the ride as she climbed down from the big rig's cab and slung her green backpack over one shoulder. The truck had been air-conditioned, and the heat of the outside world enfolded her like a dry, old blanket. A hot afternoon breeze stirred the ends of her shoulder-length brown hair but did little to cool the sweat popping up like pimples on her face.

Taking shallow breaths, she started across the parking lot where the trucker had dropped her off toward the door of a rough-looking bar that at least promised a return to cooler air. Behind her, the truck pulled back onto the highway with a huff of air brakes and the low grinding of the big engine. It left her feeling alone although she'd only met the trucker half an hour earlier when she'd thumbed a ride.

An unlighted sign gave the name of the bar—Hot, Blue and Righteous. She was only twenty-two. If she'd grown up anywhere else but Texas she probably wouldn't have recognized the phrase as a reference to the three-piece rock band ZZ Top. But she did. Even through the walls, she could hear the heavy blues of that little ol' band from Texas as "I Gotsta Get Paid" rumbled on the jukebox.

Pushing through the door, she stepped inside. The interior was dimly lit, except in the back section where the fluorescent lights bloomed brightly over two pool tables, and several bikers played eight-ball while they drank and smoked. It wasn't particularly cool temperature-wise. She couldn't hear any AC running. But at least she was out of the direct sun. The smells of stale, spilled beer and cigarette-charred air were not unpleasant though. She'd grown accustomed to them.

The bartender IDed her but the fake license she showed listed her age correctly. It listed her name as Catherine James. It wasn't correct but it was what she was used to going by.

The cheapest drink written on the wallboard behind the bar was a Coors Light. She ordered one. Footsteps alerted her to someone approaching. A man slipped onto the stool next to hers.

"Buy you that drink?" the man asked.

She turned her head and smiled prettily. The fellow was at least fifteen years older than her. He wore a dingy white shirt and dress pants that had seen better days. He'd gone too long between baths. He smelled sour. A former white-collar worker who'd fallen on hard days, she imagined.

"I'm sorry but I'm waiting on someone," she said.

The man smiled back with nicotine-stained teeth. "Too bad. If he doesn't show…"

"I'll know where to find you."

The man nodded, rose, and drifted away. She nursed her beer. The song on the jukebox changed to "One Bourbon, One Scotch, One Beer" by George Thorogood. Places such as this were nothing if not predictable—at least for the music.

To the left of the bar were the doors to the restrooms, complete with signs announcing "Señor" and "Señora." To the right stood another door with a black plaque on it reading "Office." That door opened and a man stepped through. The woman at the bar stiffened.

The man had to be at least 6' 6" and heavily muscled under his black, sleeveless, nylon T-shirt. His face was strongly masculine, with broad cheekbones, a wide jaw, and a cleft chin. His hair was sandy-brown. Catherine watched him, feeling the first stirrings of uncertainty about her chosen course of action.

The bartender approached the big man. They whispered together, and then the man walked over to her. He pushed two stools together and sat on both. He didn't speak. She glanced over to meet his gaze and looked quickly away. His eyes were an odd color, a dark amber, and completely devoid of expression as they scanned over her body like a machine.

Her fingers worked at the beer can in front of her, turning it around and around. To keep from blushing at the frankness of the man's gaze as he mentally stripped her of her jeans and white V-necked T-shirt, she tried to imagine more pleasant times. It wasn't easy, especially since the fellow smelled of Old Spice, her father's scent.

Finally, she said, "I was…uhm, looking for Mason French."

"That would be me," the man said, his voice almost toneless.

"So…you know what I want."

"The important thing right now is who sent you."

"I…uh, told the fellow on the phone. Anne…gave me your name."

"Anne's in jail."

"That's why I need what I need."

The man stared at her, then shrugged. He got up from the stool. "Follow me," he said.

Catherine nodded but Mason French wasn't watching. He walked toward his office. She rose hastily and hurried after him, leaving three-quarters of her beer behind. French held the door to his office open for her. She skittered past into a small room containing little more than a desk, a chair, and two filing cabinets.

French closed the door, and Catherine smiled as she turned back toward him. She used the same smile she'd put on for the man who'd tried to pick her up at the bar. It often worked to calm the male of the species.

It didn't work on Mason French. His hand shot out and locked around her throat.

***

At 6:35 PM, Concho's doorbell rang. He smiled. The T-bone steaks were grilled. Two baked potatoes wrapped in tinfoil stood ready to go. Salad waited in the crisper. He rinsed his hands quickly before answering the door.

Maria Morales stood on his doorstep when he opened up, still dressed from her day's work at the mall. She wore a business suit with charcoal gray pants and a stylish jacket buttoned over a deep blue satin blouse. Sensible heels adorned her feet, and in one hand dangled a six-pack of Shiner Bock beer.

"Be wary of mall managers bearing gifts," Maria said holding up the six-pack.

"Wary is not in my nature," Concho replied. "I'm inviting you in. Sure hope you don't abuse my hospitality."

Maria chuckled as she stepped inside. "No promises."

Concho took the six-pack from her as she lifted up on her toes and kissed him on the corner of the mouth. His nose picked up lavender and honeysuckle, and the scent of her hair just barely dampened as she'd walked from her car to his door through the late summer day's heat.

"Mmmm, something smells good," she whispered against his cheek. "Not sure if it's you or the steaks."

"It's me," Concho said. "I rubbed steak juice behind my ears."

Maria laughed and gave a quick nibble to his ear before she dropped back down on her heels and walked past him into the kitchen. She stopped in front of his bar and took her purse off her shoulder to set it down. She pulled the tie from her hair and stretched, lifting and straightening her back as she shook her head and her long dark hair brushed across her lower spine.

Concho set the Shiner on the bar and slid his arms around Maria's belly from behind. He slowly unbuttoned her jacket and let his large hands slip inside to brush across her satin blouse. She gasped as his fingers found her breasts and caged them gently.

Her body arched into his as he nuzzled his face into her hair and nipped at the back of her neck.

She turned to face him and they kissed. Concho grasped her hips and lifted her up to sit on the bar. He teased her neck with his lips, then nuzzled his way downward. She cupped the back of his head with one hand, her fingers twining through his long black hair. Her voice rose slightly as she whispered: "Let dinner wait a little longer."

CHAPTER 9

The woman who went by the name Catherine James kicked wildly at Mason French's legs as he held her by the throat. Her tennis shoes connected but didn't faze the big man. She fumbled to reach her backpack, and he tore it off of her and tossed it aside. He pushed her back across the small office and up against the wall. She tried to scream for help but only a croak emerged as French's grip tightened.

"Shhh!" he said. "If I wanted to kill you, your neck would already be broken."

Catherine heard him and understood. She fought fear for control of her body. She strained to breathe through her nose, forced herself to relax against the wall. She stopped kicking. Mason French loosened his grip slightly but did not release her.

"Anne knows better than to give anyone my name," French said. "Who really sent you?"

"It was Anne," she gasped out. "I swear! She… We're friends."

A faint smile twisted French's lips as he finally let go of her and stepped back. "Anne doesn't have any friends but me," he said. "Lift up your shirt."

"What?" Catherine asked. "I—"

"Lift up your damn shirt! So I can see if you're wearing a wire!"

Understanding the man's intent now, Catherine grasped the bottom of her T-shirt and tugged it out of her jeans. She drew it all the way up to her neck. French stepped toward her; she flinched back against the wall but didn't pull down the garment.

French stuck a thick finger in the strap of her black bra and pulled it away from her chest. She gritted her teeth but said nothing. The man popped the strap, then ordered her to "Turn around!"

She did as she was told, feeling his hands on her as he patted her down from waist to ankles. After a moment, he stepped back. She didn't dare turn without being told. A chair creaked as French sat down. A drawer slid open on the desk.

"All right," French said.

Catherine jerked her T-shirt down and turned to face him. The man leaned back slightly in his desk chair. A semiautomatic pistol with a silencer screwed onto the barrel rested in his lap.

"Tell me everything," French said in a conversational tone. "If I believe you, you live. If I don't, you end up in a dumpster."

***

It was nearly 9:00 PM when Concho reheated the steaks and potatoes and set them on his dining room table for himself and Maria Morales. Maria wore a black satin lounging robe she'd hung in his closet for just such occasions. Concho tried not to stare at her too much in the robe. He was very hungry but if he looked at Maria too long in this outfit the food would get cold again.

Maria was well aware of Concho's thoughts and kept doing little things to attract his attention, such as flipping her hair over her shoulder, or brushing an imaginary crumb off the front of her robe, or nibbling provocatively at the food on her fork.

"You're quite a witch," Concho eventually stated. "Do you want me to starve to death?"

Maria laughed. "You've already inhaled most of your steak and half your potato. I hardly think you're starving. In fact, I'm beginning to fear for my own meal. I'm trying to eat as fast as I can before you pillage mine too."

"I'll wrestle you for it," Concho said with a fake leer.

Maria gave him a grin and wink. "Later. For now, maybe we should remember why I really came over here tonight."

Drawing a blank, Concho frowned. "Uhm, right. Why was that?"

Maria shook her head. "The pictures. Of the book signing! You wanted to see if you might be able to identify your mystery 'Katniss' in them!"

Concho felt himself flushing. He really had forgotten. He scratched his head. "Yeah, I remember. Where are they?"

"Still in my car. They were stored digitally. I printed a few I thought you might be most interested in seeing. The rest are on a data stick."

"Great," Concho said. "I can get them." He started to stand.

"No, no," Maria said, putting a slender hand on his wrist. "I wouldn't want you to starve while making the great trek." She took a last bite of her steak and pushed to her feet. Talking around her food, she added, "It'll only take a sec but my food better be here when I get back or you won't be in any shape to sleep tonight."

"Threats, threats," Concho said.

Maria chuckled and blew him a kiss. Concho watched her walk away in her robe and the pretty pair of beaded moccasins he'd bought for her from a woman who made them on the reservation. He shook his head as he considered what a lucky man he was. The front door opened. He heard the sound of the outside light switch being flicked on. A minute passed. He was seriously considering stealing a bite of Maria's steak when her voice called out:

"Concho!"

A chill coursed across Concho's back. Maria sounded frightened. He leaped to his feet, sprinted through the house toward the front door. Maria had left the door open. He rushed through it onto his small front porch. No moon yet. Night lay heavy in the yard. The yellowish outside light cast strange shadows across the ground.

Maria stood by her car, a 2017 Ford Focus. In the glow of the flashlight she held, her body was rigid, and she stared off to her right through the darkness toward the big spreading mesquite tree where Concho kept a few lawn chairs and his fire pit. He couldn't see anything there to have disturbed Maria but that didn't stop him from running barefooted over to his lover.

"What is it?" he questioned. "Are you OK?"

"I…" Maria started. Then, "There was something there. Something big."

Concho took the flashlight and directed its light toward the mesquite. The tree's twisted branches raked the darkness. A few other smaller trees and bushes loomed behind the bigger tree. He could only see their shadowy shapes and nothing else.

Listening, he heard only the usual night sounds of birds and frogs, though it was quieter in the direction Maria had indicated. He couldn't smell anything unusual either but the breeze blew from behind him toward the mesquite.

"Did you see it? Or just hear it?"

"Saw it. But just for an instant. It was…tall. Human-shaped. I didn't get a good look before it faded into the background. But…" Maria looked at Concho and he could see she was frightened of the unknown, "it had purple eyes."

The chill Concho had felt before came back. Purple eyes! Like whatever it was George Night-Run had seen on his farm and reported to Roberto Echabarri? He'd not mentioned that to Maria. It couldn't have been some kind of "suggestion" from him.

"All right," he said. "Let's go back inside. You got the photos?"

Maria cleared her throat. "Yes." Her voice sounded almost normal as she held up a manilla envelope.

"Good. After we get back in the house, I'll put on some shoes and fetch my gun and have a look to see if I can find any tracks of whatever it was."

"No!" Maria said as she grasped his wrist, her voice scared again. "Let it…go. At least until morning."

Concho could see she was still badly frightened by her encounter. Given the situation, he didn't feel exactly comfortable himself. "OK," he said. "Morning it is."

He slipped his arm around Maria's shoulders as they started back to the trailer. They'd reached the porch when something in the near distance howled. The sound rose, wavered, echoed, faded.

"That…wasn't a coyote. Was it?" Maria asked, her voice shaking slightly.

Concho let out a deep breath. He didn't like to lie, even if it meant scaring Maria a little more. "I don't think so," he said. "Maybe a wolf. Although there aren't supposed to be any around here anymore." In his head, he was thinking the howl didn't sound exactly like a wolf either but he decided not to share that tidbit.

Maria stepped on through the door into the house. Concho glanced back toward the darkness. He half expected a purple eye to wink at him but only the stars stared back coldly.

CHAPTER 10

Concho cleaned away the dinner dishes while Maria spread out printed copies of four photographs on the dining room table. The Ranger sat down with a magnifying glass to study the images. The photos all showed a group of fifty or so children and adults—almost all of them female—sitting on folding chairs or on the floor in front of a small stage in the Eagle Pass Mall. You couldn't see who was on the stage in the pictures but Concho knew it was Suzanne Collins, the author of The Hunger Games Trilogy.

As Concho passed the magnifying glass over the first picture, he recognized a much younger Maria Morales sitting in the third row with her twelve-year-old niece, Angelina, scrunched up on her lap. Maria had even longer hair in those days, as did Angelina. The two looked a lot alike.

Maria had printed the images on her work copier. It was an expensive machine and the pictures were clear and in color. The names of the subjects had been written in the bottom margins of the photos but Maria said she wasn't sure of the accuracy.

Concho scanned for a girl of fourteen or so with brown hair and pleasantly symmetrical features. That was how he remembered the bank robber who called herself "Katniss," though he'd only gotten a good look at her for a few seconds. Unfortunately, he found three different girls who fit his general criteria.

He checked the other three pictures but, other than the angle of the photo, they were all much the same. Then, one of the names at the bottom of the photo caught his attention—Anne Reese.

Excitedly, he scanned the picture until he found someone who resembled the Anne Reese he'd met at the bank robbery. She looked about sixteen here. She had longer hair, still reddish-orange in color. It was clearly the same person.

His excitement grew when he realized that one of the three girls he'd pegged as a possible "Katniss" was sitting on the floor right in front of Anne Reese. The name there read Katy Delchamp.

"Katy equals Katniss," he murmured.

"You got something?" Maria asked, leaning toward him.

Concho showed her. "Looks like Katy knew Anne for years before they robbed a bank together."

"Why don't we get on the net and see what we can find about Katy Delchamp," Maria said.

Maria's face was close to Concho's. He reached a hand to her cheek, brushed it lightly with his knuckles. He kissed her sharp little chin and murmured, "Let the internet wait a while longer."

***

As soon as morning light peeked through the window into his bedroom, Concho slid out of bed without waking Maria and got dressed. He slipped out the front door and closed it gently behind him, then strode over to the big mesquite tree where Maria had seen something the night before with purple eyes.

Two cooing doves sat close together on one of the mesquite's branches, bobbing their heads up and down. They were more interested in each other than in him, though, and didn't fly. That brought him a smile and a thought. He was quite in love with Maria Morales.

Trying to focus more on the task at hand than on the woman inside, he began to search around by the mesquite for any signs of what might have frightened Maria. The ground was mostly dirt, with only scattered clumps of dried grass. A few bushes glistened with yellowish dust in the morning sun. No dew. It had been dry for several weeks. The earth had grown hard; it wouldn't take tracks easily. They needed rain.

One low bush had the dust knocked off a limb. He found a few scuffs in the dirt but no discernable footprints. Something had passed through here but he couldn't tell how big it was or what it might have been.

Concho knew Maria. He believed her about last night. But what had she seen? If it had been a man, he'd dragged his feet to avoid leaving footprints. That suggested sinister intent. But he couldn't rule out a wild pig. They typically rooted with their snouts as they walked. The scuffs might have been left by such, although only the boars typically traveled alone and a sounder would have torn up the whole area.

Stepping back into his yard with a frustrated sigh, Concho sat down in one of the three lawn chairs he'd placed underneath the shade of the big mesquite. A small circle of stones marked his fire pit. The ashes within were old and nearly colorless. He often enjoyed sitting out here at night with a small blaze but it had been weeks since he'd used his pit—in large part because of the dry conditions and the fear of wildfire.

A rattle in the brush made Concho sit up straight. His heartbeat sped up. Then he relaxed as a human form stepped into the open. He knew this form—Meskwaa, a Kickapoo elder and friend whose name meant "red."

Meskwaa was old, though no one knew how old. Yet, he was spry and could move as silently as any panther when he chose to. The rattle he'd made in the bushes had to have been deliberate, a warning to Concho so he wouldn't be surprised. Meskwaa remained one of the very few people that Concho knew who could surprise him.

"Uncle!" Concho said as Meskwaa approached. "Join me and

sit. I wish I had a dipper of water to provide you."

The old man nodded as he moved over and sat in one of the free lawn chairs. He crossed thin legs in trousers of fringed buckskin and took a match and a filterless cigarette out of the pocket of his red cotton shirt. After offering the smoke to Concho and hearing a polite "No, thanks," Meskwaa flicked the match alight with his thumbnail and set fire to the cigarette. He drew deep and released, letting the smoke curl up through the branches of the mesquite to disperse.

Concho studied Meskwaa as the man smoked. Beneath a stained, broad-brimmed hat, braids of long white hair hung down across each shoulder. The face was lined and expressionless but the deep-set eyes missed nothing and the mind behind them was as keen as a freshly sharpened blade.

"What brings you here this morning, uncle?" Concho asked after a bit.

Meskwaa pinched the glowing tip of his cigarette out with his fingers, then tucked the remnant back into his pocket. He tipped the hat on his head back and let his gaze focus on the Ranger.

"Trouble here. Last night," Meskwaa said.

Concho did not ask how the old man knew. Meskwaa saw things others didn't.

"Nothing too serious," Concho replied. "Maria. She saw something." He jerked his chin toward the big mesquite. "Near the tree." Concho watched the old Kickapoo carefully as he added, "She said it stood like a man and had purple eyes."

Meskwaa nodded. He did not seem surprised.

"You know of this thing?" Concho asked.

"I know it is not the first time it has been seen of late on the reservation."

"Yeah. George Night-Run and his son, Manuel, saw it. Near their barn where a wild pig had been slaughtered."

"There are others. Bearfoot is one."

Bearfoot was the husband of Estrella Deer-Run whose murdered father, Ben, had been the chief of the tribal police before Roberto Echabarri.

"What is it?" Concho asked. "Or should I ask, who?"

Meskwaa said nothing for a moment. And when he did it seemed he spoke of unrelated things. "Do you remember the vision from your naming ceremony?"

"Yes."

"Do you remember when you awoke in the council wickiup? The circle of elders was present."

"I remember. I didn't understand how I'd gotten there. I only remembered the creek where I had fallen. But I recall, you were in the circle."

"And what happened then?"

"You asked If I'd had a vision. I said I did."

"And?"

"You spoke with the other members of the circle." Concho frowned. "At least I think you did. I remember hearing voices but, in my memory, I can't see your mouths moving. I was still hallucinating, I guess."

"You were still experiencing. Yes. What happened next?"

"You said the circle was in agreement. I would be gifted the name Ten-Wolves."

"Did you think that odd?"

Concho nodded. "I did. Because I never told you, or any of them, what was in my vision. But, I already knew, from my grandmother, that you saw things. She called you a naataineniiha."

Meskwaa made no acknowledgment of the word, which was Kickapoo for 'Medicine Man.' He only said, "You were one in a pack of wolves. A leader. And yet, you were all of them too."

"A pack of ten," Concho said.

"The pack was running."

Concho nodded. "We were pursuing something. Prey."

"What manner of prey?"

A long breath sighed from Concho's lips. "I don't know. I

never saw it."

"But you felt it!"

Concho strained to remember something that had happened nearly twenty years ago. "I knew it was dangerous," he said finally. "That it was a thing to cause fear. I knew it could harm the pack."

"Did you sense it as evil?"

Concho shook his head. "Not exactly. Not evil. More…savage. Primal. I don't know how else to describe it."

Meskwaa let his gaze link to Concho's. His brown eyes were quiet like undisturbed water. But the voice, when it came, rang with intensity. "The force you were chasing in your vision. That is what is here now. On the reservation."

Surprise rocked Concho, both at what Meskwaa had said and at the tension in his old friend's voice. Meskwaa was normally as laid back as a cat sunning itself in a window, but now his words snapped with emotion. And their meaning…

Choosing his words carefully, Concho said, "That's…hard to believe."

"Many things are hard to believe. And yet are true."

"I suppose so."

"There is, another thing."

"What?"

"Do you remember the gift I gave you before you left the Elders' wickiup?"

"A white shield. Of buffalo hide stretched across a frame of Osage orange wood. I always kept it hung on the wall above my bed. But it burned when my house burned. A month ago. I ache for its loss."

"And…a power has come onto the reservation that should not be here."

Spontaneously, Concho laughed. The idea that a wood and hide shield given to a teenager in a naming ceremony had been protecting the reservation from danger for two decades struck him as ridiculous. He could not believe in such things.

Meskwaa rose from his chair and walked a few steps away. Concho feared he'd offended his friend but the old Kickapoo turned at the big mesquite and looked back with kindly concern.

"You must remake the shield. Soon. You will need it and I cannot do it for you this time."

Concho's mouth opened but he couldn't think of anything to say. Meskwaa turned away into the brush and disappeared like a twist of smoke in a breeze. Concho sat alone with the morning and his thoughts.

CHAPTER 11

Eventually, Concho returned to his trailer. The sound of the shower running told him Maria was stirring. He quickly threw an iron skillet on the stove and began frying bacon and eggs. He also started the coffeepot which had been a gift from Maria but one meant more for herself than for him. He seldom drank coffee; Maria did not go without.

By the time Maria came out of the bathroom tousling her hair dry and smelling clean and beautiful, breakfast was served. Wearing one of Concho's T-shirts, which hung on her like a dress, Maria kissed him on the chin and immediately sat and grabbed her cup of coffee. Two huge sips later, without the slightest indication that the black liquid had been steaming hot, she put the cup down and spoke.

"There," she said, "my urge to kill has abated."

"Whew!" Concho said as he sat and tucked into his own breakfast of three over-easy eggs with eight slices of bacon and two pieces of buttered toast. Orange juice was his drink of choice.

"I checked on our visitor this morning," he said around a mouthful of toast. "Unfortunately, the ground is too dry and hard to take much in the way of tracks. There were some scuff marks. Nothing identifiable."

Maria's dark eyes studied Concho over her cup and her plate with its single egg and a lonely strip of bacon. He'd had to work to get her to eat anything for breakfast. She was one of those strange folks—to him—who normally just drank coffee.

"Thank you for believing me," Maria said.

"You wouldn't make it up. But what it was remains to be seen." He didn't tell her what Meskwaa had said about the thing with purple eyes. He needed to process that information himself before he shared.

After breakfast, Concho dressed for work in blue jeans, a long-sleeved white western shirt, and his gun belt. Maria slipped back into the outfit she'd worn over here the night before.

Seeing her frown over a spot on the sleeve of her jacket, Concho said, "Maybe you should just leave a few work outfits over here for emergencies."

Maria glanced at him. She seemed to carefully consider her next words. Concho and Maria had broken up originally because they'd moved too fast. They'd both determined to take it slower this time and they, generally, had. Often, Concho felt it was too slow but he worried now he'd said the wrong thing.

But Maria smiled and everything was OK. "You're right," she said. "No reason I shouldn't. I'll bring some. It won't be tonight though. I'm helping mom cook for a wedding this weekend."

"Oh? Anyone I know?"

Maria grinned and patted him on the cheek. "An old friend of the family. But don't worry, I wouldn't subject you to a get together like that. I know how you are in crowds and this will be a big one."

"Thanks for looking out for me."

"You!" Maria said. "I'm looking out for the crowd. Some of them I actually like too much to see 'em in the hospital."

Concho shook his head and gave her a playful shove, sprawling her face first across the bed. She rolled over and sent him a glare, which she let segue into a wicked leer.

"Really!" she said. "Again?"

Concho gave a mock groan and grasped Maria's arm to pull her to her feet. "No, no, no. I couldn't handle it. Besides, we'll both be late for work."

"Your loss, big man," she said but she slung her purse over a shoulder and sauntered to the door.

Concho trailed her out and locked it behind them. He followed Maria to her Ford Focus, giving her a last, lingering kiss before climbing into his pickup. He drove behind her all way into Eagle Pass but when she turned down Bibb Avenue toward the Mall de las Aguilas, where she worked, Concho continued on through town toward one of the most exclusive neighborhoods in Maverick County.

Last night, after he and Maria had made love a third time, Concho had finally gone to the internet for information about Katy Delchamp, aka Katniss. Through the Texas Rangers' databases, which he was able to connect to remotely through his laptop, he had access to information most people couldn't easily get. He'd found Katy's parents and was headed to their house for questions and, he hoped, answers.

***

It was a big house on a street of big houses—at least a three-bedroom with a long front porch and what looked like a fenced-in back yard. The stylish black mailbox had the name Delchamp painted on it in large white letters. Two cars filled the driveway so he parked his truck at the curb.

William Delchamp owned several up-scale fitness and health centers in Eagle Pass and Maverick County, as well as a couple of the places folks just call "gyms." It looked like business was good. From the outside at least. Both the Delchamp's vehicles were expensive: a QX60 SUV from Infinity, which Concho suspected belonged to the wife, and a Lexus LC convertible, which started at over a hundred grand and was likely the husband's mid-life-crisis car.

The landscaping around the house had been expensive too. Beds of hibiscus flowers spread their colors and scent in the air. A row of Texas Gold Columbine wasn't in bloom but he could still smell them and a few orange and lemon trees which were getting a morning misting from a sprinkler.

As Concho walked up the driveway, the curtains in one of the upstairs bedrooms twitched. He knew he was being watched as he strode up to the front door and rang the bell.

Footsteps sounded from inside and the door opened a few inches with the chain-lock still engaged. A woman's face peered through the gap. She appeared to be in her early fifties, rather heavily made up and with the kind of brassy blonde hair that shrieks of dyes and visits to beauty parlors. The hazel eyes and the face, while puckered slightly with age, were still attractive.

"Yes?" the woman asked.

"Mrs. Delchamp," Concho began. "I'm with the Texas Rangers. Is your daughter, Katy, at home by any chance?"

The woman's pupils dilated. "Katy? Katy! No, she's not here. Has something happened to her? What's wrong? Is she OK?"

Concho held up his hands to stem the rush of questions. "Honestly, Mrs. Delchamp, I don't know how Katy is. I spoke to her on the phone twice and she was all right both times. I hope she still is but she seemed a little scared. I need to talk to her."

"Scared! Of what?"

"You probably have a better idea than I do," he said.

The woman shook her head. "I don't. I don't have any idea. Why are the police involved?"

The woman sounded sincere in her question. If so, it must mean she knew nothing of her daughter's involvement with the IBC bank robbery. Katy's name had certainly never been mentioned in association with it on the news. Of course, Delchamp might be lying to protect her daughter. Concho needed to proceed with caution.

"Right now," he said, "I'm the only one involved and that's because your daughter called me. I want to talk to her but, first and foremost, I want to make sure she's safe. Do you know how I could get in touch with her? Or where she might be?"

Mrs. Delchamp put both hands over her mouth and held them there for a moment. Finally, she shook her head and dropped her hands to speak. "I haven't seen her in several days. I—"

"Maureen! Who is it?" a voice called from within the house.

"Maureen" had a rather strange reaction to the voice. At first, her face furrowed and her mouth narrowed in what looked like irritation. Then, she glanced at Concho and the anger was replaced with something more like trepidation or calculation. That look disappeared, in turn, as a man's face materialized in the background behind the woman. Mrs. Delchamp unhooked the chain-lock and pulled the door back. Concho got his first clear look at William Delchamp.

The man was tall and fit, well-toned and muscular as if he regularly used his own gyms. He had to be a year or two younger than his wife but his short hair was still graying at the temples. He wore a white dress shirt and slacks, without a tie.

"What do you want?" the businessman asked, his lips thinning into a narrow line as he studied Concho and noted the Ranger badge.

"As I was telling your wife," Concho said patiently, "I really need to speak to your daughter, Katy. I've gotten some calls from her and I want to see she's all right."

"Don't tell me you're dating my daughter!" the gym owner said. "That would be ridiculous!"

Concho blinked. He couldn't think of a thing to say. Maureen abruptly excused herself and almost fled from the door. Her husband took a step closer to Concho. "I will call your supervisor about this!" he snapped.

Concho shook his head. "That's not what any of this is about. I've never met your daughter. She called me as an officer of the law. She sounded worried. I think she's gotten into something over her head. I want to find her. Help her."

"And you expect me to believe you? You just show up here out of the blue!"

Concho's patience had worn away. "I expected you to be concerned about your daughter!" he snapped. "Apparently, it's not the case. Call Texas Ranger headquarters. Company D. Ask about Concho Ten-Wolves. Shouldn't be too hard to remember. I'll come back later, when you've had a chance to process the information. And I'll expect more cooperation or you're gonna have a whole lot of officers showing up on your doorstep."

Concho turned on his heels and stalked away. A pause followed before the door slammed behind him. He heard the primary engaging. From the corner of one eye, he saw the curtains flick again in the room upstairs.

Returning to his truck, Concho hesitated. He'd let himself be made angry. Yes, Katy's father had acted like an asshole but Concho was the one who allowed the words and ridiculous insinuations to get under his skin. He wasn't going to go back quite yet, though. It would be good for the Delchamps to check with Ranger headquarters. They'd almost certainly be more cooperative after.

Something else kept Concho hanging around, though—a feeling, an intuition, that whoever had been watching him through the upstairs window might want to talk to him. He was sure it wasn't Katy but the database entry on the Delchamps had mentioned a second daughter, a younger girl named Vera. And, Concho remembered, in The Hunger Games books, Katniss had a younger sister she'd been close to.

Concho glanced back at the house. The upstairs curtains hung closed and still now. But whoever had stood behind them would need time to get downstairs and get to him. He fiddled with his phone for a few moments, then climbed in his truck and started it up. Making a slow U-turn in the street, he eased back up the block fifty yards before pulling over to the curb.

Acting purely on instinct, he sat in his truck with the engine running and waited.

Five minutes passed. Furtive movement in his rearview mirror caught the Ranger's attention. The handle on the passenger side door clicked. Concho's right hand rested close to his pistol. The truck door opened.

CHAPTER 12

Concho relaxed as a skinny girl of fifteen or so climbed into his truck. She had short, brown hair, a pale face drawn with tension, and wore a baggy gray T-shirt over jeans. It was exactly who Concho had expected. He took his hand away from his gun.

"You're Vera, aren't you?" Concho asked. "Katy's sister?"

"Yeah. Is…is Katy OK?"

"Honestly, Vera, I can't be sure. She called me yesterday. She was OK but it sounded like she was worried about something. Maybe she was scared. You know anything about that?"

Vera shook her head. "Not really. I mean, I guess you're here because," Vera's gaze darted to Concho and away again, "Katy robbed a bank."

Concho felt a spurt of surprise. "How did you know?"

Vera twisted her fingers together in her lap. "I saw…on the TV. The news. About four women robbing a bank."

"They didn't say anything about Katy on the news."

Vera shook her head again. "No. But they showed a picture of Anne Reese. And said one robber got away. Anne is Katy's friend." She shrugged. "Sort of."

"Sort of?"

"Anne uses people. I'm not sure she thinks of Katy as a friend.

But Katy never wants to hear it."

Concho nodded. "So, because Anne was involved, that made you think Katy was the fourth member of the gang?"

"Katy has been...well...living with Anne. For a while now."

"Do your parents know Katy was likely involved in the robbery?"

Vera nodded a weak affirmative but her words were less sure. "I...I think so. They saw the news report too. I could tell it bothered them but they didn't say anything to me. Could be why they were weirder than usual when you spoke to them though."

"You overheard?"

"Most of it. There's a...echo, I guess. Where I was standing. Some pipe. Plus, I've got really good hearing."

Concho smiled. "So do I."

"Are you Katy's friend? I mean, if she called you and all?"

"I'll tell you up front, I haven't met Katy directly and I'm a law officer. I'll have to arrest her for her part in the robbery. But, I think there's more to it than just a bank robbery. And I doubt Katy knew about the secret agenda. I think she's in trouble because of it. I want to find her and make sure she's all right."

"And you can protect her?"

"I'll do my best. I'll make sure she's in a safe place with myself or people I trust to watch over her. She'll have to be charged with the robbery but I didn't find any history of criminal activity for her. And she's young. She's likely to get a light sentence."

Vera nodded. "I'm going to trust you because I get a good feeling about you. And I'm worried about Katy. And because my parents won't do anything. And I...I can't do anything!"

"I appreciate your trust," Concho said.

"I don't know a lot. Katy doesn't live at home anymore. She... calls me sometimes. She's always worried about me. She told me Wednesday she'd be out of touch a while but not to worry. And the robbery was on Thursday. I knew she was staying at Anne's place. I can tell you where it is. But I don't guess she's still there right now. But maybe it will help."

"It'll certainly help, Vera."

"714 Butcher Street. It's an apartment complex. Anne was on the third floor. Number 316."

Concho etched it in his memory, then plucked up his cell phone from the holding slot beneath the radio. "Let me give you my cell phone number," he said. "If there's anything else you need to talk to me about, you can call me. And I'll get yours too, so I can call you if I have news about Katy."

Vera nodded and took out her own phone. They exchanged numbers.

"I'm sending you a recent picture of Katy," Vera said as she worked her fingers across her keypad.

Concho's cell chimed. He saw the message from Vera and opened it to find a picture attached. It showed the young woman who'd thrown him a kiss from the back of a getaway car. Clearly, it was a selfie of a very pretty young woman with a lot on her mind."

"I better go," Vera said.

"All right. And thanks."

Vera's gaze finally met his directly. "I hope you're not lying to me. Most adults lie."

Concho nodded. "A lot of 'em do," he said. "But I'm not one of those."

Without saying anything else, Vera opened the door of the Ford and slipped out. Concho saw her in the mirror walking quickly toward the back of her house. He called Isaac Parkland to tell him that Katy Delchamp was the last of the four bank robbers but asked him to keep it quiet to the public for now. Slipping his truck into gear, he headed for Butcher Street.

***

Butcher Street ran through one of the poorest and rough-est neighborhoods in Eagle Pass, a huge contrast to the street on which the Delchamps lived. Concho pulled his truck to the curb at 714 Butcher Street, in front of an apartment building called Pueblo

Luna. A pueblo was usually built of adobe but this three-story complex had been constructed of dull yellow brick with fake red shutters around the front windows and tiny iron-railed balconies hanging off the back of the apartments. The place had seen better days.

More than a dozen loiterers in front of the building watched Concho intently as he climbed out of his Ford F-150. All were Hispanic, men and women, or boys and girls judging by their ages. Most were surely law-abiding citizens but a few were likely gang-bangers who wouldn't be happy to have a lawman visiting.

For the edification of the latter, Concho let them all see him lock his truck and set the alarm. He also made sure they noticed the circle-and-star badge on his chest and the two Colt Double Eagle semiautomatics holstered at his hips. He offered them a smile as he walked past and took the stairs up toward the third floor.

Apartment 316 lay just past mid-way along the level. The yellow paint on the door was cracked and flaking, like mud in a dried-up creek. A cell phone rang inside the apartment as Concho reached the room. No doubt, someone was being warned of his approach.

A dark circle on the door's faded paint indicated where there'd once been a knocker. It was gone. Concho stood to one side of the door, behind the bricks, and banged on the particle board three times with the knuckles of his left hand. His right hand was wrapped around the butt of a Colt .45.

The door opened six inches. No chain lock hung on this door which would make it easy to kick in if he needed to. The face that showed in the gap was male, Hispanic, late twenties, with bristle cut hair and an eagle tattoo on the neck.

"Whatcha want, man?" the fellow demanded.

"I'm looking to talk to either Anne Reese or Katy Delchamp," Concho said.

"Don't know 'em."

The door started to close and Concho stuck his boot in the crack to keep it open. "Anne Reese lives here," he said calmly, "so if you don't know her, maybe you better get out of her apartment."

The man smirked. "Oh, Anne. Reese, did you say?" He snapped his fingers. "Yeah, yeah, she lives here. Or did until a couple days ago. She gone now. She asked us to watch her place for her."

Concho could see at least three other men in the apartment behind the fellow at the door. "Looks like you brought a whole crew to help you," he said.

"Yeah, man. This a rough neighborhood. Us law abiding citizens gotta watch out for each other."

"Did Anne have another woman living here with her?"

"Not that I know, man."

"Well, I'd like to come in and have a look around if you don't mind. Then I'll get right out of your hair."

The man grinned. "But I do mind, Officer Ranger. Maybe you show me your warrant, right?"

"I don't need a warrant given the fact you don't own the apartment. I also suspect a crime is being committed inside at this moment."

"Crime?" the fellow said indignantly. "What you talkin' about crime?"

"I smell methamphetamine residue."

The gangbanger's grin turned to a feral snarl. He shouted, "To hell with you, man!" and started to slam the door.

Concho lunged with his left shoulder, striking the door and sending it hammering back into the face behind it. The impact sounded like a drum being hit by a baseball bat. The fellow staggered backward, tripped over a rug and fell. Concho stepped inside.

Four other young men occupied the room. Two of them leaped up from the couch and hurled themselves at Concho. A third, standing beside the couch, froze. The fourth fled.

Though Concho's hand rested on his pistol, he didn't draw it. Instead, he launched himself to meet the two men charging at him. His long arms swept out and clotheslined them both, sweeping them off their feet before slamming them down with an earthquake crash to the floor. Each of them released an aborted cry as the impact stole their breath. As Concho rose, they struggled for air and forgot about fighting.

The frozen gangbanger unfroze long enough to draw a knife and hold it up in front of him. Concho walked toward him. The fellow shook. He shoved the knife awkwardly toward Concho who slapped it out of his hand. The Ranger grabbed the fellow by the collar of his oversize T-shirt. Jerking the young man around, Concho shoved him stumbling backward onto the couch.

"Sit down and stay down!" Concho ordered.

The gangbanger who'd manned the door had climbed groggily back to his feet. He was shaking his head to clear it when Concho turned toward him. He glimpsed fear and anger leap together into the youth's latte-brown eyes. He knew what that meant.

The man's hand snaked behind his back as he yanked a revolver from his belt and brought it slinging around toward Concho.

CHAPTER 13

"Tell it to me again," Mason French said slowly as if he were dealing with an imbecile.

From the cot in the room serving as her cell, Catherine James stared up at the tall shape standing over her. She rubbed her cheek where he'd struck her with the back of his hand but she wouldn't let any tears flow.

Yesterday, she'd told this man about the robbery and its setup and aftermath more than once. He hadn't liked what she'd said, or, more importantly, what she hadn't said—what she didn't know.

He'd dragged her out the back door of his bar and locked her in a sparsely furnished bedroom of a nearby trailer with a couple of gallon water jugs, a plastic washing basin, and a bucket with a roll of toilet paper for her physical needs. He'd choked her yesterday but hadn't hit her until today. She didn't imagine this was the last time she'd feel his hand.

Overnight, she'd sought ways to escape. The door was locked and reinforced with some heavy weight pushed against it. She could have broken the window glass but she'd have to get through the bars beyond. There had been a small screwdriver set in her backpack but that had been taken away and an examination of her prison had revealed nothing of use as a tool or a weapon. She had only a camouflage-colored hammock for a cot, the bucket, and one big candle, which French had lit and let burn.

Catherine had considered using the candle to set fire to the room but decided against it. She had no reason to believe that French wouldn't let her burn to death. He'd made it clear her life meant nothing to him. She felt lucky not to have been significantly beaten yet. She could live with the bruises she'd picked up so far.

"I..." Catherine started. "I wasn't told about the robbery until just a few days before it happened. Anne had been planning it with Tessa. And maybe with Cindy—"

"That's Tessa Mercadel and Cindy Barnes," French interrupted.

Catherine recognized French testing her. She knew she couldn't fail or there'd be punishment. "No," she said. "Cindy Karnes. She was our driver. She stayed in the car. Tessa and Anne went in first. I came in next. We wore ski masks.

"As soon as we were inside, Tessa pulled her gun. She had one of those...machine pistols. She didn't shoot it but she waved it around. There were a few screams and then everything got quiet. Anne and I had sacks for the loot. Anne went to the tellers on the left and motioned me to the right. We both said the same thing as we handed the tellers the sacks. 'Put all the greenbacks in the bags. No coins. No tricks.' We'd practiced it."

"How much did you get?"

"I told you, I don't know. There was a lot of money in the sacks when we left the bank. It felt like thousands but there was no chance to count it. And I didn't see how much Anne got."

"What about the guard?"

Catherine nodded. "I was coming to that. We knew he was there. Tessa focused on him first. She had him under control. I couldn't tell you exactly what happened. We left the bank one by one. I went first. I was outside when I heard the gunshot. Anne came running out saying the guard tried to grab Tessa's gun and she'd grazed his arm with a warning shot. I guess he was hurt a little worse than that."

"What happened after you left the bank?"

"Tessa covered us. We ran to the car. I handed Anne my sacks of loot. Once we were in the car, she stuck everything into a big gray gym bag. She had it with her from then on.

"The ski masks were hot. Uncomfortable. I think we all pulled ours off once we were in the car and going. We knew there weren't cameras on us anymore. But as we pulled out of the parking lot, a big white pickup tried to cut us off. It had lights and sirens so we realized it was an unmarked police vehicle. Cindy managed to avoid the truck at first. We got on the road but it followed right behind us. We were so close I could see the driver. He looked like a big dude. Big as you. But black. Or maybe Indian.

"Anne shot at him with her pistol but I don't think she hit anything. He rammed us. What I think they call a...pit maneuver. Ran us off the road. When we crashed, I ran one way and Anne ran the other. She had the money bag. I saw the big cop running after her and that was the last I saw."

Catherine fought an urge to look away from Mason French. Everything else she'd said had been the truth. But here she'd lied. She'd actually seen the big trooper capture Anne. She'd watched a Cadillac Escalade charge at the two as they crossed a road after. Whoever had been in the Cadillac had gotten the bag full of money.

Catherine had assumed, at the time, it was Mason French or his allies in the Escalade. She knew Anne had told the bar owner about the robbery, figured he'd followed them as backup. But French acted as if he had no idea what happened to the cash and was grilling her to find out. That meant the information was valuable and dangerous. She had to hang onto it as long as possible.

"You didn't have a gun?" French asked.

"I...well, I did. But Anne took it and put it in the gym bag with the money after we left the bank. It wasn't loaded anyway. I could never have shot anyone."

"Why'd you leave that part out?"

"I didn't mean to. I just didn't think of it."

French smirked as if he didn't believe her words. He didn't hit her again, though. "How did you manage to get away?"

Catherine shrugged. "I just ran and kept on running. The cop went after Anne. He was the only policeman there at first. I didn't see the others but I heard a whole lot of sirens. Eventually, I made it to where we'd stashed another vehicle. An old oil well off 277. We had a change of clothes there and some wigs. I didn't have a wig but put on a cap. We'd left the car unlocked but only Anne had the keys to start it. I took my clothes and hiked away on foot."

French shook his head. He lifted his hand which looked as big as a football. His whole body was huge, like a mountain. He leaned closer to her and Catherine shrank back. Her heart began to pound and a brassy taste filled her mouth.

"That's not exactly what you told me yesterday," French said softly, almost whispering.

"I…uh, sorry, I…yes, I waited a while. Hoping one of the others might make it. But they didn't show up. I probably waited an hour. Maybe a little more."

"Then, somehow, you made your way here."

"No! Not at first. I…I spent the night in a barn. But I remembered Anne mentioning you to us. Saying that if anything went really wrong, we should go to Mason French at a bar called 'Hot, Blue and Righteous.' She said it was about forty miles outside Eagle Pass. Down 277. I hitched a ride with a trucker. You know the rest."

"Who else did you talk to besides the trucker?"

"I didn't even talk to him. I mean, I didn't tell him anything about the bank robbery. I just rode with him."

"But surely you called someone during your lonely night in the barn. Who?"

Catherine's heart had calmed but it began to thud again as French asked her this question. Again, she was about to lie. She prayed he wouldn't find out.

"We had…burner phones. For emergencies. I tried calling

Anne and Tessa. When they didn't answer after a few rings I hung up. I figured they'd been caught. I broke the phone. Pounded it with a rock and threw it away."

"Who told you to do that?"

"Anne."

French shook his head. "You can't be giving me the whole story. The robbery was on the news already on Thursday night. Anne's name was mentioned. And her arrest. But nothing about the money. And nothing since. Officially. So, the cops didn't get it back. That means Anne managed to hide it. Or, your whole story is a pile of steaming crap.

"And, now, I hear," he continued, "unofficially from certain sources, that some heavyweights are looking for you. People who wouldn't give a shit about the kind of money you'd get robbing a small bank branch. So, what are they looking for? What else did you all take?"

"Nothing! I promise. I mean, nothing I know of. Anne and Tessa were running everythi—"

French flicked her with a big finger against her already bruised cheek. It stung and she flinched back. Catherine's jailer brought his hands together, cracked his knuckles in front of her face. Fear brought words pouring out of her.

"I swear I don't know about anything else. But I think you must be right. Anne had to be behind it. Maybe Tessa knew too. It must have been something one of the teller's gave Anne. But me," she shook her head. "I was just," and she didn't have to fake the tinge of bitterness filling her words, "cannon fodder."

French tsk tsked but straightened and moved away from her. "And yet you're the only one who is still free," he said. "Odd."

Catherine shrugged. "I can't tell you why."

French grinned. It wasn't a humorous expression. "Can't, or won't."

"Please," Catherine begged. "Just…let me go. I won't tell anyone anything. I'll forget everything about you. I don't really know anything anyway."

"I let you go and you'll get your cute little ass arrested ten minutes later. And the cops will break you. You'll lead 'em right to my door."

"Then help me. I came here for help. Like Anne told me. You could help me get across the border. Get set up somewhere safe."

"Costs money, little lady."

"I can pay you back. Over time. I just need a stake. You would have helped Anne," she finished accusingly.

French grinned again, with more humor, albeit a sly humor. "Maybe. Anne owed me a lot of money. She would have had to pay that off first. But, if she'd helped ole French out a bit. Like she used to. I might have been lenient. Of course," he leered, "you could help ole French out yourself."

Catherine suppressed the shudder she felt. "Please, I…I'm not really like that."

"Hmph," French said. "then I guess you sit right here shitting in a bucket until I find out what I need to know."

He turned away and slammed the door behind him as he left. She heard the sound of something heavy being pushed against the door. And she was alone again with her nightmare worries.

CHAPTER 14

The gangbanger's pistol swung toward Concho, with a finger already on the trigger. The Ranger snapped a kick into the wrist behind the pistol, knocking the hand upward and driving the hammer of the gun back into the fellow's face. The weapon discharged harmlessly into the ceiling as the fellow cried out.

In one stride, Concho reached the would-be gunman, grabbed the barrel of the pistol and twisted it downward. The young man screamed as his finger was caught inside the trigger guard and bent backward. Concho smashed a left jab into the fellow's chin, and he wilted in his tracks. The Ranger jerked the revolver away, snapped the cylinder open and dumped the cartridges on the floor in a slow rain of brass-jacketed bullets.

Another of the gang started to push himself up from the floor where he'd been slammed down. Concho kicked his elbow, collapsing the arm and dropping him back to the carpet.

"Stay down!" Concho ordered, his voice harsh.

Something crashed in the bathroom, where one of the gang members had fled. Concho rushed toward the sound, bulled the door open as he leaped inside. A young man was halfway out the window but the opening had proven too small for his hips and he was stuck with his legs flailing wildly.

Concho grabbed the young man by his ankles and jerked. The fellow came free and fell into the porcelain tub, cracking his elbow and chin in the descent. Concho pulled the moaning gangbanger across the bathroom floor and out into the living room where he slung him down among the other injured and half-conscious bad boys.

"You can't do this, man! You can't do this," one of the trouble-makers shouted.

"Just did," Concho said. "I didn't have the slightest interest in you boys. And maybe I still won't, if you answer my questions and don't give me any more crap. What do you say?"

Concho studied the sullen faces in front of him. He began to see nods.

"Who was the woman living with Anne Reese?" he demanded.

The young man who'd tried to flee through the bathroom window looked barely eighteen. He was rubbing his chin with his left hand and rubbing the elbow of that arm with his right. He answered Concho in a whiney voice.

"She went by Catherine James."

Concho pulled his phone out of his pocket and called up the picture Vera Delchamp had sent him of her sister. He enlarged the image and held the phone out for the men to see.

"Her?"

"Yeah, man, that's her," another gang member said, who was pinching his bloody nose closed with two fingers.

So, Concho mused, Katy Delchamp had been going by Catherine James and, on the phone, she'd given him yet another alias, albeit a pretty obvious one. Why? What did a twenty-two-year-old woman need with multiple names?

"Which room was she in?" Concho asked.

The fellow with the damaged nose gestured to the hallway leading to the apartment's two bedrooms. "On the right," he muttered.

"Anyone seen her since yesterday?"

Negative head shakes made the rounds.

Concho nodded as he studied the group. "All right, anyone who is not out of here in the next three minutes is going to jail. And if I see you outside when I leave, or if there's anything been done to my vehicle, I'm gonna hunt all of you down and put a bullet in you. We clear?"

This time affirmative nods made the rounds.

"What about my gun?" asked the fellow who'd pulled the revolver on Concho.

The lawman gave him a look. "You didn't just seriously ask that, did you?"

"Come on, man!" another of the gangbangers said as he climbed to his feet. "Let's just get outta here. Before he changes his mind."

"And I can feel the winds of change coming," Concho said, which earned him a few dirty looks but a much faster-paced exit by the gang members.

After the apartment had cleared, Concho tucked the confiscated revolver into his belt at the small of his back and walked down the hall to Katy Delchamp's—alias Catherine James's—room.

The door was open, the bed unmade. No posters hung on the wall. A small white writing desk with attached bookshelves stood in front of the lone window. The shelves held just three books, The Hunger Games Trilogy. A glance at the flyleaf in each book showed they'd been signed to Katy by Suzanne Collins, the author.

A plastic shopping bag from JCPenney rested on the shelf beneath the books and Concho slipped all three novels into the bag. He'd take them with him though he couldn't quite say why.

The closet held a few T-shirts, a short-set, and a couple of pairs of jeans. There was only one dress, a white cotton piece for casualwear. Concho checked pockets in the clothes but found nothing. Nor did he find anything in the two pairs of shoes on the floor. He turned to the bed.

Nothing had been hidden under the pillow or mattress or under the bed itself. A small bedside table held a clock radio and a book of matches with a green cover. Concho picked up the matches. It showed a bar on the front side and gave a name on the back—Hot, Blue and Righteous. The address lay along Highway 277 out of Eagle Pass, the same highway where the bank robbery had occurred, though much farther out.

When Concho opened the matchbook, he found not a single one had been used. That brought a frown to his face. He tucked the matches into his shirt pocket. A quick reconnaissance of the rest of the apartment revealed no useful information. Concho picked up the bullets he'd dumped from the gangbanger's revolver and stuck them in a pocket before leaving the building.

No one remained in sight, not even the loiterers from earlier. And his truck stood unmolested. He smiled as he climbed in, after placing the book bag on the floor in the Ford's extended cab area. Reloading the revolver, he stashed it in his glove box, then radioed Texas Ranger headquarters.

After reporting on his day's activities and findings so far, he asked for everything they had on Hot, Blue and Righteous. He'd decided to give that bar a visit.

***

Concho was using his phone to map out a trip to Hot, Blue and Righteous when an idea occurred to him that might solve one of the smaller mysteries of the bank robbery—how the people in the Escalade had known where Concho and Anne Reese would be with the money in order to steal it. He quickly dialed the number for Terrill Hoight, the first Maverick County deputy to arrive at the scene where the bank robbers crashed their car and who Concho had turned Anne Reese over to at the wreck site.

"Ten-Wolves," Hoight said as he answered his cell. "What can I do you for?"

"Quick question about the woman Anne Reese."

"Shoot."

"Did she have a cell phone on her when you patted her down?"

"Uhm, yeah, yeah she did. Why?"

"Because that's how the folks in the Escalade knew where to find her and steal the duffle bag of loot back from us. They were using her phone like a GPS. Means she was probably working with them. She had to have given them the number to trace."

"Right!" Hoight said. "Didn't even think of that. Don't reckon we can get her to verify it now, though."

"No," Concho said. "But it may be one of the reasons someone had her killed. Did you get anything helpful from the two women involved?"

"No. They've both clammed up like constipated turtles."

"Colorful simile," Concho said.

"Should I be insulted by what you just called me?"

Concho laughed. "You need to join my book club," he said. "But hey, I'd still like to question those two at some point."

"Right. Sheriff Parkland mentioned you wanted to. I don't guess he's had a chance to call you. He's been busy dealing with reporters. He wants to keep Reese's murder out of the news until we can get a few answers but the newshounds are getting restless. They wanna know how we could let something like that happen right under our noses. I'd take them in and introduce them personally to some of our fine inmates if it were me but the Sheriff is a bit more diplomatic."

"Yeah. I imagine he's wading through it all and calling it brown. Thanks for the information."

"No problem. Stay safe."

"Afraid that ship has sailed," Concho said as he ended the call.

CHAPTER 15

Concho was on Highway 277, already headed for Hot, Blue and Righteous, when the radio squawked and the dispatcher came on with information for him. This dispatcher's name was Raul Molina. Concho and Raul had been members of the same Texas Ranger class and Molina was his best friend on the force although they didn't get to see each other very often. Molina had a sense of humor and, as a clan, the Rangers tended toward serious types.

"You decent?" Molina asked through the radio.

"Never have been," Concho replied. "But what have you got for me?"

"Mason French," Molina said. "He's the guy who owns and operates Hot, Blue and Righteous. Age 39. Listed as 6'6" and 290. He's a big dude, bigger than you, Ten-Wolves."

"Hard to believe."

"Ain't it, though. Oh, and conveniently, his address is a trailer right behind his bar."

"Easy to find. What about his background?"

Concho heard rustling through the mic and knew Raul was shuffling papers around.

"Not much. Been arrested once. For assault. The charges were dropped. He's been questioned a few times for fights at his bar."

"Nothing unusual about that," Concho said.

"Nope. The assault charge was from a woman though. Looking it over now, I'd say she might have dropped the charges out of fear."

"Not good!"

"No. If there was one, you can bet there've been others."

"Probably."

"The bar itself looks to be something of a biker hangout," Molina continued. "I guess you caught the reference dropped in the place's name?"

"ZZ Top."

"Indeed.

"'La Grange' is the best driving song of the ages."

"Afraid not, big fellow. It's 'Radar Love.'"

"You never did have good sense, Molina."

"Got both the sense and the taste. Better than yours."

Concho chuckled.

"But hey," Molina said. "Something about this guy sets off the old alarm bells. Be careful with this one, you hear!"

"Sure thing, Mama Hen."

"Hmmm." Molina clicked off and Concho rehung his mic.

Another twenty-five minutes on and Concho sighted a big unlit pole sign advertising "Hot, Blue and Righteous: A Blues Bar." Just past the sign lay a cinder top parking lot and a metal-sided, one-story building about the length of two train cars. The place had an industrial feel and stood in an area zoned for industry but, even at 3:00 in the afternoon, it looked busy.

Concho turned into the parking lot and selected a space about three rows back from the building. The row was empty of vehicles, giving him room to maneuver if he needed to leave quickly.

Right in front of the building, to either side of the incongruous forest green front door, leaned a dozen motorcycles, a mix of cruisers to the left and crotch rockets to the right. Elsewhere, he saw several country boy pickups and one big tractor-trailer taking up several parking spaces. Next to a side door, on the left of the building, sat a dirty white panel van that screamed serial killer.

As Concho stepped out onto the parking lot's blacktop, the heat hit him from all directions and he began to sweat. A fitful breeze rang an occasional snap out of the American flag flying on a wooden pole next to the bar's door. The same breeze brought him the smells of hot tar and exhaust and a whiff of stale urine.

Concho wondered what exactly he expected to find here. That Katy Delchamp had a matchbook with this bar's address on it in her room didn't mean much. People shared those around. But the fact that none of the matches had been used intrigued him. It was as if whoever had taken the matches had done so more for the address of the bar than the practicality of carrying fire with them. And, Concho had a feeling. He'd been getting a lot of those with this case.

Opening the bar's door, he stepped inside. The interior was shadowy and dim but not much cooler than outside. He guessed the AC either wasn't working or had been set high to save money. The place didn't look terribly prosperous: The floor was sticky, the tables battered, the faux-leather covered bar stools patched.

But, almost a dozen bikers clustered around a couple of pool tables to one side, and plenty of barstools had drinkers firmly seated. The right side of the bar, farthest from the bikers and closest to a room bearing the sign 'Office,' was the least crowded. Concho pushed aside a stool there and leaned his elbows on the scuffed surface of the bar as he looked toward the bartender who was polishing glasses and chatting with a patron.

Bartenders in such places tended to either be attractive women or big, burly guys. This one was male, of the burly type, with a thick wiry beard and the beginnings of a significant gut. He ignored Concho. The Ranger wondered whether it was his badge or the color of his skin. When he gazed around the place again, he decided it was likely the skin. Except for one biker who looked like he might have some Mexican ancestry, there weren't any brown-toned folks here.

After waiting another minute and still not being acknowledged, Concho strode down the length of the bar and stopped directly in front of the bartender. The man looked up with hostile eyes. Concho showed him his best shark smile.

"I won't trouble you with having to tell me you don't serve my kind here," he said. "But you need to get your boss out here before I decide to check around and see what local ordinances you might be breaking."

"What boss you talkin' about, boy? Several folks around, I call boss. None of 'em are you."

Concho grinned at the collection of insults. "That would be Mason French."

"He ain't here."

"Not in the room over there, eh?" Concho said, nodding his head toward the door marked 'Office.'

"That's what I said. You hard of hearin', boy?"

Concho grinned again, then slowly and deliberately let the grin fade while the man watched him.

"That's twice," Concho said evenly. "So you've showed everyone what a helluva man you are but you don't get a third. Now, go knock on the office door and tell whatever boss is inside that a Texas Ranger wants to see him."

The patron who the bartender had been talking to looked up from his stool as if about to say something. He thought better of it when he noted Concho's size and took a sip of his drink instead. Meanwhile, the bartender was fighting an inner war revealed only by the tightening of every muscle in his face.

Finally, the crowfeet around the bartender's eyes loosened and he responded with a "Hmph" and a "You ain't gonna much like what you get."

"I'm adaptable."

The bartender stared for just an instant longer before doing as he was told. The office opened at the knock and a second man, who had to bend down to get his eyes below the top of the door, looked out. He was big enough to fill the whole doorframe, and his smile held a bit of shark too as he listened to his employee's whisper and then looked toward Concho and said,

"Hello, Officer. I'm Mason French. What can I do for you?"

Concho approached French. He wasn't used to having to look up to meet anyone's gaze but he didn't let it bother him.

"We can talk out here or in your office," Concho said. "Whichever you prefer."

French shrugged, but stepped back from the door and held it open for Concho to pass through. The Ranger stepped inside but made sure not to turn his back. Now he understood what Raul Molina had meant about "alarm bells." In his bones, he felt it; Mason French was a dangerous fellow and it was far more than just his height and weight.

Both chairs in French's office were big enough to accommodate men of size. Concho felt grateful as he dropped into the visitor's chair and it didn't even creak underneath him. French walked his way around the battered wooden desk and lowered himself into his own seat. He wasted no time with niceties.

"Why are you here, Ranger?"

A cherry red bowl full of green matchbooks rested on French's desk. Concho picked up a book. "One of these led me here," he replied. "A woman I'm looking for had it."

French's glance flicked to the matchbook and back to Concho. "We distribute a thousand of those a year."

"I figured," Concho said as he slid his phone out of his pocket and called up the image Vera Delchamp had given him of her sister, Katy. "But I'm only interested in the one this woman took." He held it out across the desk for French to study.

French leaned forward to examine the picture. It's difficult for even trained liars to avoid showing the flash of recognition in their eyes when they see someone they know. The pupils dilate to the familiar. But the room was relatively dim and maybe French was really good. Concho thought he saw a brief flicker in the dark, amber-colored irises but couldn't be absolutely sure.

"Don't recognize her," French said, leaning back in his chair again. "What's her name?"

Concho watched the man carefully as he said, "Catherine James."

"Hum, don't recognize the name either but it sounds made up."

Concho saw no flash in French's eyes this time. He was sure. Maybe it just meant the bar owner was ready for the name.

"Oh? Why do you say it's fake?"

French offered a half smile, a half smirk. "I own a bar. I've seen a whole lot of fake IDs. You pick up certain things."

"I suppose so." The Ranger slid his phone into his shirt pocket. "Let me run some other names by you."

"OK."

"Tessa Mercadel?"

"Nope."

"Cindy Karnes?"

"Nada."

"How about Anne Reese?"

There was no flash in French's eyes at mention of the red-headed bank robber but there was just the faintest hesitation before he replied. Concho smiled to himself, though he didn't let it show on the outside. French knew Anne Reese, or at least knew of her.

French was quick witted, though. He must have realized what his hesitation had cost him and tried to recover.

"Weise, did you say? I know an Anna Marie Weise."

"Anne Reese," Concho repeated carefully.

"Ah," French said. "Afraid not. An Anna Weise used to come in here but I haven't seen her in a while."

Concho nodded and rose from his chair. "Maybe I'll show the picture around to some of your patrons," he said.

French shrugged. "Be careful around Jack. He's the bartender. Seems like you two didn't hit it off."

"I think I'm off his Christmas list."

French laughed. "Yeah, he's a racist son-of-a-bitch but he makes a helluva Bloody Mary."

"Glad to see you have your hiring priorities straight," Concho replied as he turned and left the room.

CHAPTER 16

Concho showed the picture of Katy Delchamp to the pa-trons of Hot, Blue and Righteous, although he gave her name as Catherine James. No one admitted they'd seen her and he believed them all—except the bartender, Jack. When he first showed the picture to Jack, the man barely glanced at it before denying any knowledge of Catherine.

"The sooner you take a real look," Concho told him, "the sooner I'll shake the dust of this place off my boots and you can get back to imagining a world where everyone looks just like you."

Jack gave Concho a glare but withheld the comment he clearly wanted to spill. Instead, he looked at the picture again and Concho got exactly what he hoped for—a little flash of recognition.

"Like I said, never seen the tail before," Jack snapped.

Concho's teeth ground together at Jack's words. He came very close to reaching over the bar and treating the fellow to what many called a "bitch-slapping." But, right now, he needed to find Katy and kicking Jack's ass wouldn't help him accomplish that even if it did make him feel better.

Concho stuck the phone in his pocket and said, "You have a

pleasant rest of the day," and walked out. He reached his truck and sat quietly in it for a bit, then started the engine and pulled out onto the highway, heading back in the direction of Eagle Pass.

He wasn't going home just yet.

***

Fifteen minutes after Concho left the bar, Mason French came out of his office and walked over to Jack.

"He gone?" Mason asked.

"Yeah," Jack said. "I watched him pull out on the road. He was headed toward Eagle Pass."

"Good. I didn't like that boy much."

Jack shrugged. "Just another dumbass spear chucker. Not much to worry about."

Mason stared at Jack, then shook his head. "If you had the brains to blow your own nose, I'd be surprised," he said.

"What?" Jack asked, his feelings clearly hurt.

"Just sling your drinks and try not to think too much," Mason snapped. "It's not a good look for you." He walked away before Jack could say anything else.

Mason made the rounds of the bar, talking to patrons and doing what he liked to call "winning friends and influencing people." He spent the most time with the bikers playing pool. They always responded well to him. He'd been one of them himself for a while and had maintained his contacts, particularly some lucrative ones.

Finally, he went into the bar's small kitchen, which seldom saw use since his cook had quit after catching Mason and his wife doing the deed in a stall of the men's room. Throwing a skillet on the stove with some butter in it, Mason turned on the burner. He took two ready-made hamburger patties out of the refrigerator and set them to frying. While they cooked, he got two plates ready with buns, Miracle Whip, and slices of tomato.

He needed to feed his prisoner. She'd had nothing to eat for over a day. That should have loosened her up. Being the bad cop hadn't gotten him anywhere though. Time for some good cop action. He'd eat with her, play nice, get her to relax, make a few promises.

He still suspected this Catherine James of lying about not knowing the full agenda of the bank robbery. "Catherine" wasn't her real name, of course. Anne Reese had been protecting her for some reason. She'd described the girl as naïve but trustworthy. Surely, Anne had told her there was more to the robbery than just cash. But it was possible she hadn't.

Anne owed Mason a considerable sum and had promised him the score from the robbery would pay her debt. If he'd been able to get his hands on her, he would have made Anne tell him the whole story herself. But she'd played it coy all along, had spoken to him only on the phone. And now she was in jail.

So, he was flying half blind but he could smell bullshit on the wind. He'd learn the truth one way or the other soon. If good cop didn't work, he'd go all the way to maniac cop. Catherine would give him what he wanted then and, if she couldn't, he'd have to find other ways for her to provide him what he needed. It had been too long since he'd let the "beast", as he called it, loose with a woman. Afterward, it would be easy enough for her body to disappear.

While the burgers sizzled in the pan, Mason French's mood began to lift. He started to whistle.

***

Half a mile down the road from Mason French's bar, Concho turned off Highway 277 and crossed a cattle grate onto a dirt road leading back to an oil well. The well was old but the pump-jack still worked with a steady kachunka, kachunka, kachunka.

A small metal frame building stood next to the wellhead and Concho parked his truck behind it where no one from the road could see it. He stepped out of his vehicle into the late afternoon heat which was at its peak for the day. Soon, the long fingers of evening would begin to feel their way across the land but, for now, the sun ruled.

Concho stripped off his white dress shirt and threw it in the truck, leaving only a black cotton T-shirt beneath. He opened the extended cab and pulled out a pair of binoculars, then started hiking across the field back toward Hot, Blue and Righteous, moving quickly but staying behind bushes and trees and hillocks whenever he could.

According to Raul Molina, the Texas Rangers' dispatcher, Mason French lived in a trailer behind his bar. Concho soon located the trailer, which looked in better repair than the bar itself. Maybe this was where French spent his money.

After examining the trailer from several angles and checking carefully for any surveillance cameras, Concho bellied down behind some big clumps of bunch grass on a hillock about seventy-five yards away. He chose a place where the sun wouldn't have a chance to refract from the lenses of his binoculars as he raised them to his eyes and began to practice the patience of a hunter.

His waiting took less patience than he'd figured it would. Ten minutes after he sat down to watch French's trailer, the man came out of the bar carrying a tray with two loaded plates and what looked like a bottle of wine stacked on it. He walked straight to his front door, unlocked it, and entered.

Immediately, Concho began to work his way closer to his target. The front of the trailer was visible to watchers from the bar but the back was hidden and he'd detected no cameras. He headed there. Reaching the corner of the trailer, he straightened. As many such structures did, French's house sat slightly elevated on stacks of concrete blocks, with a tin skirt around the base to keep out critters.

Concho couldn't be sure what the inside of the trailer looked like but imagined it was probably similar to his own. That meant he'd be outside the master bathroom and bedroom here, with two smaller bedrooms at the other end. About two-thirds of the way along stood a back door with a set of four wooden steps leading up to it.

Trailer walls were thin, he knew. If there'd been anyone in the bathroom he would have heard them moving around. But only silence met his keen ears. He began to work his way along the back of the trailer, listening as he went. It soon paid off as he heard muffled voices coming through the walls in what he guessed was a back bedroom.

A man and a woman were talking. The man must be Mason French. But who was the woman? Concho felt sure he knew. And although he couldn't quite make out the words, he could pick up tones. The male voice sounded calm and smooth. The woman's words were ragged, perhaps afraid.

Concho let his right hand drop to his Colt. He considered forcing his way inside through the back door but, so far, the woman didn't sound as if she were in pain or immediate danger. He hesitated and, a moment later, felt glad he had.

A cell phone rang inside. The man's voice answered. Concho made out the word "Dammit" amid more muffled talking. Footsteps rang on the floor of the trailer. A door opened and closed, followed by the scuffing noise of something heavy being pushed across the floor. The footsteps continued across the trailer, fading into a more distant sound of the front door opening and shutting.

Mason French had been called away. Now was Concho's chance. But how long would he have before the bar owner returned?

CHAPTER 17

Returning to the trailer's back steps, Concho eased up them to the door. A quick peek through the window showed him a laundry room with a washer and dryer. The place was dusty and empty.

Concho's hand found the doorknob. It was locked as he'd expected. He squeezed the knob tight, started to twist. Concho had shoulders nearly as wide as the horns of a Texas bull. His arms were sheathed with muscle packed tight to the bone. He exerted that strength. The tendons corded along his arm.

The doorknob began to turn against its lock, then snapped off in his hand. The lock mechanism fell out to clang on the wooden floor inside. Concho tossed the broken knob away and drew his pistol. A rustle of movement sounded from the room where he'd heard the voices.

Pushing the door open, Concho stepped inside. Silence met his ears. The house seemed to hold its breath. He moved out of the laundry room. Across a narrow hallway stood a bathroom, open and empty. It smelled of Lysol, with an undercurrent of toothpaste and Old Spice aftershave. Apparently, Mason French did believe in hygiene.

To Concho's right were two doors. One of these also stood

open, revealing a small bedroom with nothing in it but an unmade cot. The other door was shut and had a chest of drawers pushed up against it to keep it that way.

Bingo! Concho thought. He leaned his head close to the door and whispered loudly, "Katy! Are you in there?"

"Oh my God, oh my God," a voice came from inside the room. "Who is it? Who's there?"

"It's the Texas Ranger you saw on the day of the robbery. I've come to get you."

"Please, yes please! Before he comes back. I think he's gonna kill me!"

"Stand back," Concho said.

The chest of drawers was heavy but Concho didn't want to risk the noise it would make if he pushed it aside. He grasped the corners and deadlifted it off the ground, then turned and set it down in the doorway of the empty bedroom. The door behind the chest of drawers was also locked. Not a surprise.

Once again, Concho took hold of a doorknob and began to exert his strength. The lock resisted. Concho didn't like that. He wrapped his other hand around the knob as well. Both arms corded with muscle and the lock broke suddenly, with the inside knob falling to the floor in a clatter. A gasp came from within.

The house wasn't quite balanced against gravity. The door creaked open on its own and Concho got his first close up look at Katy Delchamp, alias Catherine James, alias Katniss. She was maybe twenty-two or twenty-three, 5' 2" and just shy of a hundred and twenty pounds. She wore jeans and a dirty white V-necked T-shirt. She looked scared and very vulnerable but not cowed, not beaten down.

"Thank God!" the young woman said as she stared at Concho with wide brown eyes. "How did you find me?"

"No time," Concho said. "Let's get out of here."

Katy nodded and came toward him. He turned and led the way to the back door.

"My backpack!" Katy said, pausing as Concho pushed the broken door open.

"Come on!" Concho replied. "We'll send the cavalry for it later."

Katy nodded and joined him on the steps.

"My truck's a half mile away," Concho said. "Follow me and stay crouched as much as you can. We'll keep low to the ground so we won't be spotted."

"OK," Katy said.

Concho led the way, moving as quickly as he dared. He'd considered waiting at the trailer to surprise Mason French and arrest him. But French wasn't alone at Hot, Blue and Righteous. Who knew how many men inside the bar worked with or for French? Being that this was Texas, most of them probably carried guns.

Katy had important information about a crime and needed to be questioned. But more, she was young and in trouble and needed to be kept safe. And so, Concho retreated, even though it galled him to do so.

In less than ten minutes, the two reached the Ford F-150 where Concho had hidden it behind the oil well. They piled in and pulled out onto Highway 277 in a cloud of dust. He punched the gas, determined to get Katy as far away from Mason French as he could.

This part of 277 was virtually deserted at the moment. The road stretched clear and empty ahead of them. Concho reached for the radio mic to report his status just as Katy spoke in a terrified voice.

"There's something coming up behind us!"

Concho glanced into his rearview mirror. Multiple winks of light were closing fast along the road. With them came a distant high-pitched whine.

"Motorcycles!" he said. "Probably from those at the bar."

"No, no, no!" Katy said. "Are they after us?"

"Likely."

"Can you outrun them?"

Concho shook his head. "Not the sport bikes."

He grabbed the radio mic, keyed it, and spoke through to the Texas Ranger's dispatcher: "Raul! It's Concho! We're a couple miles down 277 from Hot, Blue and Righteous. Headed to Eagle Pass. We've got pursuit. Need backup now!"

He rehung the mic without waiting for an answer, punched his foot to the floor. As the truck leaped forward in response, Concho glanced over at Katy.

"You know how to shoot a gun?"

"I...yes."

"Good! There's a pistol in the glovebox. Loaded. Take it out and get ready! But don't fire it unless you have to."

Concho heard Katy fumbling with the glovebox but he was glancing into his rearview mirror again. Flickers of light closed fast on their position. Sunlight, he imagined, reflecting off the windshields of the big sport bikes he'd seen in the parking lot of Hot, Blue and Righteous.

With his face grim, Concho turned back to the highway and tried to milk another bit of speed from his Ford. The hounds were on the hunt but they had a wolf for their prey.

***

Mason French furiously stuffed clothes, weapons, cash, and Catherine James's green backpack into a gym bag for a possible emergency getaway as he relived the last half hour of his day. He'd been looking forward to playing "good cop" with the woman—and maybe much more—when Jack from the bar called to tell him someone needed to see him immediately.

The someone turned out to be a certain cop of his acquaintance, a man Mason generally called "Scout." Scout had given him information that changed everything. Anne Reese was dead, murdered yesterday morning in jail by a couple of prostitutes. The Sheriff's Department had kept it quiet so it was good for Mason to have friends among the police even if the news disappointed and angered him. Scout also let him know that the woman who called herself Catherine James was really Katy Delchamp, whose father, supposedly, had loads of dough.

Seeing one potential big score about to fall through, but another opportunity looming, he'd stormed back to his trailer only to find the back door broken open. He always kept a Glock 9-millimeter taped under the bar in the kitchen. He'd pulled it out and checked the loads.

A quick look out the back of his trailer showed nothing and when he turned to the room where he'd locked Catherine James, aka Katy Delchamp, he found it empty. His fists clenched; the Glock shook in his hand from rage.

His mind asked "who," and immediately answered itself. Ten-Wolves! It was no coincidence the Texas Ranger had just visited him with questions about Katy. Though how the man had discovered her hidden in his trailer, Mason didn't know.

What he did know was that he wanted Katy Delchamp for more than just the promise of money—although he always had a place in his pocket for green. The girl's vulnerability excited him, and his mouth had started to fill with the brassy taste of "need." Concho Ten-Wolves would pay for interrupting his fun.

Rushing back into the bar, Mason had pulled aside the leader of the motorcyclists and told him what had happened and what he wanted. He handed over six thousand dollars with orders to "Bring the girl back to me alive. Kill the Ranger! Make him hurt!"

CHAPTER 18

The next glance Concho threw into the rearview mirror showed four big sport-type motorcycles closing on his Ford. They were within two hundred yards now, eating the asphalt like candy. The drivers, in leathers and bright helmets, leaned forward and low behind their windshields. Each bike carried a passenger and Concho saw the flash of guns in gloved hands.

Katy had turned to look at them too, out the back windshield. She held the Smith & Wesson .38 revolver the Ranger had taken from the gangbanger at Anne Reese's apartment in her lap but didn't look like she wanted to use it. Her eyes were huge in a pale face.

"Don't look out the window!" Concho snapped. "Keep your head down. Keep your eyes closed. We've got a truck bed, a tool chest, and an extended cab between us and them. Their bullets won't cut through all that but they'll take out the back glass."

Katy gasped but ducked low as Concho ordered.

Concho reached up to his sun visor. A black strap around it held a brown leather case for sunglasses. He flipped the case open, took out a pair of mirror shades and put them on as protection from potential flying glass.

This stretch of 277 ran straight. A glance at the Ford's speedometer showed them doing better than 120 but the engine was starting to strain. Concho eased up slightly on the gas. He glanced into the mirror. The bikes were closer. A hundred yards away. Then fifty. Twenty-five. Twenty! One of the motorcycle passengers swung up his gun.

"Hold on!" Concho shouted to Katy and he hit the brakes.

The closest bike, almost directly behind Concho, was a big orange Yamaha. The driver must have seen the white smoke come boiling up from under Concho's tires. But he was too close. By the time he heard the shriek of the Ford's brakes, he and his passenger were dead men riding. He tried to swerve and didn't make it as the bike slammed like a heat-seeking missile into the bed of the pickup. A gas line ruptured on the motorcycle; a spark ignited. The Yamaha erupted in a ball of fire as its rear end flipped upward in the air.

Katy screamed. Concho both heard and felt the explosion. The push of displaced air slammed against the back of the truck. He fought the Ford as it tried to swap ends. One man, most likely the motorcycle's passenger, came flying through the fiery cloud and crashed down into the bed of the truck. Flames and smoke ran in rivulets across his leathers. His helmet had twisted sideways with his head inside. He wasn't a danger anymore.

The other three cycles had been far enough back to avoid their leader's fate. Their riders leaned. The bikes swept like colored streamers past to either side of the Ford. Gunfire erupted from their passengers and stitched holes along both sides of the pickup.

Machine pistols, Concho thought. Tec-9s or Uzis.

Katy screamed again.

At still better than eighty miles an hour, Concho swerved the pickup as he tried to clip the motorcycle passing on his left. The bike was too nimble. It slid past. The passenger swung his weapon behind him and fired again. Concho had no time to duck. The front windshield vaporized, shedding safety glass like confetti.

Inadvertently, he threw up a hand, but the sunglasses protected his eyes as the glass shrapnel flew past. The skin of his face stung. Cuts, he imagined. He didn't seem to be shot.

Fighting the pummeling force of the wind, Concho yelled to Katy. "Are you hurt? Are you shot?"

"No!" the woman screamed back, barely audible over the shriek of the wind.

Concho glanced toward the motorcycles, out in front of him now. They pulled away but surely weren't breaking off. They'd return.

With a teeth-rattling boom, the right front tire blew out. The truck lurched drunkenly toward the ditch.

***

Raul Molina, a dispatcher for the Texas Rangers Com-pany D, registered the urgency in Concho's voice before his friend disconnected radio contact. He didn't try calling back. Time was critical. For a second, his mind considered the threat of Mason French and how he'd been afraid something like this would happen. For the next second, he considered his immediate options for getting Concho help.

No other Texas Ranger was within fifty miles of Concho's position. He immediately radioed the dispatcher for the Maverick County Sheriff's office, which had jurisdiction in the emergency area. That dispatcher put Molina into direct contact with her deputies in the field. With calm urgency, Molina stated the problem and asked for someone to respond. A deputy named Terrill Hoight answered.

"I'm on Highway 277. Responding. But I'm twenty to twenty-five minutes away."

"Roger." Molina acknowledged, while his mind shouted, "Please hurry!"

Fear for his friend kept roiling in the back of Raul Molina's mind but he didn't let it stop him from contacting every other police agency he knew of for assistance. He had to get the big Ranger all the help he could, as soon as he could. Every tick of the clock was a gold coin of survival slipping through Concho's fingers.

***

Terrill Hoight snapped on his siren and lights and punched the gas on his police interceptor. The tires squealed as he accelerated down Highway 277 in the direction of a bar called Hot, Blue and Righteous. Concho Ten-Wolves was in trouble.

Terrill liked Concho, respected him, though the man wasn't easy to get to know. Ten-Wolves wouldn't call for help if it weren't desperately needed. But right now, the Texas Ranger was a long way away and on his own for at least twenty minutes.

Hoight buried his gas pedal to the floor in an attempt to shave time off that deadline.

***

The right-front tire on Concho's pickup must have been clipped by a bullet when the motorcyclist strafed them in passing. It exploded like a bomb and there was no way to keep the vehicle on the road.

Fortunately, the ditch here was U-shaped rather than V-shaped. They hit it hard and bounced. Concho fought the nearly useless wheel for control while Katy Delchamp cried out in shock. The dead biker in the pickup's bed went flying.

A barbed-wire fence bordered the ditch. They smashed through it, ripping the wires loose in a wild symphony of snaps and spangs. Carrying part of the fence and several metal poles with them, the Ford churned on into the field beyond and slewed sideways before coming to halt in a pall of dust. Something metallic clacked under the vehicle's hood and the engine sputtered and died. Steam boiled up through the grill. Concho feared the truck was about to catch fire.

"Get out!" he snapped at Katy. "Quickly!"

The woman fumbled at the door latch, got it open, and tried to climb out without taking off her seatbelt. Concho snapped it loose for her and she bailed and ducked behind the truck.

Concho followed out of the passenger side after throwing a look back toward the highway. The motorcycles were gone; the whine of their engines fading. The Ranger couldn't imagine the attack was over. Mason French must want Katy back very badly to have his men open fire on a Texas Ranger in the middle of the day. He wasn't going to give up now that his targets had been cornered in an empty field with a broken-down truck.

Concho glanced at Katy. She shook. Tear tracks furrowed the dust on her face. But she still held her revolver. He put his hand on her shoulder.

"I don't think it's over," he said. "Stay ready but don't shoot unless you have a clear target."

Katy nodded, then dashed the tears angrily from her face with the back of a hand.

The steam rising from the big Ford's ruined engine dissipated. Relieved they weren't about to lose their vehicle shield to fire, Concho stepped around Katy and opened the door on the truck's extended cab.

Reaching in, he pulled out a long leather gun case from which he removed a Remington .30-06 hunting rifle with a scope on it. The case had a slot for three extra magazines and Concho stuck these in his pockets. He also snagged a couple of smoke grenades.

After leaning the rifle against the truck, the Ranger grabbed his police body armor. Turning to Katy, he had her stand up while he slid the armor over her head. It hung huge on her, swallowing her upper body and dangling nearly to her knees.

"Keep your arms inside the vest as much as you can," Concho told her.

She nodded.

Concho picked up his rifle and turned back toward the highway. He saw why the motorcycles had kept going. They were only the first round of the assault, meant to stop the Ford and set the Ranger and his passenger up for the second round.

The white panel van he'd seen parked at Mason French's bar skidded to a halt on the shoulder of the road. Concho heard the doors open on the opposite side of the van and caught the movement of men disgorging. He heard slides being racked as guns were readied.

Moving to the front of his truck, Concho lined the Remington up across the hood and squinted through the scope. He waited. Seconds ticked past. Each one seemed to last forever.

Other than their attackers, Concho had not spotted a single vehicle on the road in the last fifteen minutes. It was as if they'd been transported to some apocalyptic future with the only people left alive on earth locked in a kill-or-be-killed scenario.

In short, help wasn't coming. At least, anytime soon. But Hell was due for a visit.

CHAPTER 19

Concho didn't know how many enemies he faced. The van could have held a dozen but he guessed there were no more than six or seven. He needed to cut those odds down if he and Katy were to survive. Fortunately, French's men had to come to him. And they'd take losses in doing so.

Concho soon got his chance to start trimming the weeds. A man's shoulder appeared at the rear of the van. Concho fired. The high velocity .30-06 slug hit meat and bone and both exploded as the gunman was knocked backward by the impact.

In the midst of agony and a scream, the injured man made the ultimate mistake of staggering into the open. Concho put a second slug into his skull and watched brain tissue and blood erupt from the exit wound. The man's body jerked like a marionette and dropped.

Now, the enemy opened fire themselves and slugs began slamming like M-80 firecrackers into the driver's side of the dead Ford. Concho ducked down; Katy sat with her back to the truck's rear tire. She scrunched forward and threw her hands over her ears. Her mouth hung open but she didn't scream.

It sounded to Concho like French's men were armed with AR-15s and similar rifles. The .223 caliber rounds fired by an AR-15 wouldn't penetrate all the way through the Ford. But the same was not true for Concho's .30-06, which he'd loaded with copper-jacketed shells. At the first lull in enemy fire, he leaped up and emptied his rifle's five-round magazine into the side of the van, aiming at a height where men might be standing on the opposite side.

A pair of shouts rewarded Concho, letting him know his shots had punched through both sides of the van, though he couldn't be sure if he'd scored any hits or just surprised them. Dropping the emptied clip from the rifle, Concho pushed a fresh one home. He slid down behind the blown-out front tire and rolled onto his belly.

Where the Ford had settled to rest in the field, the front end sat up a little higher than the rear. Concho could see underneath through the scope on the Remington. He glimpsed gun barrels poking around and over the van and a flurry of unaimed shots hurled his way. None came close enough to do any damage.

Two men tried to use the shooting as cover to rush around the front of the van and throw themselves into the ditch. Concho fired. He hit a target but not the one he wanted. The slug from his Remington smashed into the rifle one man carried and tore it spinning out of his grasp.

The would-be shooter cried out in pain from the sting to his hands but Concho didn't think he'd been seriously harmed. The fellow with him opened fire from a position flat in the ditch. The bullets walked their way toward the lawman and he rolled back behind the pickup's steel wheel just as they stabbed the ground in front of and under the Ford. The ping and whine of ricochets filled the world.

The sun watched from a bright, coppery sky. The heat stomped down as Concho lay in the dirt. He smelled dust and the bitter pollen of ragweed. A scratch on his hand bled; he had no idea how it had been cut. Laying the rifle down, he drew one of his Colts and rolled over to empty the magazine in the direction of the van.

The barrage of fire bought a pause from the enemy as they ducked low to avoid the Ranger's bullets. Concho shoved the Colt back into its holster and grabbed up the rifle again, stealing a glance through the scope toward the ditch.

He thought at least four men hid in the ditch now. The first two must have been joined by others while Concho had his head down. Even as he watched, the grass and wildflowers along the edge of the ditch began to sway back and forth in both directions away from the van. He knew what that meant. At least two of French's gunmen were crawling down the ditch in an effort to flank their position. If they succeeded, it would all be over.

An idea flashed into Concho's mind. He acted on it. Squinting through his scope, he put five rounds into the back, lower section of the van, right where he suspected the gas tank of being located. At least one shot must have punctured the tank. A thin reddish spurt of gas arced out of the van and splashed into the ditch. More gas dripped from underneath the vehicle.

"What the hell!" a man shouted. "He hit the damn gas tank! It's all over the place."

"Stay calm, stay calm!" another voice called. "It ain't gonna hurt you."

But Concho thought it would. He'd reloaded his rifle already but a gunshot would be highly unlikely to set spilled gasoline on fire. He had something better than a bullet for that purpose. Picking up one of the smoke grenades he'd taken from his truck, he rose to his knees, activated the grenade, and hurled it over the hood of his Ford toward the van.

The grenade hit the side of the van with a loud clunk and ignited as it bounced off into the ditch. A white cloud of hexachloroethane-zinc and granular aluminum boiled up. Modern smoke grenades weren't supposed to make a lot of sparks but most still produced some. And the sparks from this one fell into a ready medium of gasoline.

A whumf sounded as the gasoline in the ditch ignited. Red-orange flames whipped up, snapping in the air like a liquid flag. A man began to scream. Concho grabbed his rifle, rose to a crouch behind his truck with his eyes just barely peering over the top of his hood. One of the gunmen in the ditch leaped to his feet, beating madly at his burning clothes. Concho shot him through the head. The screams stopped.

A second man rolled away from the source of the flames but, in his panic, came up on his hands and knees. Concho twisted the rifle barrel toward him and fired. The heavy slug of the .30-06 smashed into the man's right collarbone and tunneled straight on into the body behind it. The fellow collapsed without a sound.

And now the fire leaped up the spitting trail of gasoline to the van. For a bare moment, the world waited. Then the vehicle went off like a bomb, kicking itself up off the asphalt in a tornado of smoke and raging flames. As it crashed back to earth, the windows bulged and shattered, and a wave of fire engulfed the bodies in the ditch and set them alight.

Concho ignored the burning vehicle. He scanned along the road wildly for any remaining enemies. He was sure two men had already been crawling along the ditch away from the van. Had they escaped the explosion? He'd heard no screaming from them but the detonation might have killed them or, more likely, stunned them.

He saw one man running madly down the highway away from the scene. He whipped his rifle up and drew a bead but, through the scope, could tell the man had thrown his gun away and was empty-handed. The Ranger's finger tightened on the trigger, then relaxed. He couldn't shoot a running, unarmed man in the back.

Behind him, Katy Delchamp screamed out his name, "Concho!"

He spun.

CHAPTER 20

As Concho twisted around, he saw what had caused Katy's scream. One of French's men had somehow reached the back of Concho's truck without the Ranger seeing him. The gunman must have lost his rifle but held a deadly-looking black semi-automatic pistol clutched in his hands and was lifting it on target.

Concho's heart slammed into high gear. He started swinging his rifle to bear but knew he'd be too late. Katy intervened. She still carried the .38 revolver but she didn't use it. Instead, she hurled herself into the gunman's legs.

The man had not expected that. His eyes widened. His weapon discharged as he fell backward. The bullet whined past Concho's head. The Ranger's finger tightened on the trigger of the .30-06 but he held his fire. Katy was in the way with her arms wrapped around the man's waist. He darted two steps toward the gunman just as the fellow fired point-blank into Katy's chest.

The young woman cried out, fell back. Concho saw the shooter's eyes, dark and evil-looking as he twisted his pistol toward the Ranger. But Concho had a clear shot and the drop. He triggered the .30-06 three times. Each bullet punched like a brass-knuckled fist into the gunman's body. Blood sprayed as the man jarred. The pistol dropped from his hand. The eyes went from dangerous to terrified and then to dead.

Concho threw a quick look toward the still burning van. No other enemies were in sight. He dropped to one knee beside Katy. She was coughing, her eyes running with tears. Her hands clutched hard at her chest.

"He shot me! He shot me!" she cried.

"Let me see!" Concho said.

Katy's gaze met his. She was scared. Concho let his rifle fall to the ground as he grasped the woman's wrists and pulled her hands apart. A breath of relief purled from his mouth.

"It's OK," he said. "OK. The bullet didn't penetrate the vest."

Katy looked down. She saw an indent in the body armor Concho had dressed her in but no hole and no blood.

"It hurts, though. So bad."

"Impact shock," Concho said. "You'll have a nasty bruise but it'll heal. I've had 'em before."

Katy's breathing began to slow as she processed Concho's words. A spurt of tears followed but she wiped them away. "Thank God," she said. "I didn't want to die."

"Pain is the voice saying you didn't die," Concho said. "But… you saved my life. Thank you."

The realization of what she'd done struck her. "I…I just… didn't know what to do."

"You did good," Concho replied.

He picked up his rifle and rose, reached a hand to help Katy up. She took it and he pulled her to her feet. She winced but flashed him a quick smile. That faded quickly as she gave more thought to their situation.

"Is…is it over?"

Concho had his head up, listening. "I think it is," he said. "I hear sirens. We're about to get some help." He looked down at Katy and grinned. "Not that we need it with you on the job."

The young woman blushed and looked away.

***

Three crotch rocket motorcycles blew past Deputy Terrill Hoight going in the opposite direction as he raced down Highway 277 to reach Concho Ten-Wolves. He ignored them, barely noticed them.

Doing better than 125, he came over a small rise and the wheels of the police interceptor he was driving grew light as he nearly went airborne. He slowed a fraction as gravity grabbed him again, then punched the gas once more as up ahead a sudden bloom of black smoke tornadoed into the sky.

In another minute, Terrill came upon the scene of the smoke. A vehicle of some kind churned furiously with flames in the ditch alongside the road. Beyond that, in the field, stood Ten-Wolves' bullet-ridden truck.

Terrill hit his brakes, swerved onto the wide shoulder of the road to go around the flaming wreckage. He screeched to a halt in the middle of the highway just past the destroyed vehicle. His lights and sirens blared. Bailing out with his pistol in his hand, he looked wildly around for any sign of Concho.

He saw the big Ranger carrying a rifle and striding across the field toward him. A young woman over a foot shorter than the Ranger walked beside him. Terrill had no idea who she might be. He raised his hand. Concho acknowledged. They all met at the edge of the highway.

"What happened?" Terrill asked.

Concho explained, then introduced the deputy to Katy, adding, "This is the last of our bank robbers from the other day. She also just saved my life while putting hers in danger."

Terrill had heard of Katy Delchamp only a little while before in a briefing from Sheriff Parkland but found himself surprised at the last pronouncement. Before he could respond, however, two other police cars screeched up with sirens wailing. The first must have followed him from Eagle Pass. In it rode one of Terrill's fellow deputies in the Maverick County Sheriff's Office, a black officer named Roland Turner.

The second car came from the other direction, from Hot, Blue and Righteous way. It bore the insignia of the State Highway Patrol on the side. A blond officer with a thick mustache slid out from behind the wheel, his hand tense on his holstered sidearm.

***

Concho's sweat-slicked hands tightened on the 30-06 he still carried. He'd met Roland Turner and had a good feeling about him, though he didn't know him well. But this newest officer? Concho didn't know how to feel about him. He'd seen him before, on the day of the bank robbery. The trooper had been interrogating the passenger in the getaway car when Concho turned Anne Reese over to Hoight. He had no reason for discomfiture around the blond officer but his gut reaction couldn't be denied.

Deputy Turner offered a distraction with a shout and a wave of his hand to Hoight and Concho. But the first action the black deputy took was to grab a fire extinguisher from his vehicle and begin foaming the grass and brush around the burning van to keep the fire from spreading in the dry environment. The blond trooper approached Concho and the others.

"Y'all all right?" he asked. He'd taken his hand off his gun.

"We're good," Concho said, relaxing. "I recognize you but don't know the name."

"Gage Herrington," the man said. "Texas Highway Patrol."

"Gage works with us in the Sheriff's Office quite a bit," Terrill Hoight said. "He's a good guy."

Concho nodded: "Saw you at the wreck after the bank robbery," he said, offering his hand. Gage shook it, then turned and held out his hand to Katy. She took it but let go quickly. Concho frowned anew.

Roland Turner had finished with his fire extinguisher and was putting out traffic cones to warn any approaching vehicles to slow down and stay out of the right lane. Not a single truck or car had passed since Concho's altercation with the motorcycles began but, eventually, someone would come along and need guidance around the wreck.

"I better get some cones up too," Herrington said as he turned back toward his cruiser.

Even as Herrington spoke, a farm truck came by and went around Gage's cruiser and past the scene with one set of wheels in the ditch. Two other police cars squealed up a moment later. Both came from the Eagle Pass direction but were state troopers rather than Maverick County deputies. Roland Turner grabbed both officers as they got out of their cars to help secure the site.

"So," Hoight said to Concho while they were without anyone other than Katy to overhear, "You needed help and didn't have it and, now, you've got it but don't need it."

"I still need it," Concho responded. "We've got to arrest Mason French at his bar. If he's still there. And I'm not gonna do it alone. But, Terrill, I need you to take Katy with you and head back to Eagle Pass."

"Wait!" Katy said, her voice rising. "You're not going to leave me. I can go with you. I'll stay in the car. I promise."

"Not possible," Concho said, turning toward the young woman. "We've got to get you somewhere safe."

"There is no place safe!" Katy protested. "Don't you realize? Except maybe with you."

"Look," Concho said. "Terrill's a friend and a very good driver with a very fast car. I'm going to have him take you to Roberto Echabarri, who is chief of the Kickapoo Tribal Police and another good friend. Once you're on the reservation, that'll be a whole other layer of protection. And I'll be there as soon as I can."

Concho turned to Hoight. "Right now, we're treating Katy as a witness rather than a prisoner. I think she's going to be a big help to us. Call Echabarri before you leave, ask him to send deputies to escort you onto the Rez."

Hoight nodded. "Will do. It's a good plan."

"Keep an eye out for anyone on a sport bike," Concho added. "They were the ones who ran us off the road. They're heavily armed."

"Saw 'em," Hoight said. "Doing all kinds of speed. Didn't realize they were involved."

"Yep," Concho said. "But if Katy lays down in the back seat of your car, they'll never know she's there. Also, there was one guy from the van who got away. He was running down the highway last I saw. Without a weapon. But you'll need to call it in."

"Gotcha," Hoight said.

Turner and Herrington had finished placing their traffic cones and joined Concho, Katy, and Hoight. The two new troopers came up, as well, and Concho explained his plan for going after Mason French.

"If French hasn't run already," he said to the others, "it'll be like trying to dig a rabid badger out of his hole. So armor yourself in mean and get ready for a fight."

CHAPTER 21

After Terrill Hoight pulled out for the Kickapoo reser-vation with Katy Delchamp lying down in the backseat of his interceptor, Concho fetched a gym bag of materials from his wrecked truck and climbed into Roland Turner's police cruiser for the race to Hot, Blue and Righteous. He'd traded an extra set of body armor from one of the other police officers to Katy and taken back his own. He reloaded his weapons as Turner burned down Highway 277 toward the bar with three other police cruisers in a line behind him.

Next, Concho took a small yellow tin container out of the bag and opened it. Turner watched from the corner of an eye while the Ranger scooped two fingerfuls of red ocher out of the tin and smeared streaks of it beneath each eye.

"War paint?" Turner said. "I'd heard you did that."

Concho glanced over at the deputy and grinned as he put the tin away and wiped his fingers on a towel from the bag. "Scares the hell out of the perps," he explained. "Makes 'em think I'm crazy."

"Sure you're not?"

"Not completely," Concho said.

The Ranger saw the sign coming up for Hot, Blue and Righteous. He drew his right-hand Colt and racked the slide to load a shell. They whipped into the parking lot. Barely fifteen minutes had passed since they'd driven away from the wreck site. They'd been running without sirens or lights so as not to warn Mason French they were coming. But they'd also radioed for backup and more cops were on the way.

The parking lot was nearly empty with no motorcycles and only a couple of rough-looking pickups present. Concho bailed out of Turner's car and ran for the front door of the bar. Turner followed with a shotgun while the other police officers circled around the sides. Concho had told them about the back door and warned them to stay ready in case Mason French was in his trailer behind the bar.

Shoving open the forest green front door, Concho leaped inside with a Colt .45 in his right fist. The only person visible in the building was Jack, the bartender. The man's hand dipped quickly beneath the bar and Concho shoved his Colt out toward him and shouted, "I'll kill you! Get your hands where I can see 'em!"

Jack froze. His face looked like he'd just swallowed a tarantula and it was trying to crawl back up his throat, but he lifted both hands into the air. Turner circled the bar, reached underneath and pulled out the sawed-off shotgun the bartender had been grabbing for. After shucking the shells, Turner tossed the gun away to clatter on the floor.

"Where's French?" Concho demanded. "In his office?"

Jack shook his head, but Concho wasn't ready to believe him. He moved to the room labeled "Office" and called through the closed door.

"French! If you're in there, come out with your hands showing. You're under arrest for kidnapping."

No answer came. Staying behind the wall next to the door, Concho reached over and grabbed the knob. It was locked. Rather than twist the knob off with his hands, Concho stepped back and launched a kick into the door plate just under the knob. The wood splintered with the sound of a shot and the door burst open.

When no bullets answered his intrusion, Concho stepped inside. The room was empty.

An explosion of weapons fire erupted from out back of the bar.

***

Terrill Hoight was ten miles outside Eagle Pass with Katy Delchamp in his back seat when a sports bike pulled out of a side road and fell in behind him. He remembered Concho's warning and his heart sped up.

Pushing his speed a little higher, he got on the radio again to Kickapoo police headquarters. Two units were en route to escort him, he was told. He'd feel better when they reached him.

After hanging up the mic, he glanced into his rearview mirror to see if the bike had dropped back. It hadn't. It was matching his speed. And now there were two.

***

At the rattle of gunfire from out back of the bar, Con-cho pointed toward Jack the bartender, who Deputy Roland Turner stood beside, and called out, "Roland, lock him down! I'll check out the firing."

Concho had marked the exits the last time he'd visited Hot, Blue and Righteous. The back door lay through the small kitchen. He headed there with his gun drawn. The door was closed but unlocked. He pushed it halfway open.

The firing had ceased for the moment. Just to the left of the door stood a metal storage shed. Two of the deputies Concho had sent to circle around the back of the bar hid behind its shelter with their weapons ready. Nearly within spitting distance stood the front of Mason French's trailer. The windows at the near end were bashed out, in the nearly empty bedroom Concho had seen inside. A faint breeze stirred the curtains there.

One of the deputies motioned frantically at Concho to join

them and, in the next instant, he saw why as a gun barrel pushed through the trailer's broken window and tracked toward him. He hurled himself out the door and into the safety of the shed just as gunfire shredded the late afternoon.

A stream of bullets tore up the dirt where Concho had been and whacked loudly into the bar's wooden siding, sending splinters flying. As quick as it had come, the gun song stopped.

"Sounds like a fully automatic rifle," Concho said into the quiet as he glanced at the other two officers. One of them, a Hispanic man in his mid-thirties with a Texas Highway Patrol badge pinned to his shirt, nodded and added,

"And he's got plenty of ammo, it seems."

"Where's Gage Herrington?" Concho asked.

The second deputy, a woman with hazel eyes and light brown hair cut short under her western-style hat, answered this question. "He went around the other side of the building. Haven't seen him since."

"All right," Concho said. "We've got to get our shooter out of there. Be ready to give me cover fire when I ask for it."

Both deputies nodded, happy to let the big Texas Ranger with the war paint across his cheeks give the orders.

Concho worked around the outside of the shed to where he could see French's trailer. From the way the curtains moved, he was sure the shooter was still in the room with the broken window.

"OK," he said to the deputies. "Fire on that window and keep it up as long as you can."

The deputies opened up with their service pistols. A hard rain of bullets slammed into the trailer and whipped through the curtains. Under cover of the barrage, Concho lunged into the open and raced toward the side of the trailer. The distance was probably thirty yards.

In college, Concho had run the 40-yard dash in 4.4 seconds. With the threat of getting shot to motivate him, he felt he'd bettered his record by the time he reached the trailer and ducked behind the protection of the wall. Congratulations weren't in order yet, though. He signaled the other cops to cease fire. As soon as they stopped shooting, the rifleman in the trailer opened up in retaliation. From the sound, he was still in the same bedroom. Exactly what Concho had hoped for.

With both his pistols drawn, Concho worked around to the rear of the trailer and slipped silently up the steps to the back door. He'd broken this door open once already today when he'd rescued Katy. Mason French hadn't bothered to repair it. It still hung loose on its hinges, giving Concho a glimpse of the laundry room inside, which was empty except for the washer and dryer he'd noted before.

The gunfire from within had stopped. Where was the shooter? Did he know Concho was coming for him? He surely must be aware of how vulnerable the damaged back door left him.

Concho used the barrel of his left-hand Colt to push the door further open. It creaked. Concho cursed, knowing he'd given himself away. Instantly, he shoved inside and ducked behind the washing machine, which was barely big enough to hide his bulk.

A man with an assault rifle in his hands and body armor covering his chest appeared at the inside doorway to the laundry room. Concho ducked his head for cover as the fellow cut loose with the rifle. In a cacophony of clangs and ricochets, bullets sprayed into the washer and dryer. Concho tried to make himself small. At the same time, he stabbed his left-hand Colt around the corner of the washer and opened fire, aiming for the gunman's legs.

A bullet burned across the skin on Concho's arm but at least one of his own shots hit its target. The shooter cried out. A crash sounded. Concho couldn't see but felt sure the man had dropped to the floor. But was he hurt? And how bad?

As the assault rifle fell silent, Concho lunged to his feet, pistols out and ready to kill. The shooter had fallen back against the wall and slid down it. Blood oozed from a wound in his right thigh. The right knee had been mangled by a second .45 slug.

The gunman had emptied his rifle and was trying to stuff a

fresh magazine up the well. Concho fired into the paneling next to the fellow's head. He flinched and froze before Concho's shout of "Don't move!" could reach him.

Concho recognized the weapon as he kicked it out of the fellow's hands, an M4A1 carbine in .223 caliber. The M4 was a fully automatic rifle carried by members of the US Special Forces, like the Army Rangers Concho had been a member of before he became a Texas Ranger.

This man, who was not Mason French, had surely never been Special Forces. He'd probably never been in the military at all. He surely wasn't much more than twenty-one, and badly out of shape, but Concho had seen him drinking at the bar when he'd been there earlier this afternoon.

Frowning, Concho questioned the man. "Where's Mason French?"

"I'm shot, man. You gotta get me a doctor. I'm shot bad!"

"Looks like you'll live," Concho said, with no sympathy. "Where's French?"

"I don't know. He…left. It hurts, man. Please! Get me a doctor!"

"Why are you shooting at cops? What's French got on you?"

"I owe him, man. Owe him big. But I didn't wanna hurt anyone."

Concho shook his head. He stepped into the doorway of the bedroom where the fellow had made his stand, calling through the busted window to the officers outside.

"It's all right! I got him. Someone call it in and get an ambulance!"

As Concho moved back to stand over the injured man, sudden footsteps echoed in the house, coming from the direction of the front door. Gage Herrington stepped into view with his pistol in a shooter's two-handed grip. The officer's gun generally pointed in Concho's direction, and the gray eyes behind it were cold and calculating.

Concho frowned. A trickle of sweat rivered down his neck.

***

Deputy Terrill Hoight, with Katy Delchamp prone in the backseat of his cruiser, checked his rearview mirror again to see the two motorcycles still behind him. Katy hadn't noticed them, of course, and Terrill was just about to warn her when two SUVs with the emblem of the Kickapoo Tribal Police on their sides came roaring down the highway past them and made U-turns to swing in behind.

Terrill waved at the reinforcements, then glanced in his mirrors once more to see that the motorcycles had dropped out of sight. Breathing a sigh of relief, he told Katy their escorts had arrived and they'd be on the Rez inside of fifteen minutes.

After riding comfortably through the town of Eagle Pass, they took Highway 1021 toward the reservation. Only after they made the final turn onto the Rez did Terrill see the motorcycles again. The same two bikes—at least he thought they were the same—continued on 1021 past the reservation turnoff. Now the riders of those bikes knew where Terrill was headed and, somehow, they must suspect he had Katy with him.

Not good.

CHAPTER 22

"You want to aim that thing somewhere else?" Concho said to Herrington, who was still pointing his gun toward the Ranger.

For a brief instant, Concho thought the Texas Highway Patrolman wasn't going to comply but the back door rattled and Concho turned to see the Hispanic officer, who'd helped supply cover fire outside, come in.

Herrington immediately holstered his gun and his face warmed with a smile. "Sure," he said. "Sorry, man. Just being careful."

"Right," Concho said. He glanced from Herrington to the second policeman and back. "Can you two keep an eye on this guy until the ambulance gets here? I need to talk to the bartender."

"No problem," Herrington said.

"Thanks. I didn't have a chance to cuff him or read him his rights."

"We'll take care of it," the second policeman said. "Officer Holland is calling it in. Probably be a bit before the ambulance gets here."

Concho nodded. Holland must be the woman officer, he figured.

"I don't think the ambulance taking a while will be a problem," Concho replied. "The guy's in pain but it doesn't look life-threatening. He says he owed Mason French a debt. See if you can find out more about that."

The policeman waved two fingers in acknowledgment as Concho stepped around him and headed back into Hot, Blue and Righteous. Jack the bartender sat with his hands cuffed behind him on a stool at his own bar. Roland Turner stood watching nearby. The Ranger walked over to them, stopping to pick up Jack's discarded sawed-off shotgun on the way. It was a double-barreled weapon with a pistol grip, cracked open to show it was unloaded.

"What kind of car does Mason French drive?" Concho asked Jack.

Jack eyed the shotgun and smirked at what he considered an empty threat. "Ask Satan when you get to Hell," he snapped.

"Creative," Concho said. A flick of a smile crossed his lips. He lifted the shotgun, grasping the barrel in one hand and the stock in the other. The muscles in his arms corded as he exerted them. The steel resisted but the bolt holding the barrel and stock together began to shriek as the Ranger twisted it. Slowly, the weapon began to bend, to fold down on itself.

Concho tossed the ruined shotgun on the bar in front of Jack. "What kind of car does Mason French drive?"

"I...I don't have to talk to you!"

"Hmm," Concho said. He leaned toward Jack and slowly let a barracuda smile spread across his face. "Satan isn't in Hell right now, by the way. He's here." With one swift move, Concho grabbed Jack's prominent ears in his powerful hands. "He's right here and about to rip your ears off for this trophy case."

Jack's features blanched; terror grew on his face.

Concho twisted the man's ears just a touch and gave one a quick tug in threat.

"A Porsche!" Jack blurted. "A Boxster. Silver."

"Headed where?"

"I don't know. I swear. He was going north. Toward Laughlin Air Force Base. That's all I know."

"How much head start does he have?"

"Half an hour. I guess."

"Is that when he got a call?"

"Yeah. Yeah! He took one. But he went into his office to talk. I didn't hear it."

Concho released Jack's ears and straightened. He let out a deep breath and said to Turner: "Someone called to tell French the attack had failed. Maybe the guy running away from the scene. Or someone we don't know yet. There's an Officer Holland out front." He gestured at Jack. "Let's turn this one over to her and get out of here."

"Not much we'll be able to hold him on."

"Don't really care," Concho said. "I want to get back to the Rez and talk to Katy Delchamp. Feels like time is getting short to solve this thing before someone else gets killed. You mind driving me?"

"Can do," Turner said. "Just as long as I don't have to check out your trophy case."

"Ain't mine," Concho said. "I'm just holding it for the Devil."

***

On the way to the Kickapoo reservation, with night closing in, Concho had Roland Turner stop by his wrecked pickup to grab a few more items. Then he called John Gray-Dove, a Kickapoo tribesman who owned his own auto repair shop on the reservation. Gray-Dove agreed to tow the truck to his shop for fixing. Concho left the key in it since it wasn't going anywhere. He'd have to figure out what he was going to do for a vehicle in the meantime.

They reached the reservation around dusk, without incident, and Turner dropped Concho off in front of Kickapoo tribal police headquarters. This was a long, low, one-story building of wood at the corner of Chick Kazan Street and Nakai Breen Avenue. A good dozen vehicles were parked outside, including Terrill Hoight's police cruiser.

In the gathering darkness, the building blazed with light. Apparently, quite a few people were still hanging around even though the day shift was over. Well, the KTTT, as the tribal police force was called, didn't get a lot of bank robbers. That made Katy something of a celebrity, he supposed.

Concho entered to find the police chief, Roberto Echabarri, and several other tribal officers sitting around chatting and laughing with Hoight. Echabarri raised his palm in acknowledgment as Concho walked over to him. Handshakes made the rounds.

"Your outlaw lady is safe in a back room," Echabarri said. "We wanted her in this building instead of the jail. She's being watched, of course. Deputy Hoight here was telling me about being followed by some motorcyclists, though. You expecting trouble?"

"I hope not," Concho said. "Sorry to put the KTTT on the spot like this. We can move the woman if you want us to."

Echabarri shook his head. "No. It's OK. I've got all my people on alert. We'll be ready if there's any trouble."

"I appreciate it."

Hoight was standing when Concho turned to him. "I better get back to the Sheriff's Department," the deputy said. "I'm sure Sheriff Parkland is still there and he'll want to hear about all this personally. You want me to have the same truck you borrowed from us last time sent over?"

Getting his truck shot out from under him had become something of a habit with Concho lately. A month previously, his F-150 had been badly shot up in another ambush on the road. Sheriff Parkland had loaned him a Dodge Ram 1500 pickup until his own Ford was repaired. Unfortunately, Concho had managed to get a few bullet holes put in the Dodge too, though apparently it had also been fixed.

"Perfect," Concho said to Hoight. "I really appreciate it. And everything else you've done."

"Happy to help," Hoight said, pushing his hat up slightly with a finger before heading out.

"Now," Concho said, turning back to Echabarri. "Where's Katy? I've got a lot to talk to her about."

***

Katy had been installed, temporarily, in the officer's lounge in the back of the Kickapoo tribal police building. Concho found her lying on the couch half watching the TV and half staring into space when he entered the room. She sat up quickly when she saw him.

She'd had a chance to shower, and all the dirt, makeup, and tears had washed off her face. She smelled of soap and shampoo. Her shoulder-length brown hair was still damp. Someone had loaned her a short red and purple sundress that made her look younger than her age and very innocent. But her eyes were hollowed after her experience and her face made a study in tension. A yellow-purple bruise covered her left cheekbone.

The only other occupant of the room was Nila Willow, who Roberto Echabarri had appointed as the first female deputy in the Texas tribal police. Another female officer had joined her since. Nila smiled at Concho as he entered and got up from the chair where she'd been reading a magazine. She offered both Katy and Concho nods before giving them the room.

"Is he…" Katy started. "Did you get him?"

Concho shook his head. "Afraid not. He'd already fled by the time we arrived."

Katy put her hand to her mouth and nibbled on a finger. "I was hoping he wouldn't have."

"Me too," Concho said. "But we've got an APB out on him. He's going to be too busy running for a while to come looking for you."

Katy nodded weakly but didn't seem convinced.

"Look, I brought you something," Concho said, handing her the plastic bag he'd picked up from his truck on the way here.

Katy frowned as she took the bag. She smiled when she opened it. "My books!" she said. "The Hunger Games Trilogy. How did you? I mean, you must have been to my apartment.

Mine and Anne's."

"Yeah. That's where I found a matchbook from Hot, Blue and Righteous."

Katy nodded again, more strongly. "I wondered why you showed up there."

"Yep. And it was all due to a tip your sister gave me."

Surprise marked Katy's face. "Vera! You talked to Vera?"

Concho nodded and pulled his phone out of his pocket. "Speaking of which," he said. He swiped to his contacts and selected the one for Vera Delchamp before handing the phone to Katy. "Give your sister a quick call to tell her you're OK. But don't tell her where you are. Better for her not to know."

Katy held the phone as a truly radiant smile spread across her features. She quickly pressed the button to call her sister. The phone rang only once before Vera answered.

"Vera! It's Katy. Are you all right?"

Concho couldn't hear the other side of the conversation, but Vera must have demanded to know how Katy was instead.

"I'm fine. Yes, I'm fine. I'm in safe hands. Ranger Ten-Wolves.

"Yes. He's here, and I'm safe. But I can't talk long. How are you?"

Vera must have answered the question because Katy spent a moment nodding and "uh-huhhing."

"No," Katy said next. "I can't tell you where I am right now. But I promise I'm safe and I'll call you again as soon as I possibly can.

"Right. Yes. I promise. And you take care of yourself. Don't tell Mom and Dad anything.

"Yes. I will.

"I love you too."

She hung up and handed the phone almost reluctantly back to Concho. "Thank you," she mouthed.

"Is Vera all right?" Concho asked.

Katy nodded, then added, "You must have made quite an impression on her."

"She was very concerned about you and didn't think your parents were going to do anything about it."

"They wouldn't. Even though they probably could. They're very rich."

"I assumed from the house and cars they had money."

"Butt loads of it."

Concho chuckled but then turned serious. "You need to tell me everything, Katy. Everything. Before someone else gets hurt or killed."

"The best person to talk to is Anne," Katy said. "She's the one planned it all. Day, time, method, everything. She knows the score. If you let me speak to her first, I think I can convince her to give you what you need."

Concho repressed the sigh building up inside him. He'd forgotten that Katy wouldn't have heard about Anne. He hated to tell her but had no choice. Maybe it would help her realize what was at stake.

"I'm afraid I can't," he said. "Anne's dead. She was murdered in a jail cell so she wouldn't talk."

Katy gasped. She bit her lower lip. Her hollow eyes grew damp with sudden grief. "I. I… Oh my God!"

CHAPTER 23

"I'm sorry about your friend," Concho said to Katy af-ter she'd recovered a bit from the trauma of hearing of Anne Reese's death.

"It's just a shock. She was so…tough. Hard to imagine her gone."

"No one is so tough they can't meet someone tougher," Concho said.

"I guess."

"I hate to pressure you," Concho continued. "But I need to understand what's going on. What do you think Anne was involved with that got her killed? And got you into trouble with Mason French?"

Katy sat on the couch with her head down and her hands clasped between her knees. She began to speak. "I thought it was just a straightforward robbery. Until that big…Escalade grabbed the money from you."

"You were watching?" Concho asked in surprise.

"Yes, I'd circled around. Mostly by accident because I didn't know where I was going. I saw you chasing Anne and you stopped her by the creek."

"So you're the one who took the gun out of the creek?"

"Yes."

"Where is it?"

"It was in my backpack. Mason French has it. My phone was in there too. My real phone."

"What can French get from that?"

The young woman shrugged. "Hopefully, nothing. It's password protected. But if he figures it out…" she glanced at Concho, "my parents' cell numbers are in there. And Vera's. I don't know what he could do with those but I'd rather he not have them."

The Ranger nodded. "Let's hope he can't crack your password. You also told me the first time we spoke on the phone that you knew who took the money. Explain."

Katy shook her head. "I only thought I did. Anne told us all that if anything went wrong we were supposed to contact Mason French. I figured he had something to do with it. Maybe he was backing Anne up. I gathered from what she told us that French was dangerous and had…connections."

"To what?"

Katy shrugged. "I just thought she meant to criminals."

"That's why you were afraid when you called me?"

"Yes. Mostly. I was getting ready to go see French. I guess I was trying to cover all my bases. But French obviously didn't have the money. And he just kept asking about what else we took besides money. At first I assumed that was nonsense but…with all that's happened…I'm starting to think he was right."

"We got a report from the bank while I was on the way here," Concho said. "They're saying your take was about twenty-three thousand. Not a big chunk of change."

Katy nodded with her head still down. "Right. See. So I started thinking. Anne and I went to different tellers. There were only like five. But maybe one of the tellers gave Anne something else besides money. Something really worth a lot more." Katy shook her head back and forth. "I have no idea what it could be."

"Nor do I."

"French said Anne owed him a lot of money," Katy continued. "From what I could tell, he was expecting a payoff from the robbery. And then he said some 'heavy hitters' were involved and they wouldn't care about the money at all. So there had to be something else."

"Whoever was in the Escalade must be those 'heavy hitters,'" Concho said.

Katy nodded.

Concho added, "The Sheriff's office probably already has a list of the tellers on duty during the robbery. I'll check it out. Sounds like one of them may have been in on it. Why did you all pick that IBC branch?"

Katy looked up to meet Concho's gaze. Her eyes shifted suddenly. He thought she was about to lie to him but when she sighed and spoke, it felt like the truth.

"Anne said it was an easy access bank," Katy said. "But the real reason, at least for me, was because my father runs his business accounts through there."

Concho felt the urge to arch an eyebrow and wished he could make that happen. It wasn't a talent he possessed though. "You wanted to hurt your father?" he asked.

A much longer sigh spilled from Katy's mouth before she spoke again. "Both my parents, I guess. Anne…knew about my…feelings. She was the one suggested using the robbery to twist the knife in my father a bit. I know it wouldn't really hurt him. I mean, banks are insured and all. But, well, getting even a little revenge can feel good."

"It sounds like a private matter," Concho said, "but since the police are involved, I have to ask: What was the problem with your father?"

Katy stared at him. He could tell she was trying to act mature about all this but the bitterness came through in her words.

"My father was a slut! Or, whatever you call a man who sleeps with just about anything with legs. He's had multiple affairs. I didn't know anything about it until about four years ago. Anne's father was like that too. Only worse. He even…" She shied away from what she was about to add, "Anne was the one who told me my father was cheating. And she was right. We caught him at it. With more than one woman."

"Does your mother know?"

"I think she does. About some of them at least. But she's made some deal with the devil for dad's money which is odd because she has money of her own. From her family."

"Did you confront your father about what you and Anne found out?"

"I wanted to but Anne said it wouldn't do any good. She knew from her own situation."

Concho kept his face neutral but inside he was curious about Anne's role in all this. "So, is this around the time you left home and moved in with Anne?"

"Not right away. It was a year or so later. I found I was just looking for reasons not to go home, not to see my parents' faces. Whenever I was at home, it was uncomfortable. I was really just there for Vera anyway."

"You and Vera seem tight."

"Yeah. She's a cool kid. A lot smarter than I was at her age. But she doesn't realize how awful the world can be. She's vulnerable, you know."

"Yes," Concho agreed. "I had the same feeling about her. What about the other two women who were with you? Cindy Karnes and Tessa Mercadel?"

Katy let out a slow breath. "Pretty sure Cindy doesn't know anything. I think she was brought in because of the getaway car, the GTO. It was hers. But Tessa? Tessa might. She's a tough one too. She was the only one of us who didn't just jump when Anne said how high."

"What was with the name Catherine James?"

Katy shrugged. "Anne's idea. She got the ID for me when we were spying on my father. For secrecy's sake. I just…kept hanging on to it."

"I'm finding it hard to believe you're the same person who robbed a bank in broad daylight just a couple of days ago. Seems like you're way too smart."

"Guess you're wrong about me," Katy said.

"I think you were wrong about Anne," Concho said roughly. "I don't think she was quite the friend you imagined."

Katy's face pruned in anger. "You don't know what you're talking about." She tapped The Hunger Games books lying on the couch beside her. "I met Anne through these books. She was older than me but she took me on as a friend. I should have been popular in high school. I had money, the clothes. But I was always too shy. Too much of an introvert and a reader. Anne brought me out of that. And she protected me more than once from bullies."

"You're right," Concho said. "I don't know the details of your life and Anne's role in it. But I know a little about people. I'm also pretty sure the 'heavy hitters' you mentioned in the Escalade were working with or for Anne. The only way they could have been there to steal that money was if they were using Anne's phone as a GPS. And they'd have to know her number for that."

Katy looked stricken. He could see her considering his words and realizing their truth. Time to let her do some thinking.

"Anyway," he said, "it's not something to deal with now. In fact, we both need some rest. Are you comfortable staying here while I run to my trailer for some things? I should be back inside an hour. I'll sleep here tonight."

Katy nodded weakly. "I guess so."

"Tomorrow I'll go talk to Tessa and see what other information I can get? You'll have to stay here."

Katy chewed her lower lip. "It's OK. The officers are nice. Nicer than I deserve. But I'll feel better when you're back."

Concho dropped his hand down to squeeze Katy's shoulder. "It'll give you time to reread the story of Katniss Everdeen," he said. "I've only made it through the first book so far, but she's someone to admire."

"I'm no Katniss," Katy said. "That's for sure."

"I don't think I can agree," Concho said. "But maybe it depends on what you do from here on out."

He left her.

CHAPTER 24

After borrowing a Kickapoo police force SUV, Concho drove home. He called Isaac Parkland on the way and was surprised to get the Sheriff's answering service. He left a message asking if he could talk to Tessa Mercadel in the morning and requested the list of tellers on duty during the robbery.

It was almost 8:00 PM when he reached his trailer. The first thing he did was shower to scrub off the sweat and grime of a long and violent day. After dressing in fresh jeans and a blue cotton work shirt over a clean black tee, he made himself a supper out of four eggs, three rashers of bacon, and two big slices of buttered bread. A couple of mason jars of tea washed down the meal. Concho's hunger was always a force to be reckoned with.

More phone calls took up the next half hour. He talked to Maria Morales and wished it could be in person. She was understanding but teased him about his new girlfriend, the "bank robber."

He also checked with John Gray-Dove to make sure he'd been able to locate Concho's bullet-battered Ford and get it towed to his shop.

"Perhaps consider a horse for your future transportation needs," John told him on the phone. "You and machines do not get along."

"You got a horse with armor plating?" Concho asked.

"No. But I have one knows better than to get shot."

"I'll take it under advisement," Concho replied. "In the meantime, please see what you can do about fixing my current ride."

"At least a week and much money," John told him before hanging up.

As Concho pocketed his phone, a scuffing noise came from his front steps. Drawing a Colt into his right hand, he pulled back the curtain over his kitchen sink and peered out. The sliver of moon in the sky didn't give much light but his front stoop lay empty of anything living.

He headed for the door, flipped on the porch light and peered out again through the small square window. Nothing moved except a breeze swirling a few leaves across his yard.

Keeping his pistol handy, Concho opened the door and stepped out on the porch. He saw what had been left for him. On the top step of his stairs lay an apparently broken stick. When he picked it up, it turned out to be an arrow instead, snapped into two halves.

Bad magic, he imagined. Placed here by someone who believed in sorcery.

The breeze teased Concho's face and hair as he studied the night. The big mesquite in his yard was just visible to his left. He could see the outlines of his lawn chairs. The dark bulk of the SUV sat straight ahead.

His eyes revealed nothing else. He smelled nothing except mesquite and wildflowers and a faint scent of gasoline from the police vehicle. His ears registered only the wind and the natural things it made dance beneath the moonlight.

Taking the arrow inside, he placed it on his bar and turned on the overhead light to study it more closely. The mystery deepened. This was not just an arrow; it was his arrow. Only the head was missing.

The Kickapoo do not mass produce arrows for their bows. Each has its personality and its markings. Concho knew every arrow he'd ever made intimately. A month ago, he'd used two arrows—and many bullets—in foiling a neo-Nazi plot to take over the Eagle Pass Mall and blow it up with hostages inside. His arrows had killed two men that day. He had not recovered them. Nor would he have reused them if he had.

However, Concho always kept his quiver full with twelve arrows. It was an important number to him. In the weeks after the mall attack, while he convalesced from his knife wound in the back, he'd replaced the two arrows he'd spent, slowly and carefully constructing them from polished wooden shafts fletched with wild turkey feathers. He'd knapped his own flints for the heads.

He'd, actually, made three new arrows because he'd lost one. A favorite place of Concho's on the Rez was an isolated canyon far from any settlement where a stream ran and trees of many varieties grew. He'd found a small stand of Texas ash there, perfect for arrows.

After making two ash wood arrows, he'd test-fired them in the canyon. Something had gone wrong with the first arrow. Its balance was off. He'd missed the target completely and had not been able to find the arrow afterward, despite a long search. Someone else had found it, though, and returned it to him tonight with the head missing and the shaft broken. He wondered why.

And who.

***

A silver Porsche Boxster crouched in the shadows of some trees cast by a streetlight at a lonely rest stop on Texas Interstate 35 outside San Antonio. Tim and Donna Sutherland, fresh from their honeymoon in Mexico, pulled into the rest stop and parked a few spaces down from the Porsche. Both got out to use the restroom, holding hands all the way until the sidewalk split for the men's and women's rooms.

Donna returned to their silver 2019 Chevy Trailblazer about ten minutes later, surprised to find that Tim had not beaten her back. Without the keys to the vehicle, she leaned against the hood and did a few stretches to loosen tendons and muscles that had tightened on their long drive.

Another five minutes passed. Donna was starting to get concerned when a very tall fellow emerged from the men's room and started down the sidewalk toward her. The man was physically rather intimidating but he offered a friendly smile as he started to walk past the front of the Chevy.

On the spur of the moment, Donna called to him. "Excuse me. Sir! Did you happen to see a young man in the bathroom while you were there? He has sandy brown hair and is wearing a green Baylor T-shirt?"

The man paused and a look of concern crossed his face. "I'm afraid I didn't. But I wasn't looking. He might have been in one of the stalls. Is he your husband?"

"Yes," Donna said. She smiled which turned her normally plain features radiant. "We're just coming home from our honeymoon. He's been in the bathroom a while."

"Well, nighttime is not a time for a new wife to be left alone. Why don't you come on along with me and I'll go in and have a look for you? I'm sure he's fine, but I'll make sure he knows his lovely wife is waiting eagerly to see him."

Donna grinned and nodded. The man's goofy-gallant humor made her feel better. "Thank you," she said. She fell in alongside him and they headed back up toward the men's bathroom.

"Nice vehicle you two have there," Mason French said. "I really like silver."

CHAPTER 25

Concho spent the night at Kickapoo tribal police head-quarters. He dosed off and on in an uncomfortable chair in the officer's lounge while Katy Delchamp slept peacefully on the couch. She'd relaxed and fallen asleep within ten minutes of him arriving back at the building.

Roberto Echabarri arrived around 7:00 AM the next morning, and the sound of him moving around finally brought Concho to full wakefulness. He left Katy sleeping and went down the hall, stopping by the bathroom before knocking light-knuckled on Echabarri's open office door.

"Come on in," Echabarri said. He was standing near a percolating coffee pot and handed Concho a big porcelain mug of steaming black. "Was just going to bring you this," he added. "I know you're not a big coffee drinker but figured you might need it."

Concho nodded, took a sip and smacked his lips. "Black with lots of sugar," he said. "Just the way I drink it whenever I do. Thanks. Wasn't sure you'd be in this morning. It being Sunday and all."

Echabarri grinned. "Not sure what you mean by Sunday. Every day is much the same when you're Chief of Police."

"I guess so," Concho nodded.

"No problems across the night, I take it?" Echabarri asked.

"No. Not here," he said. "Something happened at my place though." He explained about finding the broken arrow.

"Hmmm," Echabarri said. "Any ideas?"

"None," Concho said, taking another big sip of his coffee. "But the weird stuff started happening after I consulted with you on that pig killing over at George Night-Run's farm. You still getting missing animal reports?"

Echabarri shook his head. "None in the last couple of days," he said. "Oh, by the way," he added, "Terrill Hoight and Roland Turner brought your replacement truck over last night while you were gone." He plucked a key off his desk and handed it to Concho.

"Same Dodge Ram as last time," the Ranger remarked. "Good."

He was sticking it on his key chain with his other keys when he heard Katy call his name.

"Looks like your charge is awake and needing attention," Echabarri said.

Concho nodded, then called back to the young woman. "I'm here. Coming. How about some coffee? We've got a lot more to talk about before I go see Mercadel and Karnes in jail."

***

A little after 9:00 AM, Concho pulled his loaner white Dodge Ram 1500 pickup into a parking space in front of the Maverick County Sheriff's Department. The place was a lot less busy today than the last time he'd stopped by. No new jail-cell murders to bring out the press.

After finishing the last bite of the drive-through breakfast biscuit he'd stopped for, Concho entered the building. Sheriff Isaac Parkland stood talking to the dispatcher. Concho wasn't surprised to see him there on a Sunday. He'd expected him to be. Since Parkland's wife had died a couple of years ago after a long illness, the Sheriff had become wedded to his job. He was normally in the office every day.

Or, maybe it was like Roberto Echabarri had suggested, every day is the same when you've got responsibilities. Come to think of it, Concho couldn't remember the last day he'd taken off.

Parkland motioned the Ranger to follow him, and they went down the hallway to his office. Parkland sat. Concho sat. The Sheriff slid a sheet of paper across his desk and, when Concho picked it up, he saw the list of bank tellers from the IBC he'd requested. The list included names with blurry, black and white photos beside them.

"Thanks," he said.

"Any particular reason you want that?" Parkland asked.

"Investigating a lead. One of the tellers may have known Anne Reese and been working with her."

"Really," Parkland said. "That's a new twist." He nodded toward the list. "We gave them a check over but maybe we better have a deeper look."

"Might be good," Concho replied.

Parkland sighed. "And you wanted to talk to the other two perps, I believe?"

"Yeah. Cindy Karnes and Tessa Mercadel. I'm most interested in Mercadel."

"Not a problem," Parkland said. "I'll call a deputy to take you back. We've got 'em both in isolation over here instead of in lock-up at the detention center. It's for their own protection. Given what happened before."

"How's that situation?" Concho asked.

Parkland made a face. He picked up a bottle of Tums off his desk, opened it and shook three into his hand. Popping them into his mouth, he chewed them like candy. Concho thought the man didn't look well. Two bright red spots danced in his cheeks. His normally immaculate white hat had a dusty crease in it. One of his shirt buttons had popped loose.

"For the first time in my life I'm seriously considering retiring,"

Parkland said. "I'm getting crap from every direction. Of course, when the media gets through flaying me over Anne Reese's death, I probably won't be able to get elected meter reader anyway."

Concho nodded. "Sorry to hear it."

Parkland shrugged. "Not your problem."

"It's a problem for all of us," Concho said. "Civilian monitoring of police affairs is an important check. But it's unfortunate when good officers get raked over the coals."

Parkland waved his hand. "It'll blow over. I've dealt with it before. Just guess I'm getting old."

Concho grinned. "True!"

Parkland shook his head, rose to his feet. "Come on, I'll take you back myself. I need the exercise."

They went down several corridors in the building, passed what looked like an officer's lounge and stopped at a metal door guarded by a rookie deputy. The man saluted and both Parkland and Concho returned it.

Beyond the door stood a short corridor with two small rooms on either side. The rooms weren't barred but were sealed in thick Plexiglas with ventilation holes cut in them. None of the rooms had windows. The first one on the right held Tessa Mercadel.

Although the name Mercadel had a French origin, this woman was Hispanic and didn't look like the rich young woman she was. She was short, maybe 5'3," and thick around the shoulders and middle. Her dark hair had been cut to about an inch all the way around her skull. Tattoos writhed their inky way up both her bare and muscled brown arms. Concho recognized some of the tats as tribal in nature though he wondered if Tessa knew their meaning.

"Karnes is in the last cell on the left," Parkland said. "I'll leave you to it. Just knock when you want out."

"Gotcha," Concho said. "Thanks."

After Parkland had gone, Concho pulled up a stool in front of Mercadel's cell while the woman inside stared at him. He remembered that the paramedics had put a splint on her left arm after the wreck of their getaway car. It was gone now. "How's the arm?" he asked. "Better?"

"Nothing but a sprain," she said with just the sullen voice he'd expected from her. "You're the asshole who ran us off the road, aren't you?"

"Guilty," Concho said.

"Well, if you expect me to talk to you, go to hell."

"Katy told me you'd say that."

"Katy?"

"Katy Delchamp. Or did you know her as Catherine James?"

Mercadel's dark eyes studied Concho. Finally, grudgingly, she offered, "I know Katy."

"How about Vera?"

"Yeah, I know Katy's sister."

"Good kid."

"What are you getting at, lawman? I don't have all day."

"Seems like you've got some time on your hands," Concho said. "But what I'm getting at is, I want to ask you a few questions. Your answers might help Katy and her sister."

"Help them what?"

"Katy was kidnapped and beaten by a man named Mason French. He got away from us and is still out there. He had an abiding interest in your robbery. I don't think he's going to quit coming for Katy. Maybe even for you."

"I don't know French."

"But you've heard of him. Anne Reese told Katy, you, and Cindy to contact Mason French if you had any problems."

"So?"

"So, I've already been to his bar, Hot, Blue and Righteous. Is there anything else you overheard Anne say about him that might help me figure out where he is and how to stop him?"

Mercadel sighed. "No. I didn't pay much attention. I wasn't expecting any problem. And there wouldn't have been except for you!"

"All right. One last question."

"I think I need my lawyer."

"You don't have to answer it. And it doesn't have anything to do with your part in the robbery. I'd like to know if you have reason to believe Anne picked up something besides money from one of the tellers."

"Besides money? What would that be?"

"I couldn't tell you. But Katy thinks Anne might have been given something by one of the tellers. Something besides cash."

"I don't… If she did, I don't know anything about it."

"All right," Concho said, rising from his stool. "Thanks."

"Go straight to hell!"

Concho tipped an imaginary hat to Mercadel, then walked down the hallway to look into a second room at Cindy Karnes, the getaway driver on the day of the bank robbery. Cindy also had dark hair but shoulder length. She was a little taller and quite a bit thinner than Tessa. Women's clothing manufacturers would call her "petite." She was also familiar.

Concho knew this woman.

CHAPTER 26

Cindy Karnes sat on the bunk in her room staring into space. A clean white rectangle of bandage clung to her forehead. A couple of yellowing bruises showed around her eyes. She didn't acknowledge Concho when he stepped into her view.

"Ms. Karnes," Concho said. "May I speak with you?"

The young woman blinked. Slowly, her gaze focused on her visitor. "Who are you?"

"Concho Ten-Wolves. I'm a Texas Ranger."

From down the hall, Tessa Mercadel yelled out, "He's the one who ran us off the road, Cindy. Don't talk to him!"

Cindy's gaze flicked toward the sound of the voice, then wandered back to Concho. "That true?"

"I used a pit maneuver to stop you," Concho agreed. "Unfortunately, you did run off the road and hit an electric pole."

Cindy gave a faint nod of her head. "You were just doing your job."

"I was."

"I probably can't answer your questions anyway," Cindy said. "I don't really know anything."

Concho pulled up a stool and sat. "First," he said, smiling, "tell me how you're feeling. You can answer that surely?"

Cindy Karnes had large and lovely hazel eyes. They blinked slowly. "I'm…all right. I only had a mild concussion, they said."

"Glad to hear it. Would you like me to arrange for you to have some books to read?"

Again, Cindy blinked. "Books?"

"Yes."

"I…I would like it."

"Who's your favorite author? I can have a couple brought to you."

"I read a book by a guy named Oppel I liked, not long ago. Called Silverwing. About bats. Anyway, I've got all three of those. But how do you know I like to read?"

"I've seen you before," Concho said. "Or a picture of you. At a book signing. I'm pretty sure."

Cindy frowned.

"A book signing at the mall. Back in 2012. For Suzanne Collins and her Hunger Games Trilogy.

Cindy's eyes brightened. "Yes. Yes. But…how did you see that picture?"

"It's actually how I identified your friend Katy," Concho said. "She was at that signing. And so was Anne Reese. But I didn't see the name Karnes on the picture. I just recognized you when I saw you now."

"I went by Cindy Taggart then. Mom's boyfriend at the time. She thought they were gonna get married."

"Right," Concho said. "I remember seeing the name Cynthia Taggart. Is that how you met Katy and Anne? Or did you know them before?"

"Katy and I were in the same class in school but I didn't really know her. My mom and Katy's mom took us to the food court after the signing. They got to be friends so we started hanging out."

"What about Anne?"

"She and Katy were already friends. From school, I think. Anne went with us to the food court. But…"

"But what?"

"Anne seemed kind of jealous of Katy having other friends. She didn't like me much, I don't think."

"But Anne recruited you to help rob the bank?"

Yeah. One of Mom's boyfriends back in the day was a race car driver. I used to hang out with him at the dirt track over in McAllen. The Rio Grande Speedway. He taught me how to drive. Plus, I had a fast car. I guess I didn't do too good a job driving against you though."

"I've had a lot of training," Concho said. "Both in the military and as a lawman."

Cindy nodded.

"Cindy," Concho said. "Katy is with me. I mean, I'm protecting her. And someone is after her. Maybe more than one person. It seems like Anne might have picked up something from the bank other than just cash. Something a lot of bad guys want. Do you know anything about that?"

Cindy licked her lips. She lowered her voice. "I…don't get what you're talking about."

Concho lowered his own voice. "Are you sure, Cindy? It could be important for Katy's safety."

Cindy turned her head as if she could see down the hall to Tessa Mercadel's cell. She sighed, leaned forward on her cot toward Concho. Her voice grew very quiet, almost a whisper.

"There was…one thing Anne said to me just before we left that morning. It was sorta odd but maybe it relates to what you're talking about."

"And what was it, Cindy?" Concho asked, keeping his own voice equally low.

"She said, 'Information is gold.'"

Concho nodded. "That helps. I appreciate it."

Cindy shrugged.

"So, has this Oppel fellow written other books?"

Light brightened in Cindy's eyes. "Oh yes. He's got like a

couple of series. One is called Airborn, I think. I'd probably like to read those." She blushed. "I know they're like…books for kids. But I still like to read that kind of stuff. Comforting, you know?"

"I do. I just read the first Hunger Games book myself."

"Really! Did you like it?"

"Quite a bit." He took a breath and pushed to his feet. "I better go, Cindy. But, as soon as I can, I'll have a look for his stuff. And try to get something over to you. Take care of yourself."

A little smile worked its way onto the young woman's face. "Thank you!" she said.

***

Concho stopped by Parkland's office to share what little information he'd gotten from Karnes and Mercadel, then headed to his truck in the parking lot. He put in a quick phone call to Maria Morales but got her voicemail. She was probably in a meeting, he imagined.

The Walmart Supercenter stood close to where Maria worked and they carried a variety of books. Concho left a message asking Maria if she could check for something called the Airborn series by a writer named Oppel and let him pay her back. He asked her to call him when she could, ending with—after a short hesitation—"Love you, bye." The hesitation was not for him. He didn't mind saying the words. He wanted to. But he wasn't absolutely sure Maria wanted to hear them yet.

Throwing his loaner into gear, he headed back for the reservation to talk to Katy. A feeling of being followed rode his shoulders, despite frequent checks in his mirrors that showed no sign of a shadow. The feeling only ended when he turned onto the reservation.

***

Katy Delchamp was eating a bowl of Fruit Loops when Concho entered the officer's lounge in the Kickapoo police station. She smiled as he sat at the scarred, Formica-covered table across from her and pushed the sheet of paper listing the bank tellers over. Looking at him curiously, she picked it up.

"It's a long shot," Concho said, "but I wanted to see if you recognized any of the tellers from the day of the robbery."

Katy nodded. She glanced at the list with its names and images. Immediately, her eyes widened and she stopped eating with the spoon halfway to her mouth.

"Oh my God!" she said. "This… Wow!"

"What is it?" Concho asked quickly.

Katy dropped her spoon into her bowl with a clink. She smoothed the paper flat on the table and pointed to one name on the list—Emily Zapatero.

"This," she said. "This woman had an affair with my father. She was the first one we…that Anne and I found out about. Crazy!"

Concho turned the paper around to face him. The picture of Emily Zapatero was grainy but showed a woman in her early thirties with medium length dark hair, though it could have been anywhere from red to brown to black in the colorless photo. She was listed as an "Assistant Manager."

"Her hair was much longer then," Katy explained. "And blonde. Kinda dirty blonde. She wasn't Zapatero either. Her last name was Clarke."

"Was she working at the bank?"

Katy shook her head. "No, she was with a temp agency. I think that's how Dad met her. His business hired her for some secretarial work. Looks like she's come up in the world a bit," Katy added bitterly. "If she married into the Zapateros I know about, they have money."

"And you didn't recognize her when you went in the bank?"

"No. But I was…nervous. Focused just on what I had to do.

On the tellers in front of me. She wasn't one of mine. And the hair's different."

"But you gotta guess Anne recognized her?"

"I imagine. Probably. Do you think… Could it be a coincidence? Her being there?"

"The chances are slim and none."

Katy almost fell against the back of her chair. "I don't understand. This doesn't make any sense."

"But it's the connection we've been looking for," Concho said. "When I talked to your friend Cindy, this morning, she mentioned something she'd heard Anne say just before the robbery. 'Information is gold.' I've heard you say the same thing."

Katy frowned. "Yeah, yeah, I got the saying from her. But she said it all the time. So what?"

"I suspect, in this case, we can take Anne's words literally. She knew Emily 'Clarke' worked at the bank but had married up in the world. She already had a connection to her. She got Emily to get some information for her and include it with the cash taken during the robbery."

Katy's tongue clicked against the inside of her teeth. "I see. Maybe, Anne blackmailed Emily? To get her to help? But what kind of information would she have that Anne wanted?"

Another possibility existed besides blackmail—a mutual deal between Anne and Emily. Concho didn't say that to Katy, who wouldn't be ready to hear it. Instead, he said, "Bank account numbers."

Katy swallowed hard. "Right. Of course. But why wouldn't Anne have told us?"

Concho said nothing, only stared. Katy blushed and looked down. She mumbled. "Anne! I can't believe Anne would cut us out."

Concho shrugged. "Maybe she intended to tell you later and didn't get the chance."

Katy nodded and Concho could see how the thought had already become gospel to her. "But if she wanted account numbers," Katy said, "and she'd blackmailed Emily into getting them for her, why the charade of the robbery?"

"One possibility," Concho said, "and this is highly speculative, of course, but maybe the accounts in question were fake."

"What do you mean?"

"Accounts set up for criminal purposes. Offshore accounts to get money out of the country. Or to launder money. Or both. If such accounts were compromised, the owners wouldn't be likely to report it for fear of involving the feds."

"But wouldn't a robbery call attention to those accounts? If they existed?"

"Exactly. And maybe that's what Anne wanted. Or part of what she wanted."

"But why would she want that?"

"Your father," Concho said.

Katy went very quiet.

After a long moment of thought, Katy looked up at Concho and said, "You think my father had some fake accounts set up and Anne got Emily to give her the account numbers? Maybe as a way to punish my father for what he did to Vera and me, and our mother?"

Concho shrugged. "It's possible. Did you ever see any sign your father might be involved in illegal activities?"

Katy shrugged. "I always assumed he was. I mean, since I found out about the affairs. You cheat in one thing, you'll cheat on others. But I imagined it was penny-ante stuff. Cooking the books a little, hiding a few hundred here and a few hundred there. I never imagined him doing anything needing offshore accounts like you're suggesting."

"Right now it's only guesswork," Concho said. "I need a lot more information. First, let me get something straight. You saw Emily Clarke years ago? You knew what she looked like? But did she ever see you or Anne?"

"I saw her. Yes. And she saw Anne, at least," Katy said. "Anne confronted her once at a restaurant. One of those places where you can eat outside. She made me stay in the car, though. I'm sure the…that Emily saw me in the car but I doubt she got a very good look."

"You have any idea what Anne said to Emily?"

Katy shook her head. "They were angry but I couldn't make out their words."

Concho nodded and sighed. "First thing I have to do is talk to Emily Zapatero. Then your father."

"Good luck with that," Katy said bitterly.

CHAPTER 27

Concho wasn't surprised when he found out where Emily Zapatero lived—on the richest street in Eagle Pass, some six blocks up from the Delchamps. He'd certainly heard the name Zapatero. Most everyone in Eagle Pass would recognize it and—as Katy had said—the name was associated with wealth.

Concho considered what he'd learned from researching the Texas Rangers' databases as he drove to the location. Emily Clarke hadn't been born rich. Her family was middle class. She'd attended Eagle Pass High School and scored well in English and the humanities. She'd been a cheerleader for the "Eagles" and a relatively popular kid, although pictures from the time showed her as long-limbed and a little gangly.

After high school, she'd attended Rio Grande College in Eagle Pass, which was a local campus of the Sul Ross State University system. Her major was listed as "General Studies." She'd worked for the university a while in the admissions office, then joined a temp agency for several years after graduation, doing mostly secretarial work.

Not quite three years ago, after a lightning courtship that set local tongues wagging, she'd married the considerably older Lucio Zapatero who'd made his money in transportation. Zapatero owned trucking interests on both sides of the border and, as happened to many whose work took them back and forth between Eagle Pass, Texas and Piedras Negras, Coahuila, there were rumors of his involvement in drug trafficking. Such rumors had never been substantiated but they remained.

As Concho pulled up in front of the Zapatero house, he found that not only was it up the street from the Delchamps, it was, in fact, the last house on the road and sat on a quadruple-sized lot. Hacienda made a better term than "house" for the large, Spanish-style mansion that partially hid behind a twelve-foot-high stone wall and was surrounded by trees and flowers mostly unsuited to the arid local climate.

A black wrought iron gate, cast with the images of two fighting bulls facing off against each other, stood open but a guard in a tan uniform held up his hand to stop Concho from driving through. Concho showed his badge and ID and asked if he could speak with Ms. Zapatero about the recent robbery she'd witnessed. The fellow didn't seem surprised and asked Concho to wait while he contacted the house with Concho's bona fides.

Eventually, Concho found himself waved through the gate into the driveway. He parked behind a white Hummer H3. It looked like a 2010, which was the last year they'd been made, but was in perfect condition—and very expensive. Past the Hummer, the garage stood open and Concho could see the rear end of a blue Maserati Gran Turismo sports car.

The Ranger stepped out of his dirty Dodge pickup and took a look around. It was a little after two in the afternoon but not as hot as you might expect. Some of the coolness might have had to do with the busy misting units hanging on trellises throughout the yard. The air was damp and full of drifting droplets of water that sketched brief rainbows over beds of roses and lilies and other exotics. Half a dozen mandarin orange bushes grew along the sidewalk leading to the front door, all heavily laden with small, hard fruits. Concho strode between them.

The door opened as he approached. An older Hispanic woman in dark stockings with a dark uniform skirt and white blouse stood waiting for him. She offered him a short bow before leading him down a tiled hallway into a large sunroom. He got his first look at Emily Zapatero. She'd grown into the gangling limbs of youth; she was strikingly lovely.

Like most men, Concho noticed beautiful women, even though he tried not to let physical appearance influence his actions or opinions toward anyone. Ms. Zapatero was tall, slender, and classically beautiful. Her slightly wavy black hair hung nearly to her waist. Her eyes, a deep, bright shade of blue, were large and artfully enhanced by just a touch of shadow. Perhaps her cheekbones were a tad high and her chin a tad sharp, but the tiny flaws worked with the rest of her face, especially with the lips, which were plump and just brushed with a sheen of crimson.

The clothing the woman had chosen highlighted every aspect of her shape. She wore high black heels at the end of long legs. A short skirt of black linen set off the legs, with a slit at one side to show even more thigh. A tight, sleeveless satin blouse in silver enhanced everything above her waist.

Emily Zapatero knew how attractive she was and wasn't above using it to her advantage. She stood near a long, polished oak table in front of a row of windows letting in a golden light to limn her. Her welcoming smile was brilliant and Concho was quite sure he'd been kept waiting at the gate just so she could frame herself for this meeting. He didn't flatter himself it was for him personally. Any police officer arriving to question her would have gotten the same display. Quite possibly, so would have any plumber or electrician.

"Officer Ten-Wolves," Emily said. Her voice was smooth, modulated, educated, calculated. "Welcome. I'd wrongly assumed the police were through with me."

"Sorry to bother you, ma'am. I have just a few questions."

Emily nodded. She waved a languid hand toward a rich,

cream-colored couch sitting against the left wall. "Please, sit! Would you care for anything to drink? I have tea. Or a beer if you'd prefer. My housekeeper might even be able to scrounge up some lemonade if you have such a craving."

Concho sat down on the couch as he'd been invited. "I'm good on the drink," he said. "Thank you though."

Emily smiled, with the wattage turned down a little, and approached him. After smoothing her skirt down, she sat at the opposite end of the couch and turned slightly toward him, crossing her legs and pointing her knees in his direction. She smelled like some of the exotic flowers growing in her yard.

"Ask whatever you want," she said.

Concho let her see him nod. "I have to say," he said, "being an assistant bank manager pays better than I expected it to."

She got the joke right away and laughed throatily in what, Concho assumed, was a practiced sensuality used to disarm men.

"I guess that means you're wondering why I'm working at a bank if my husband is rich enough to afford this place?"

"None of my business, of course. But it does arouse the curiosity."

"Of course. Well, I'm only part-time. It's just bad luck I was there on the day of the robbery. And working as a teller. I normally work a couple of days a week at a different branch. Setting up accounts and stuff. But someone from there called in sick that day."

"I see."

The woman slid her right hand along her stockinged leg and cupped her knee. "All I really know is that working part-time helps my husband with his taxes. Something to do with him having interests on both sides of the Mexican-United States border." She shrugged. "I'm not versed in the details."

Concho nodded.

"Surely that wasn't what brought you all the way out here to see me?" Her voice was subtlety flirtatious but carefully nuanced.

Emily Zapatero was no ingenue.

"All the way out here?" Concho asked, making sure to mold his facial expression into the inscrutable look that so often disconcerted non-Indians.

It worked. Ms. Zapatero looked flustered as a quick blush of color leaped into her face.

"I mean…from the reservation. Isn't it a long drive?"

"What makes you think I came from the reservation?" Concho asked, keeping up the verbal pressure while staring straight into her blue-eyed gaze with his own dark one.

Again, Ms. Zapatero blushed. "Well…I just…assumed. Everyone knows the great Concho Ten-Wolves lives on the Eagle Pass reservation. You're quite famous locally. Since the mall incident where you sho…stopped those terrorists."

"Ah," Concho said. "I did have another question for you. I wondered if you knew any of the bank robbers?"

Ms. Zapatero blinked. He could see she hadn't expected this question.

"Well…I mean, I didn't really see them. They wore ski masks."

Concho had her off balance and had no intention of letting up the pressure. "But you saw pictures of them later, didn't you? On the news? Of three of them at least?"

The woman made one more attempt to discombobulate Concho and gain control of the situation. She uncrossed her legs and leaned toward him, resting one arm along the back of the couch with her hand to her mouth. While nibbling at a red-nailed finger, she casually stretched her finely toned left leg out and arched the foot, then drew it back up on the couch to tuck beneath her short skirt.

"Yes, of course," she said, her gaze focused on him as if he were the most important thing in her world. "But I didn't know any of them. Why would you think I might?"

"Not even Anne Reese?" Concho asked.

A short pause silenced the day. Emily straightened abruptly

on the couch. In a scramble for time, she replied, "Anne Reese, did you say?"

"Yes."

"Uhm, the name sounds vaguely familiar but I'm…not sure where I heard it."

Concho smiled, letting a little bit of the shark slip into his grin. "Oh? She wasn't the one who confronted you a few years back about your affair with William Delchamp?"

The pause now was palpable. And every pretense of friendliness and flirtation fled from Emily Zapatero. She was angry.

"You seem well informed of things that are none of your business," Zapatero snapped as she leaned away from him. "And which have nothing to do with the fact I was working in the IBC bank and might have been shot when it was robbed."

"I'm pretty sure it did have something to do with the robbery, though not exactly how. At least, I don't know yet. And I doubt you were in real danger of being shot."

Zapatero stormed to her feet. "This is ridiculous. Baseless accusations. I think you should leave."

Concho didn't bother to rise. "I reckon it's too late to ask for the lemonade," he said.

"Get out!"

"Not just yet," Concho said. "Did you know Anne Reese was murdered?"

Concho watched Emily Zapatero very closely as he spoke. Reese had been killed Friday morning. It was now Sunday afternoon. The information hadn't shown up in the news yet. The only private citizens who would know of Anne's death were likely involved in it.

Zapatero's face drained of color at Concho's words. She shook. If she were pretending, she was wasting her life in Eagle Pass, Texas. She should have been in Hollywood winning Oscars.

"I. Murdered! But wasn't she…weren't the robbers in jail?"

"Two other inmates killed her," Concho said.

“I didn’t…hear anything about this.”

Concho rose now. “It’ll likely be in the news this evening.” He tried to catch Emily Zapatero’s gaze but she wouldn’t look at him. “I believe she was killed for what she knew about the robbery. Not good to know secrets about that, it seems. Sure you don’t have anything you’d like to tell me?”

Zapatero licked her lower lip but it was an unconscious move this time, without calculation. She shook her head, straightened her shoulders, and made eye contact. Back in control. She adapted quickly. And perhaps her anger had been tempered with just a touch of empathy for the dead? He thought so and had to respect that. Her words gave nothing away, though.

“I don’t know what you’re talking about, and I think you should leave. Please.”

Concho nodded. “Sure,” he said. He reached into his shirt pocket and pulled out the business card he’d stuck there for just this purpose. Leaning over, he placed it on the low table in front of the couch, then offered Ms. Zapatero a polite nod as he turned and walked out.

CHAPTER 28

Seeing as how the Delchamps and Zapateros lived on the same street, Concho decided to stop and question William Delchamp after leaving Ms. Zapatero. No gate or guard here. He pulled into the driveway directly behind William Delchamp's blue Lexus LC convertible. Maureen Delchamp's green Infinity QX60 was gone. Perhaps the matriarch of the family was shopping. Nor did he see the curtains twitch on the second floor, despite revving his engine as he pulled in. Maybe Vera had gone with her mother.

Good, Concho thought. Best to talk to William in private at first. Until it became necessary to go public.

Delchamp must have heard Concho's Dodge. He came out of the house to meet the Ranger, looking physically fit but not as put together emotionally as the last time the lawman had seen him. Maybe it was a good sign.

"What do you want?" Delchamp demanded. Apparently, his rudeness remained intact.

"I assume you've checked my credentials, so I thought we might have a more pleasant conversation than we did last time."

"I know who you are," Delchamp said. "I still want to hear why you're here."

"I thought you might like to know, your daughter, Katy, is safe at the moment."

"Katy! She's safe! Where is she?"

"I'm not at liberty to say but she's OK and in police protection."

"For what it's worth," Delchamp snapped.

"What do you mean?" Concho asked calmly although his heartbeat sped up just a tad. Could Delchamp be referring to Anne Reese's death in police custody? He shouldn't know about that. If he did…

Delchamp blinked and paused which might mean nothing or might mean he knew he'd said too much. He changed the subject.

"Can we talk to Katy?"

Concho countered with, "If you give me your cell phone number, I'll have her call you. If she wants to."

"I…better give you her mother's number. She's more likely to call that."

Concho nodded and took out his phone, tapped in and saved the number Delchamp gave him, storing it under the name M. Delchamp. He also gave the man his number.

"You and your daughter don't get along well," Concho said as he tucked his phone away.

"I don't know what you're talking about," Delchamp said.

"Lot of that going around," Concho replied. "But I'm talking about your daughter being angry because you cheated on her mother."

Concho wasn't expecting the response he got. Delchamp snorted a laugh. "All men cheat," he said. "My wife is aware of my past peccadilloes. It shouldn't concern my daughter."

"It does. It also seems, strangely enough, to have been a concern of Anne Reese."

"Anne Reese is not a nice person," Delchamp snapped. "And I doubt she's any kind of true friend to my daughter. After all, she involved Katy in a bank robbery. You shouldn't believe anything she says."

A chime from Concho's pocket indicated the arrival of a text.

He glanced down.

"You might as well take that," Delchamp said. "I believe our conversation is over." He turned to go and Concho let him start walking away although he had no intention of ending this interview yet. A strange feeling inside told him the text was important. He pulled out his phone and read the message. The number he did not recognize but he had a feeling he knew who'd sent it. He'd just left her house a few minutes ago.

"Wow," he murmured to himself. He called out loudly to William Delchamp. "I think there's one more question you're going to want to hear."

Delchamp had almost reached the door of his house. He turned with his face pruning in irritation. "I doubt it," he said.

Concho smiled. He held up his phone, though he knew Delchamp couldn't read it at this distance, and spoke again in a voice loud enough to be heard by the neighbors if they were listening.

"Oh, we'll see. How long did your affair with Anne Reese last?"

***

Driving a silver 2019 Chevy Trailblazer instead of his Porsche, Mason French pulled into an abandoned gas station just south of Eagle Pass, Texas. It had been a long day of running the road.

Two sport bikes—1000cc Suzuki GSXs—stood on their stands on barren concrete where the gas pumps had been pulled up. One bike was black and red, the other purple. Their riders, in twin black leather outfits, gave Mason a nod as he got out and joined them. Both men smelled of exhaust and sweat and the need for a shower.

"So she's still on the reservation," Mason said, referring to Katy Delchamp.

One of the two bikers had very curly brown hair. The other was a ginger, with a face full of freckles and hair a dull red in color. Both men were in their mid-twenties. Mason knew the curly-haired one as TJ and the other as Drew.

TJ shrugged. “We haven’t seen her come out the main entrance but none of us really know this place. Could be any number of back roads and we’d never see her brought out that way.”

Mason bit back a retort. He knew the men were right and couldn’t expect any more of them. It galled though.

“What about Ten-Wolves?” he asked.

“Yeah, we saw him,” TJ said. “He came out early this morning, headed toward Eagle Pass. Then he went back to the reservation a while. He’s out again now. Been out a couple of hours. Driving a white Dodge Ram 1500. Got an extended cab.”

“Anybody follow him?”

Drew offered a derisive snort in answer. “Hell no!” he said. “He’s already wasted half a dozen friends of ours. He knows our bikes and I ain’t takin’ him on without you payin’ me a helluva lot more money.”

“Speaking of which,” TJ said.

Mason felt the urge to bash both bikers’ heads in but he needed them for now. Pulling a fat wallet out of his back pocket, he opened it and counted out three crisp hundred dollar bills to each of the men. This particular money meant nothing to him; it was leftover honeymoon cash from Tim and Donna Sutherland, the same folks he’d gotten his new Chevy Trailblazer from. Tim and Donna couldn’t use either anymore.

“Where are the others?” Mason asked.

“Donny’s watching the reservation,” TJ said. “A couple more of the boys are over at the Motel 6.”

“All right,” Mason said. “Lead the way. I’ll give them their money. And we need to rent a couple cars so we can trail this law dog when he leaves his zoo. I want to know what he’s up to.”

Drew laughed at the “zoo” reference; TJ didn’t. Both men climbed on their bikes. As they were putting on their helmets, Mason returned to his vehicle and started it up. He pulled out behind the bikers as they headed back into Eagle Pass.

Mason’s thoughts turned to Katy Delchamp as they’d been doing more and more. He'd begun to care less and less about any cash score he might make off her. He hadn't realized it clearly until she was gone but she reminded him of the first woman he'd showed his real self to—back when he was nineteen on a trip into Mexico. A silly young American girl who thought she was slumming and found out what that really meant.

Maybe Katy could help him relive the excitement of those hours. In more ways than one, she was unfinished business. And Concho Ten-Wolves had put himself squarely in the middle of that business. It couldn't be allowed to stand. He didn't like to leave any details hanging.

***

William Delchamp's face went through a series of con-tortions that would have left a protean-faced actor like Jim Carrey tied in knots. In reading the changes, Concho became convinced it was true. Delchamp had had an affair with Anne Reese, who'd supposedly been his daughter's friend.

Delchamp stormed over to him, his face watermelon red. "You're about to earn yourself a lawsuit!" he snapped, his voice angry but low. "Who told you such trash? It's nonsense! Not a word of truth in it!"

"I don't know," Concho said, still speaking loudly. "It makes sense out of a bunch of things."

"Keep your voice down!"

"Oops," Concho said. "Guess I've just got a naturally loud speaking voice. Maybe we should talk inside. I'm guessing your wife and daughter are gone?"

"Thankfully. They don't need to be upset by such filthy lies."

"Whose filthy lies would that be?" Concho asked. "Anne Reese's, or yours?"

CHAPTER 29

Delchamp glared at Concho. His face turned even bright-er red. His fists clenched. He clearly didn't like being called a liar. But Concho wasn't in the mood to go easy on the businessman. He simply didn't like him. And he did like both Katy and Vera.

Despite his anger, Delchamp maintained control. "Inside!" he said.

Concho followed as they entered the house. As expected, all was neat and orderly within. Maureen Delchamp seemed the type to control her home as tightly as she apparently controlled her anger at her husband. Of course, she probably had a maid. Most folks living along this street would have help for the housework and, usually, for cooking and childcare.

A hallway floored in hardwood led into a kitchen and dining area at the end of the house. Concho could see the corner of a refrigerator and half of a modern-looking steel breakfast table with steel chairs.

Cold, he thought.

On the left side of the hall stood a closed room and the stairs leading up to the second-floor bedrooms. Beneath the stairs was a gun cabinet holding several expensive-looking shotguns.

Delchamp turned right, however, and entered what looked like a formal sitting room that didn't appear to get much use. It smelled stale. Everything seemed decorative, from the small antique tables holding antique lamps to the large, glass-fronted armoire, which mostly displayed trophies for women's softball and tennis. No books could be seen, not even old collectible ones.

Delchamp strode across the room and sank onto a small white loveseat. Immediately, his demeanor changed. His shoulders slumped and his face aged a dozen years.

"Does Katy know?" he asked, in a quiet voice.

Concho felt surprise at the sudden collapse of Delchamp's defenses but didn't let it show in his face. For all he knew, everything the gym owner did could be an act. He glanced around for a seat. The few chairs in the room were antiques and he had his doubts they'd bear his weight. He certainly didn't want to join Delchamp on the couch. He stood.

"She doesn't," he replied.

"I don't want her or Vera to know."

"Not under my control," Concho said.

Delchamp looked up, with maybe a little fire back in his grayish eyes. "You don't have to tell them."

"Doubt I'd talk to Vera. Or would tell her if I did. As for Katy, I've no reason to tell her at present but if she asks me a direct question, I'm not going to lie for you."

"It's important for you to understand. Anne Reese is a first-class bitch and she came on to me. She started it. And she was of age."

Concho wanted to spit but the floor was innocent. "I'm sure that would be a great comfort to Katy," he said from behind twisted lips.

"You've destroyed my life!" Delchamp whined. "Even my wife won't forgive me for this one. Not for Katy's friend."

"If your life is destroyed," Concho said, "it's from your ability to blame other people besides yourself for your weaknesses. But I didn't come to talk to you about your affairs. There's something else."

"What?" Delchamp asked warily.

"The robbery Katy and Anne were involved in. Something was taken besides a few thousand in cash. Something worth a lot more than the cash itself to someone who is willing to kill over it."

"Like what?"

"Maybe account numbers. For hidden accounts. Offshore accounts. The kind that wouldn't get reported if they were emptied suddenly."

Concho watched Delchamp closely, looking for any kind of slip or accidental acknowledgment that such accounts existed. He didn't get it. It might not mean they didn't exist but it certainly weakened the loose theory Concho had been working on. Still, with both Anne Reese and Emily Zapatero involved, both of whom had had affairs with William Delchamp, the safest bet was that he was somehow the focus.

"You mean like money laundering," Delchamp said.

"Yeah."

"You can't pin any such thing on me." He vented a low, humorless laugh. "Hell, my business is mortgaged to the hilt."

Interesting, Concho thought, but what he said was, "You had most of your business accounts at that bank. The fact Anne Reese targeted it specifically is telling. Clearly, you two didn't end it well. Maybe she wanted to get even. Can you think of any way she might have been able to do so by robbing that particular bank?"

Again, Concho was fishing. This time he got a bite, a small one. Delchamp's face flushed slightly but he quickly regained his equilibrium.

"I don't..." He shook his head. His next words came quickly. "Can't see how she could hurt me. The bank's insured. The customers wouldn't be held responsible for any loss."

Concho knew the man was withholding information but he had only one more bit of leverage to bring to bear.

"Have you arranged for Vera and your wife to leave town?"

Concho asked.

Delchamp glanced up, startled. "What? What are you talking about? Why would they leave town?"

"I'm going to tell you something you don't appear to know," Concho said. "Anne Reese has been murdered. In her jail cell. It'll likely be on the news this evening."

Delchamp startled. He sat up straight. Concho couldn't tell if he were acting. "What? My God!"

"She was almost certainly murdered because of the robbery," Concho continued. "Whoever killed her is likely to go after everyone else who knows anything about it. If you're such a one, you better make sure Vera and your wife are not in the line of fire. Of course, you could come clean with me right now and we'll get all of you into police protection."

Delchamp shook his head. He'd calmed and even offered Concho a small sneer. "I couldn't care less that Anne Reese is dead. I told you, she was a bitch. She probably pissed off the wrong person with her nonsense and they killed her. I doubt it had anything to do with the bank robbery. More likely, wrong place, at the wrong time, with the wrong attitude."

"In my experience, it doesn't usually work that way."

Delchamp snorted. "You'll forgive me if I'm not overawed by your 'experience'!"

"Didn't think you would be," Concho said. "I thought you might be worried about your family. I see, again, I was wrong. Well, you have my number if you change your mind. Better not wait too long, though. Until it's too late."

"As the saying goes, don't let the door hit you in the ass on the way out!"

Concho let Delchamp see him smile. "You're a riot," he said. "But another saying might fit here."

"Oh! Do tell."

"One riot, one Ranger."

***

After leaving Delchamp's house, Concho sat in his truck a moment. He made a radio report updating Texas Ranger headquarters on his progress, then called Isaac Parkland to tell him what he'd found out. The call went to voicemail and he felt relieved. Maybe his friend was taking things a little easier. The sheriff had certainly been working too hard lately and didn't need any more stress.

"Isaac," Concho said into the recorder, "when this is over, I'm taking you fishing. Get your gear ready. I know a great place down along the Rio Grande."

Concho tucked away his cell, started his truck, and headed back for the reservation. He had just driven by the Eagle Pass Mall and was reaching to turn on some music when he realized he'd picked up a follower. And they weren't being any too coy about letting him know they were on his tail. He hung a left at the next turnaround and made another turn into the mall lot, staying well away from the building as he parked his truck and got out.

The afternoon grew late; the sun was still hot, baking down on the asphalt of the parking lot. He could smell tar and see the stains of dripped oil and other automobile fluids. Sweat started on his face. All in all, he'd rather be home.

An ivory-colored Lincoln Continental pulled into the lot and parked across from him. The driver and front-seat passenger got out. These were large gentlemen of the bodyguard persuasion. Both were Hispanic, with shaved heads and shoulder holsters under their matching expensive gray suits.

One man opened the rear door of the Lincoln and his boss slid across the seat and out. The boss wore a much more expensive linen suit the same color as the car. He appeared fiftyish but already had iron-gray hair, carefully curled and styled. He looked quite a bit like Ricardo Montalban, Concho thought, but he felt sure he was about to speak to Lucio Zapatero.

The man approached, stopping a polite few feet away. "Officer Ten-Wolves," he said. "I'm sorry to accost you in such a fashion." The voice was practiced, meant to exhibit both cultural refinement and a mastery of English, but the practice couldn't completely hide the distinct accent undercurrent, indicating Spanish as this man's first language.

Concho shrugged. "I've got time. Mr. Zapatero."

Zapatero smiled. "I see you recognize me. That saves us some effort." He steepled his fingers in front of him. "But I'm afraid you've upset my wife terribly."

"Not my intent. But things like that happen in my line of work."

Zapatero gave a small, "Hmph!" Then, "You're a very big man, Mr. Concho. But I have two very big men who work for me also."

The two bodyguards took a step forward in concert to stand at Zapatero's shoulders. Concho gave them a once over and said in a flat and controlled voice:

"I see. If you want to keep them, better have 'em take a step back so I don't feel so crowded."

For a moment, the tableau held. Tension thrummed the air. Zapatero smiled and lifted a hand with one finger raised. In unison, his guards took a step back and relaxed into what someone with military experience would call "at ease" posture.

Concho smiled. "Good. Now we can all be friendly again."

"You do not seem a friendly man at all, Mr. Concho," Zapatero said. "I can see why my wife is not fond of you."

"Sometimes I grow on people," Concho said.

"I rather hope we don't see each other that often," Zapatero said.

Concho shrugged.

Slowly, Zapatero grasped the left side of his jacket with two fingers and lifted it away from his body. His other hand slid beneath the jacket while Concho watched and withdrew a cell phone.

"Let me give you my direct number," Zapatero said. "Should you need to speak to my wife again, I hope you'll do me the courtesy of giving me a call first."

"If I can, I will," Concho said.

Zapatero's nearly black eyes burned into the even darker ones of Concho. Finally, the man realized he'd gotten the best he could expect to get.

"All right," he said. "I suppose it will have to be sufficient. For now."

Concho took out his own phone and tapped in the number Zapatero gave him. "We done?" he asked next.

"I sincerely hope we are," Zapatero said. "For both our sakes." He tucked the phone back into an inside pocket of his suit and strode back to his car.

One of Zapatero's guards held the door for his boss, then closed it. Concho watched the two war-hounds as they returned to the vehicle themselves and the Lincoln pulled back onto the highway and headed toward home. He hid away his own phone.

A glance across the parking lot took in the mall. Most likely, Maria Morales would still be in her office. Concho smiled as he strode off in that direction.

CHAPTER 30

As Concho entered the Mall de las Aguilas, or the Eagle Pass Mall as many called it, he saw no overt signs that just a month previously a group of Aryan Brotherhood members under the command of the neo-Nazi Darrell Fallon had seized control of the building. Fallon and his men had threatened hundreds of hostages and killed a few. They'd planned to blow up the building and kill many more.

As a Texas Ranger, Concho had responded to the call. He'd taken out more than half a dozen Brotherhood members with varied weaponry, including a bow and arrows. He'd captured Fallon after a fistfight in the mall's parking lot as the Brotherhood leader tried to commandeer an ambulance dispatched to help care for the injured.

During the incident, two of the mall's entrances had been blown open. Stores had been robbed and vandalized, glass windows and storefronts shattered, and one of the bathrooms torn up. In the past month, businesses and kiosks had been renewed. Entrances had been repaired and bloodstains scrubbed away.

For the knowledgeable visitor, however, the signs of the invasion and its results were still clear. For example, as Concho arrived at Maria Morales's office, he found the door locked and a brand new intercom installed. He thumbed the intercom button and heard a corresponding buzz inside.

"Who is it?" Maria answered.

"Texas Rangers, ma'am," Concho said in his 'official' voice. "I'm here to ask you a few questions."

"Uh oh," Maria said. "I bet it has to do with that awful fellow named Concho Ten-Wolves."

Concho grinned but kept his voice stern. "It does indeed, ma'am. We have reason to suspect you've been cavorting with this Ten-Wolves which is against community standards."

Maria tried to maintain character but lost it in laughter. "Cavorting even!" she said after she caught her breath.

"I thought the 'community standards' thing was funnier."

Maria chuckled again and unlocked her door remotely. Concho heard it buzz and pulled it open, then stepped inside to see a narrow stairway leading up to the second floor. He started up the steps and a vision appeared at the top. At least, Concho often thought such when he saw Maria.

She wore a black, pencil skirt with stockings and low heels, and a long-sleeved blouse in pale gold. Her long black hair was up in a ponytail but various strands had escaped and framed her face. She wore only a trace of makeup. She didn't need any.

Concho's mouth dried; his body tingled. He sped his pace up the steps and Maria met him halfway. She pushed her way into his arms and he wrapped them around her. Her scent flooded his nostrils. A kiss melted their mouths together and left them both shaking.

Concho slid one arm beneath Maria's legs; he picked her up and carried her the rest of the way up the stairs while she laughed raucously. He sat her on her feet next to the office desk and she immediately shoved her skirt down and kicked it off. She grabbed Concho's arm and pulled him toward the black leather couch positioned against one wall.

He resisted only long enough to unbuckle his gun belt and

lay it across Maria's desk, then let himself be pulled, and pushed down onto the couch. The leather crackled under him. For a long breath, Maria stood over him. Her dark eyes were dilated; she licked her lips. She kicked off her heels and started to strip away her underwear and stockings.

Concho fumbled at his jeans and started to push them and his own underwear down. Maria took hold of his left leg and worked his boot off. After repeating that with the right, she grabbed the bottoms of his jeans and started jerking. Concho lifted his hips to help her, and she got him undressed and threw the jeans across the room. She fell on top of him.

Their mouths met again. Their teeth clicked once together but they didn't care. Maria shifted her lower body and took Concho inside of her. Her hands shoved his shirt up, her nails scraping across his belly and chest.

Concho's hands enfolded her hips, spanning from front to back. He held tight while they made love quickly, almost savagely, their mouths clinging, their bodies thrusting. In a few wild minutes, it was over, leaving them both sated and sighing.

Slowly, Maria sat upright, with Concho still inside of her. She smiled and pushed the long sheave of her ponytail back over a shoulder. "I'm afraid, Officer," she said, "that I've been 'cavorting' with Ten-Wolves again."

Concho laughed and lightly stroked her hip. "All charges have been dropped," he said. "The investigating officer has been compromised."

"Oh, indeed, he has," Maria said as she slid off him and scooped up her stockings, underwear, and skirt.

Concho sat up on the couch and watched her start to dress in front of him, completely unselfconsciously. He suppressed a little groan of pleasure at her beauty, then got up and headed across the room to retrieve his jeans and underwear. Feeling a little self-conscious himself, he pulled them on with his back to his lover.

When he turned around to face Maria again, she was completely dressed, with her blouse tucked neatly into her skirt and her stockings and heels on. She looked cool and unruffled, with only a faint blush on her cheeks to indicate that anything unusual had happened. In contrast, he knew he was a complete mess, with his shirt hanging out, his belt askew, his white socks dirty.

"You're beautiful," he blurted, feeling like a fifteen-year-old crushing on a girl.

"Thank you," she said as she walked over and pecked him on the cheek. "So, tell me, Officer Ten-Wolves, was this just a booty call or did you come to see me for some other reason?"

Concho shook his head as the feeling of being a teenager dissipated. "Booty call? Ever the romantic, aren't you?"

She laughed. "You're romantic enough for both of us." The laugh segued into a fond and loving smile. "And I appreciate it. But I also know you're a busy fellow. Solving crimes and busting bad guys. And bad girl bank robbers. So…"

"So," Concho said, "mainly I just wanted to see you. I think I'm addicted."

"Mmmm," she murmured. She kissed him again. No peck this time but a lingering exploration of his mouth. "See how romantic you are," she said.

"A regular Romeo," he murmured.

"By the way, I've got those books you asked for. It's a trilogy. The writer is Kenneth Oppel. They're YA. Pretty popular apparently."

"Oh! I didn't figure you'd had a chance to pick them up yet. I was gonna tell you that since I was in town, I'd stop for them."

"I had business over at Walmart this morning anyway. Got them then but they're still in my car. You want me to bring them to your place this evening?" She wriggled her eyebrows at him.

Concho groaned in mock agony. "I wish," he said. "But I'll likely stay at the Kickapoo police station again. Besides, I'm actually going to deliver the books to Isaac Parkland over at the sheriff's office. They're for someone in a cell there named Cindy Karnes."

"Oh? What's that about?"

"She's one of the bank robbers. And a reader. Turns out she was at the same Hunger Games signing with Katy Delchamp and Anne Reese. That's how Reese knew her to recruit her."

"Wow!"

"Yeah, you finding those pictures cracked the case open."

"When do I get a badge and a gun?"

"You've already got a Texas Ranger in your pocket."

Maria shrugged. "Meh. He's OK."

Concho grinned and kissed her. "Anyway," he said, "I thought the promise of books might put Cindy at ease."

"Did it work?"

"A little. She was friendly enough but doesn't really know anything helpful. At least, I don't think she does. She's pretty much an innocent actually." He frowned. "That's one thing that bothers me. Both Cindy Karnes and Katy Delchamp seem to be good kids. The other two, Anne Reese and Tessa Mercadel, they're different stories. Both rough customers. Anne, in particular. She also had some kind of hold over both Cindy and Katy. I don't understand it."

"Some mothers and fathers do that to their children," Maria said. "Particularly their daughters. It happens when you start out being overprotected and suddenly see through the sham. Young women like that, they get disillusioned. They start looking around for someone older and 'cooler' to replace their parents in esteem. Maybe these two girls settled on Anne Reese."

Concho nodded. "From what I've picked up about Katy, that sounds exactly right. I'll have to look into Cindy's parents."

Maria nodded. "Tell you what, Parkland's office is close along my drive home. I know you're busy so I'll drop the books off to him right after work. How's that sound? For Cindy Karnes, right?"

"Yes, but I hate for you to have to go to any trouble."

Maria grinned. "Seeing as how I've already been ruined by the evil Concho Ten-Wolves, I might as well get used to seeing the inside of a police station. Don't you think?"

Concho answered with his best leer.

CHAPTER 31

Concho had almost reached the turnoff for the reservation when he realized he'd picked up another tail. Unlike Zapatero and his goons, this one wanted to stay hidden. They were following well back in a nondescript vehicle.

The Ranger's lips tightened. He was getting a little tired of people pushing him. Maybe it was time to push back. An idea sprang fully formed into his mind and he pulled a U-turn and started back to Eagle Pass as if he'd forgotten something.

Taking out his phone, he held it up to his ear and acted like he was talking into it as he passed his hangers-on. There were two of them, though he didn't take a good look because he didn't want to spook them. The car was a brown Ford Taurus, an older model.

Concho kept an eye on his rear-view mirror as he continued on into Eagle Pass but now he made an actual call—to Terrill Hoight.

"Yo!" Hoight answered. "I was just about to call you."

"Oh?"

"Just heard. A trooper out of San Antonio located Mason French's Porsche Boxster. Hidden among some trees and abandoned near a rest top off Interstate 35. Two bodies were found in the men's bathroom. Tim and Donna Sutherland. Newlyweds, apparently. The woman was raped."

Concho's hands tightened brutally on his steering wheel. "No sign of French, I take it," he snarled.

"No."

"He took their car? The newlyweds?"

"That's what the trooper figured. Apparently, they were registered to own a Chevy Trailblazer. 2019. Silver. The Sheriff has already put an APB out on it."

"We might have a shot," Concho said. "I'll bet anything he's coming here. In fact, I suspect he's already here. And maybe involved with why I'm calling you."

"Speak it!"

"It's not an emergency but I need your help again. I've picked up a tail and want to set a trap for them."

"You figure it's French?"

"I doubt it's him personally. But I bet he's behind it. He wanted Katy Delchamp bad enough before to send his killers after a Texas Ranger in the middle of the day along a highway. I doubt he's given up. And if he wants to find Katy, he's got to know I'm the way."

"I'm in."

"You think you could get ahold of Roland Turner and bring him in on it?"

"Don't see why not."

"All right. Here's what I'll need you to do."

***

Concho drove back through town and out along Highway 277. He drove as if he had a purpose and his tail kept pace with him. They were mediocre at the business and he felt sure they didn't know he was on to them.

A couple of miles outside Eagle Pass proper, Concho turned off 277 onto a dirt and gravel side road leading toward the Rio Grande. He didn't plan to go far. The road was wider than most and carefully maintained as it ran between fields full of scrub brush and dried brown grass where a few cattle grazed.

He passed a working oil well on his right, then came to a sharp curve that cut off his view of the highway behind him. Right around the curve stood a fenced-off compound where the Texas Department of Transportation, TxDOT, kept some of its road graders and mowing equipment. The gate was open. Terrill Hoight had arranged that as Concho had requested.

The Ranger pulled his Dodge into the compound and parked behind a pile of gravel the size of the Titanic. He left the engine running but got out. The light had yellowed as the day began to fade. Less than forty-five minutes remained until dark. A fitful breeze, stirred by the falling temperatures of evening, moaned with a lonely sound through the parked machinery.

Concho positioned himself where he could see the road without being seen from it. No vehicles showed but he was patient. The men tailing him would avoid making themselves obvious and would first have stayed on 277 past Concho's turnoff. When he didn't reappear, however, they'd likely come along for a look. And he doubted they'd be overly patient themselves.

Five minutes passed. He returned to his truck and took a second to streak red ocher on his cheeks before returning to his watch. Another ten minutes passed. The crunch of gravel came echoing along the road.

A brown Ford Taurus passed the compound, kept going. Concho smiled and darted back to his truck. Shifting into drive, he pulled out from behind the gravel pile without revving his engine. Exiting the compound, he turned down the road behind the Taurus. The Ford was about a hundred yards ahead of Concho when blue lights flared in front of it. The amplified voice of Terrill Hoight blasted the air.

"Halt your vehicle and exit!"

First, the brake lights on the Taurus flashed. Then the backup lights came on. Gravels flew as the Ford's tires spun backwards. Concho hit his own police lights and punched the gas on his Dodge, quickly closing the gap between the two vehicles.

With nowhere to go, the Ford slid to a stop. But it didn't end there. The passenger door thrust open. A red-haired man bailed out with both hands full of guns—what looked like Mac-10 machine pistols or a knockoff of such. He was trying to aim them in both directions, at Concho and at Terrill Hoight.

Concho had started to slow to avoid ramming the Ford but, now, he accelerated again. His left front bumper slammed into the right side of the Ford, sending it slewing around. The car clipped the gunman, sending him flying just as he opened fire. Bullets sprayed the air and ground but didn't hit any soft targets.

Now, the driver of the Taurus bailed. He didn't try to shoot. He ran toward the fenced-in field to the left, going to his belly to slip under the lowest strand of barbed wire, which caught and ripped his shirt before he surged back to his feet and raced off.

Concho threw his truck into park and leaped out. He couldn't see into the ditch on the other side of the Ford where the gunman had landed but he heard Terrill Hoight shouting at the man to, "Stay on the ground." He heard the crack of a shot from what had to be Hoight's service pistol.

A hoarse voice cried out in response to the shot, "Don't shoot, man! Don't shoot! I give up."

The shooter was out of the picture but the second man was getting away. Concho rushed toward the fence. Afternoon shadows were turning to evening darkness but, in the dying light, he could see the runner churning across the field, his feet kicking up dust and dead leaves of grass.

"Stop!" Concho shouted.

The racing man glanced over his shoulder, his face fearful. But maybe he saw that Concho didn't have a gun in his hand. He didn't stop but redoubled his efforts. Concho growled in irritation as he grabbed the capped top of a steel fence post and used it as leverage to help him vault over the top wire of the fence. He landed running, some twenty yards behind the fleeing driver.

"Stop!" he shouted again.

This shout didn't work any better than the first so the Ranger gave up on talk and concentrated on the run. The fleeing man was younger than he was but probably not in as good of shape. And he didn't have Concho's long legs. Quickly, the gap began to close.

The runner took another glance over his shoulder; his face showed startlement as he realized how close Concho was to catching him. He tried to redouble his efforts again but didn't have it in him. A stumble nearly felled him; he swung around with an oath to face his pursuer. His hand grabbed at his belt where a sleek semiautomatic pistol waited. The gun came free.

Concho didn't slow down; he plowed straight into the man in a move he'd learned playing football in college. It was called "running through your target." The impact sounded like a watermelon being slammed into a concrete wall.

The man's gun went flying one way, his body the other. He hit the ground and rolled through the dust. By the time he got himself into a sitting position, Concho loomed above him.

"You're finished!" the lawman said.

The downed man's nose was bloody. He wiped it on the back of his hand and his shoulders sagged. Concho grasped his arm and jerked him to his feet, then pulled his arms behind him and handcuffed him. Dragging the fellow around to face him, Concho made sure the slashes of warpaint were clearly visible as he leaned in close and offered his best predator's smile.

"It's almost dark out here," he said with soft menace. "The others can't see from the road. And before we go back to that safe haven, you're going to tell me who sent you to tail me. Or else!"

The man had brown eyes. Concho could read the thoughts behind them. Something like, who is this crazy Indian? What's he going to do to me? The gaze dropped and the shoulders slumped, signifying defeat. He gave the answer Concho expected.

"Mason French," he said wearily.

CHAPTER 32

Night now. Concho's Dodge Ram sped swiftly back into Eagle Pass, headed for the Motel 6 at 2338 E Main Street, not far from the Mall de las Aguilas. Roland Turner, one of Isaac Parkland's deputies, sat in the passenger seat of the truck. His dark face was calm, even though they were likely on their way to dispense and receive violence.

Once the man Concho had run down in the field admitted surrender, he'd been free with information. Mason French and three additional men were staying at the Motel 6, room 223. French wanted revenge on Concho and to get Katy Delchamp back in his grasp. Seems like things had become personal rather than business.

Terrill Hoight had complained at not being included in the motel raid but accepted his role of escorting the two prisoners to jail. Concho promised Hoight he'd get his turn at more bad guys in the future. He'd also called Roberto Echabarri at KTTT headquarters and asked him to inform Katy he'd be late seeing about her tonight.

Wheeling into the Motel 6 parking lot, Concho immediately sighted three big sport bikes on their stands. He couldn't be sure but they looked like some of the same ones that had been parked outside Mason French's Hot, Blue and Righteous. Had it been just yesterday? Much had happened since.

Concho let Turner out by the front door, then pulled around the back and got out. To either side of the motel's rear entrance stood a small fenced-off area to hide the business's trash cans. Right above it was a wooden awning and two windows. According to Roland Turner, the window on the left marked room 223. The deputy had arrested a drug dealer there just a few weeks earlier.

The parking lot was well lit but empty of observers. Balancing on a pair of short yellow poles just outside the modesty fence, Concho reached up and grasped the edge of the awning. From there, it was an easy swing to the top of the wooden structure. The brown awning hung supported by two metal poles attached to the motel wall and creaked dangerously under Concho's weight. He held his breath as he tiptoed to the window.

From within 223 came a dim and flickering light, the moving shadows cast by the TV. Concho heard Matt Dillon's voice warning an evildoer that drawing on him would be a mistake. Gunsmoke made an appropriate background for what was very likely to happen in the next few minutes.

After waiting against the wall to make sure his movements outside had not been heard or recognized, Concho peeked surreptitiously through the window. Three men lounged inside. One sat in a chair; the other two lay stretched across the beds, one single and one double. All had weapons close to hand. He couldn't see Mason French but maybe he was in the bathroom which was closed.

The face of one man was clearly limned by the light of a dim bedside lamp. Concho remembered faces better than motorcycles. This fellow had been in Hot, Blue, and Righteous playing pool when Concho had visited. It was evidence enough. These were the men Ten-Wolves sought.

A few more minutes passed. Concho waited patiently with a Colt Double Eagle .45 in his right hand. A knock banged on the door. The men inside were instantly alert, their hands seeking the comfort of weapons. The man in the chair moved toward the door carrying a machine pistol.

"Who is it?" he called through the door.

Roland Turner's voice answered. "Police!" he said. "Open up!"

The tension in the three men spiked into the stratosphere. Concho ducked back from the window as one man turned and rushed toward it.

"Sure, Officer!" one of the three called. "Just a sec."

The window slid upward from inside the room. A head poked out, followed by the upper body of one of the bikers.

"Coming, Officer!" the fellow near the door called.

Concho tensed. He hoped Roland Turner had moved away from the door. He had to trust in the officer's intelligence and training. The criminal climbing through the window must have sensed Concho standing over him. Or maybe he caught the lawman's shadow pinned by the overhead streetlights. He turned his head and looked up. His eyes showed surprise.

Concho slammed the barrel of his pistol down across the man's skull. The biker collapsed, unconscious, halfway in and halfway out of the room. Someone shouted inside the room. Gunfire opened up as a voice shouted, "Screw you, cop!"

The bullets must have been flung toward the door, toward Roland Turner. Concho stepped into the framing of the window. One man fired at the door. The other rushed toward the window but paused as he saw his partner's body draped across the windowsill and the big bulk of the Ranger standing over him.

"Freeze!" Concho shouted.

The man swung up the pistol in his hand but Concho fired first, through the upper pane of the window. Glass shattered inward. Concho's first shot missed, whizzing past the gunman's head. The man flinched and, by that time, Concho had fired twice more. Both bullets struck the biker square in the body, flinging him backward and down.

Concho palmed his left-hand Colt. The gunman who'd been

shooting through the door spun toward the window, swinging his machine pistol to bear. Concho fired once with his second Colt. The bullet caught the man just above the nose and exploded through his skull, dropping him to the floor like a torn sack of wet groceries.

Using his forearm, Concho chopped the wooden frame out of the window and lunged through, his pistols tracking toward the bathroom where he expected Mason French to be hiding. No sound came from that room. The Ranger moved toward it while gun smoke tingled in his nostrils. He called outside to Deputy Turner.

"Roland! They're down! French may have barricaded himself in the toilet!"

Concho half expected shots from the bathroom to track his voice but nothing happened. Turner came through the bullet-riddled front door with his gun drawn.

"How many?" the deputy asked.

"Two dead," Concho replied. "The one in the window is unconscious. Could you check him?"

"Right," Turner said.

Concho eased over to the bathroom door. "French!" he said. "If you're in there, give it up."

Silence answered him and the place had a feeling of barrenness. Concho reached to the doorknob and twisted it open. The light was on inside but the room was empty. Mason French was nowhere to be found. Again.

***

Five blocks away from the Motel 6, Mason French, the man Concho was looking for, stood on the roof of a closed law office and studied the back parking lot of the motel through a pair of binoculars. He'd used the dumpster behind the office to climb up to his vantage point and now followed the events unfolding before his eyes.

Beneath the glow of sodium vapor lights, he saw a tall man he figured to be Concho Ten-Wolves park and exit his truck. He watched the officer clamber up on an awning behind the motel, which was just outside the window of the room Mason's men had previously rented. A few minutes later, a spate of gunfire rattled the air. The sound rose like firecrackers on New Year's Eve, then faded into silence.

Concho disappeared into the hotel through the window, into the room where Mason French himself would have been hanging out if he hadn't got a phone call half an hour earlier from the fellow designated as "Scout" on his contact list. Scout had previously given him the news of Anne Reese's death. Now it looked like he might have saved Mason's life, making him well worth the small "retainer" Mason paid.

"French!" the voice on the line had said.

"Yeah?"

"Something's working. I don't know what but that Texas Ranger is involved. And a couple of Parkland's deputies are here in town. It might be about you."

"That it?" he'd asked.

"Ain't it enough?"

"For now," Mason said as he hung up.

He'd told his men he was going on a "scouting" expedition and to stay alert. He'd laughed to himself at the inside joke. It was certainly a good thing he'd gotten out of the motel when he did. Damn Ten-Wolves! The man kept getting on his last nerve and needed to pay.

Climbing down from the roof, Mason tossed the binoculars into his Chevy Trailblazer and abandoned it. He left the vehicle unlocked with the keys in it as he made away on foot through the night. With any luck, someone would abscond with it and help cover his tracks. He'd have to steal another car himself but that shouldn't be too much trouble.

Sirens began to wail in the distance and he spotted blue lights headed for the motel as local police responded to the shooting. None of them came anywhere close to him but he didn't tarry. When he felt safe, he called Scout.

"You were right," he said. "Ten-Wolves raided my room. Don't know how he found out about it, but it is what it is."

"He's smart," Scout said.

"Or lucky. Anyway, he'll be dead soon enough. I've had it with him."

"Glad to hear it. You still want the girl?"

"If you're talking about Katy Delchamp, you're damn right, I do."

"Then I've got someone you ought to talk to. Big guy locally. Rich. You two have some goals in common."

"All right," Mason said. "Give me his number."

"He's gonna have to call you. If that's OK?"

Mason considered. Every instinct told him to cut his losses and run. But to Hell with it!

"Let him call," he said.

CHAPTER 33

It was after 11:00 PM when Concho pulled into the park-ing lot of Kickapoo Tribal Police headquarters. The building was dim except for one light blazing in the front office belonging to Roberto Echabarri.

The Ranger climbed out of his truck and stretched wearily. It always took it out of him to deal with the aftermath of a shooting, the questions and scrutiny from the coroner and other police—even if generally sympathetic—the scrounging by reporters on the scene for every scrap of potentially incriminating evidence, the personal toll of having taken a life. He'd taken more than he cared to dwell on, both as a soldier in war overseas, and as an officer of the law in the United States. It was never an easy thing.

The building was unlocked and Concho stepped into the shadowy interior. Nila Willow had drawn night watch and sat at the dispatcher's desk. Only a focused desk lamp guided her pen across the paperwork she filled out. She smiled at Concho as he entered. The Ranger gestured across the hall toward Echabarri's office.

"I hope he didn't wait up on my account," he said quietly.

Nila shrugged and pointed over his shoulder. Concho turned to find Echabarri standing in the door of his office.

"Long day, I take it?" the head of the tribal police asked.

"Way too long. Three men in cuffs. Two more dead."

"Sorry to hear."

Concho nodded.

"Come in," Echabarri said, turning back into his office and moving across to a small table beside his desk. A coffee pot and a stack of red styrofoam cups stood on the table. "Care for some?" Echabarri asked as he poured himself half a cup.

Concho shook his head. "Nope. I need sleep if anything."

The police chief sipped his coffee, made a face. "Right. Well, I'm about to call it a day myself, but Nila can help you with anything you need."

"Didn't mean to keep you up past your bedtime," Concho said.

Echabarri chuckled and waved the comment away.

"Katy asleep?" Concho asked.

"Yep."

"Nope," a voice said from the hallway and both men turned to find Katy standing in the doorway of the office looking at them. Her hair was tangled, her face full of sleep. She looked eighteen if she were a day, although she was four years older in reality.

"Sorry I'm so late getting here," Concho said.

"Doesn't matter. Did you get him?"

"You mean Mason French?"

"Yes."

"Who told you I was trying for him?"

"Just didn't imagine it could be anyone else. I knew he wouldn't run."

"Guess you know him better than I do."

"You spend a day with a maniac who wants to kill you or…do other things to you, and you'd get to know him too."

"I see your point," Concho said.

Katy sighed. Echabarri finished his half cup of coffee and grabbed the hat he'd taken to wearing, a flat-crowned gray Stetson. Roberto was very young for a police chief. Maybe he thought the hat added some needed gravitas. It sort of did.

"Gotta get home," Echabarri said. He slapped Concho lightly on the shoulder as he passed. He offered Katy a nod and a gentle "Miss Delchamp," before heading out the door.

Katy and Concho stared at each other. Then, "I have to get out of here!" Katy said. "Just for a little while. I can't...stand it. It's. Everyone's so nice but..." Her words trailed away

Concho considered the dangers. He didn't foresee any if they stayed on the reservation. "All right," he said. "Let's go."

Surprise blanked Katy's face. She clearly hadn't expected him to agree. But very quickly a smile crossed her lips and her eyes brightened. "Lead the way," she said.

They headed for the truck and Concho helped Katy climb in before getting in and starting the engine. Not far off could be seen the lights of the Kickapoo Lucky Eagle Casino which was still doing a booming business.

"Can we...could we go to the casino?" Katy asked.

Concho sighed and shook his head. "Afraid not. I can't imagine Mason French would be there but more of his men might be around. We can drive, though." He pressed the button to roll both windows down. "And get some fresh air."

Katy nodded and sat back in her seat with a satisfied smile.

They turned away from the casino and headed deeper into the reservation along a wide dirt road. Houses rose on either side of them, silent under the moon. Some were brick and looked like any other suburban home. Others were trailers or what were called "manufactured" homes. Here, close to the casino and its heavy tourist population, most yards were kept neat and tidy, even down to lawns and flower beds.

The more isolated homes on the Rez were often very different, with yards full of wrecked machinery, junker cars, broken toys, chicken coops, and sometimes a wickiup, the traditional lodge of the Kickapoo people. Concho rather preferred the latter houses to the former. In a strange way, they looked more alive.

Concho kept his speed down. Katy trailed her hand out the

window as they drove. The breeze stirred her hair, which looked like it had grown longer in just the last couple of days. The scent of mesquite and night flowers filtered through the truck. The air was naturally cool in a way air conditioning could never achieve.

"I have a question," Concho said.

"Ask."

"Do you know if your father had a safety deposit box at the bank?"

Katy glanced over. "I imagine he did. Don't know for sure. Why?"

"When I talked to your father, I asked him about any offshore accounts. He denied it. Acted like it was funny."

"You believe him? He's a liar, you know."

"Yes, but this didn't sound like a lie. So I'm thinking something else. Maybe he had something in a safety deposit box and that's what Anne was after, and what Emily Zapatero could supply."

"You mean something like…blackmail material?"

"Maybe."

Katy sat silently for a minute. "That…could be. How would you ever find out? Especially if they took it? And how would they have gotten access? Wouldn't they have to have my father's key to get in?"

"Emily worked there. Maybe she knew a way. Or they somehow made a copy of your father's key."

"Seems unlikely."

"Did Anne ever come to your house?"

Katy looked startled. "You think Anne could have made a copy?"

"Do you?"

Katy took a deep breath and sighed. "I guess. Maybe it's possible. Anne stayed over when we were both younger but," she looked away from Concho and out the window, "she was only there with me a couple of times in the last two years. She did…."

"Did what?"

"Once. About eight months ago. My parents were gone and I went over to see Vera. Anne went with me and…she searched my dad's office. She was looking for evidence regarding his cheating. At least, that's what she told me."

Concho nodded. "I think we're on to something."

Katy said nothing and her good mood evaporated. Concho felt guilty. "We're almost there," he said as they turned onto a one-lane dirt road.

Katy looked interested again. "Almost where?"

"My place," Concho said. "Don't you want to see how a wild Indian lives?"

CHAPTER 34

Mason French's cell phone rang. He didn't recognize the number but it was local. It was likely the contact that Scout had told him about.

"Yeah?" he said as he answered.

"Mr. French," a man's voice said. "I've been told we two may have common ground on a certain sticky…issue."

Mason took an instant dislike to the voice. It was too artificial, like an actor's voice playing a role. He could hear the Mexican peasant underlying it. He didn't much care for Mexican peasants. Or any Mexicans for that matter.

But his immediate thoughts were, beggars can't be choosers. He'd lost his own personal army. He had limited cash to hire another. This Mexican peasant on the phone supposedly had gobs of money which meant guns and men to do what Mason French wanted them to do—kill Concho Ten-Wolves and take Katy Delchamp.

"I believe you're right," Mason said. "Let's talk! Mister Zapatero."

***

Fifty yards down the dirt track leading to Concho's trail-er, the Ranger slammed on his brakes and the truck slid to a gravel-crunching stop. Katy gasped in fear as the headlights flashed out and showed something very big facing them in the road.

"What in the world!" Katy said.

"Wild hog," Concho replied. "A boar. And a big one."

"Are they…dangerous?"

Concho nodded. "See those tusks in its jaws. Those will tear a person up if they get at you. He won't be able to hurt us in the truck though."

Katy still looked scared. She hit the button to roll up her window. "I didn't know wild hogs were around here. I mean, I've heard about them other places."

"They're all through Texas," Concho explained. "And becoming a serious nuisance. We've only just started having problems with them on the reservation."

Bristly black hair covered the boar blocking their path. The beast probably weighed close to four hundred pounds which was very large for a feral pig. It's mean-looking eyes squinted into the headlights. Its almost shovel-shaped snout was up, sniffing the air and apparently finding an enemy. Four tusks jutted out from its jaw, two from the bottom and two from the top that curved up the thick flesh of its lips. Each knife-bladed tooth was at least six or seven inches long.

A flurry of movement from the right caught the humans' attention. A flood of feral hogs rushed out from the cover of some mesquite bushes and spilled across the road right behind the boar. There were at least ten adult sows and about the same number of striped piglets and shoats. The sows ranged in color from black, to gray, to a brown and white one.

"A sounder!" Concho exclaimed.

"Is that what they call a group of wild hogs?" Katy asked.

"Yeah. Boars don't usually travel with them but this one must be trying to mate."

As soon as the sounder flowed into the brush on the opposite side of the road, the boar turned and lunged after them. Concho eased up on the brake and they resumed their drive.

"I was going to ask you how you could live out here all alone?" Katy said. "But it looks like you have the pigs for company."

Concho chuckled. "Pigs, coyotes, wild cats, rabbits, mice, owls, hawks, buzzards, doves, crows, bats, roadrunners, tortoises, frogs, snakes, spiders, and assorted bugs. I'm not often alone."

They pulled up in front of Concho's trailer. Midnight neared. The moon hung full overhead, dressing the trees and bushes and land with silver. The Ranger held the trailer door open for Katy. After following her in, he flipped on the living room light.

"Books!" Katy exclaimed.

A smile creased her face and she immediately walked over to a set of four bookshelves bracketing his TV. She began scanning the titles, which were mostly fiction in the mystery and historical genres.

Concho smiled at Katy's smile. He often did the same thing when he saw books in people's houses. He was always disappointed when there weren't any, or when folks had shelves full of knickknacks and DVDs instead of books.

"I used to have a lot more volumes," Concho said. "There's only eighty or so there. Mostly repurchases. Lost every book I had in a fire a little over a month ago."

Katy glanced sympathetically at him. "Ow!" she said. "Sorry to hear that."

She walked toward him.

"Would you like something to eat besides cereal?" Concho asked.

Her eyes brightened. "I might kill for it."

He grinned. "Bacon and eggs OK?"

"Not from…one of those wild pigs like we just saw, is it?"

"No. Regular old store-bought bacon."

"I'd love it. But I hate to put you to any trouble."

"Haven't eaten this evening myself, so I'm gonna fix some anyway."

"All right, I'll have two eggs and a couple slices of bacon."

"How you want 'em?"

"However you make yours will be fine."

Concho nodded and headed for the kitchen, saying, "Mi casa es su casa. There's tea and sodas in the fridge if you want one. Help yourself."

Slapping his cast iron skillet on the stove, Concho slathered in some butter and set it to heating. He took six eggs out of the fridge, as well as a box of microwavable bacon he'd bought recently out of curiosity. It wasn't as tasty as the real stuff but it was quicker. And he had hunger issues.

"Would it be possible to borrow your phone and call Vera?" Katy asked.

"She won't be in bed this late?"

"Unlikely, she's a real night owl."

Concho handed her the phone and she walked a few paces away to make her call. No one answered though, and she returned the phone to him. Her face showed puzzlement.

"Everything OK?" Concho asked.

Katy shrugged. "Guess she's asleep. Or maybe her phone battery's dead. Not like her though. I'll try again in the morning."

Concho handed Katy two forks and a couple of cloth napkins. "You could set the table for me," he said, nodding toward the glass-topped table in the den which was separated from the kitchen only by a long counter. "Our late-night breakfast supper is almost ready."

"Sure," she said. "What do you want to drink?"

"A big glass of ice tea will do me."

A couple minutes later, Concho carried two steaming plates to the table and placed one in front of Katy and the other by his own chair. Katy had poured him a glass of tea and selected a Cola for herself. She was already seated and Concho joined her and tucked into his meal.

Katy stared at the four eggs and pile of bacon on Concho's plate and raised an eyebrow. "Feeling peckish?" she asked.

Concho met her gaze and grinned. "One might think I was inspired by those hogs we saw. But really, this is just a light bedtime snack for a Kickapoo. Did you ever read The Lord of the Rings?"

"Only The Hobbit, so far."

"Well, we Kickapoo are like hobbits. First breakfast. Second breakfast. Elevenses."

Katy chuckled and took a bite of her own eggs. "Good," she said. She finished the first one quickly but began picking at the other. Her thoughts seemed elsewhere.

"You OK?" Concho asked, washing some bacon down with a big draught of tea.

She nodded, but added, "I guess I'm just wondering why you're being so nice to me. I don't see how I deserve it."

"I think you do. You're a good kid. Though maybe you listen to others too much instead of yourself."

Katy sat silently, then said, "I'm not a kid!"

Concho wiped his mouth on his napkin. "You're right," he said. "I apologize."

Katy turned her chair slightly to face him. Her gaze sought his. Concho saw her intent coming before the young woman herself knew it was happening. She practically lunged toward him, her mouth seeking a kiss.

Concho caught her shoulders and held her back. "That can't happen, Katy," he said quietly.

She slumped against his hands before pulling away to lean back in her chair. "I'm…sorry. I… Is it because I'm a witness in a case you're investigating?"

"That's part of it. But the main reason is, I'm seeing someone."

"Who?"

"I don't talk about her because my job could put her at risk. But it's been going on a while."

"And you wouldn't cheat on her? Most men would."

"I like to think that's not true."

Katy made a bitter face; clearly her thoughts were on her father.

"Do you love her?" she asked.

"I do."

"And how does she feel?"

He smiled. "I can't speak for her but I'm pretty sure she's fond of me, at least."

Katy smiled back, weakly. "I hope she treats you well."

"She does."

Katy rose, taking her plate with about half of her second egg on it and carrying it and her empty soda can to the kitchen. She returned a moment later. "I guess we have to go back to the police station," she said.

Concho started on his fourth egg. "I've got an extra room. I thought maybe you'd prefer to sleep in a bed tonight instead of a couch."

Katy nodded. "Just not your bed."

"No."

"I guess you're getting tired of sleeping in a chair too."

Concho forked the last bit of his late-night breakfast into his mouth, chewed and swallowed before saying. "Absolutely."

"I need to use your bathroom first," Katy said.

Concho rose, showed her the bathroom and the guest bedroom just beyond. He flipped on the lights for her.

"I'm going to bed too. If you need anything, I'm at the other end of the house."

Katy nodded, stepped into the bathroom and closed the door. Concho returned to the kitchen and rinsed the dishes, then headed for his own room. He heard Katy's bedroom door click shut.

The young woman was clearly hurt and he blamed himself for not realizing what was happening with her. She'd been through a lot in the last few days. He'd pulled her out of a bad place and he had been nice to her. He genuinely liked her. No wonder she'd become a bit overwhelmed by it all. Nothing he could do about it now but hope she'd feel better in the morning.

While these thoughts were running through his head, exhaustion kicked in and he fell deeply asleep. As happened to him sometimes during peak periods of stress, an experience from his past coalesced into a dream that illuminated his present. This time he returned to adolescence, to the moment in Kickapoo tradition when he transitioned from child to man. He was sixteen years old, on his vision quest, and dying.

CHAPTER 35

He has been running but now there's no strength for that. He walks. Occasionally, he stumbles. He crosses the reservation, between the low brown hills, through the scrub. A rocky stream finds him. He drinks and follows it. At some point, he is no longer on Kickapoo lands but it does not matter. He seeks and who knows where the thing he seeks hides.

He is not supposed to sleep. He does not. That is easier than fasting. It has been four days since anything but water crossed his lips. He is a big young man—even at sixteen. He loves food and it is denied him.

He must fast for another seventy-two hours but the hunger is a gnawing beast threatening to eat itself. His body is tired but restless, his throat tight and dry. Sometimes his belly growls a vicious symphony. Sometimes it rests as quiet as the grave.

On the fifth day, he begins to eye his deer-skin moccasins with a desire that bursts salivation in his mouth. Finally, he must kick them off and go barefooted among the rocks unless they tempt him to gorge.

The sun burns. A mesquite tree beckons with shade. He moves toward it but dares not sit or he will sleep. A buzzing sound catches his ear. He leaps back just as a rattlesnake in hiding strikes at him. It misses. He thinks. He moves on, knowing the shade is not for such as him.

The day grows and dies, turns into the sixth morning. Out beneath the sky, beneath the brass sun, he moves back and forth along the stream. It is here; he knows it is here. The thing he seeks. Why won't it reveal itself?

The hunger rides his shoulders now like an entity separate from himself. It is never silent but it never shouts. He sings to entertain it, to keep it quiescent. He sings in the language of scorpions and crows which he did not know until last night's moon taught him. The stream sings with him in its own voice.

At noon, when the sun hangs like a cross in the sky, he begins to dance. As he has been told, by someone, by some thing. Power grows in his world. Now, it is he who is sought. The thing he wants is coming. He must draw it closer, close enough to merge.

Hunger leaves. It spreads its wings and flies. He kneels by the stream and cups water to his mouth. It drips like glistening honey through his fingers. It flows like fog down his throat.

At times, over the last few days, he has doubted he has the magic to find what the elders expect him to find. He is Kickapoo, but he is also a product of the "civilized" world. He is a good student in school. He has studied biology and physics and astronomy. He knows the European names for the stars, as well as the Kickapoo names. But by the evening of this sixth day, he does not doubt that he has drawn magic to him.

He lies down by the stream, no longer afraid he will sleep. His body has become a cavern into which many things pour—saw-edged winds and the ringing sound of light breaking. The bed of stone he lies on becomes the softest blanket of beaver fur, the softest thing he has ever felt. Until it becomes glass.

He looks down and it is like looking up. The first stars leap into existence, painted suddenly on the blackening sky by spirit fingers. He can see all around, in an entire circle around his body, above and beneath. The stars become a swarm of blazing insects swirling close above him. Or perhaps he has been captured by a tiny sentient race of embers. They surround him in a phosphorescent wave.

He lies there with his eyes peeled wide. Between the silken dusk and the promise of dawn come the hours of wraths and wraiths, when the membranes of memory and experience are torn to shreds and reassembled into visions and truth. Concho begins to pray. The universe answers.

A pack of wolves, black as oil, polished as obsidian blades, comes rushing across the sky, their paws scattering stars like pebbles. Ten beasts make the pack. Concho watches them run. Yet, he is one of them too. He is both the leader and all those who follow.

They give chase, silently, to some vast prey that sweeps ahead of them through the Milky Way. The pack neither gains nor loses ground. Concho feels as if the chase will go on forever. He wants it to, for he is both excited and afraid of the prey leading their hunt. And he knows: when the chase ends, the greatest danger will birth.

But now something from the ground fights him. The rhythm of movement changes. The stars wink out to be replaced by flickering firelight inside a wickiup. Someone holds his head and dribbles a few drops of warm liquid into his mouth. Soup, he wants to say. But he dares not speak. Not first.

Meskwaa leans over him, neither older nor younger than he has ever been. But there are other elders in the background. Stern faces reveal nothing. He wonders if he has failed in his task. He wants to protest. But Meskwaa asks the question then, the only question of importance.

"Tell us if you had a vision."

Concho nods weakly but then gathers strength in his voice to shout, "Yes!"

Meskwaa does not look at the other elders but some communication passes between them—like a hum, like a throb, like a thunder.

"You have a name," Meskwaa tells him. "Ten-Wolves. Carry it as a man of the tribe."

***

Concho awoke. The clock by his bed said it was 6:00 in the morning but he already knew the time. It was the moment when he always awoke. And, as usual, he was wide awake when his eyes opened. He'd always been this way, even as a child. It had served him well in the military and it served him now. Because something was different about his world, and it wasn't just the aftermath of the dream.

Sitting up and pushing the covers back, he listened to his house. Nothing unusual. Of course, the house felt different because Katy Delchamp slept in his guest room but that wasn't what disturbed him. This feeling came from outside rather than inside. And as he processed it, his body relaxed. This wasn't a dangerous thing. And then he understood.

Slipping into jeans and a T-shirt, and sticking his big feet into the moccasins he kept by his bed for nocturnal activities, he opened the front door and stepped outside. As he expected, Meskwaa the Elder sat in one of the lawn chairs by Concho's firepit. The old man's presence would partially explain his dream of last night.

Concho approached the firepit. "Uncle!" he said. "Good morning."

Meskwaa let smoke from the filterless cigarette he smoked trickle from his nostrils. He acknowledged the greeting with a wave of his gnarled hand and indicated a second lawn chair nearby as if inviting Concho to sit. Concho had to smile at being invited to sit in his own yard but remained standing anyway. As always, if given a chance, Meskwaa had taken the biggest of the lawn chairs, the only one of the three that fitted Concho comfortably.

"You are sleeping late today," Meskwaa said. "I suppose it is inevitable that a little bit of laziness would creep in after such an injury as you suffered recently."

Meskwaa was probably referring to the knife wound which had come close to paralyzing Concho a little over a month previously but one could never be sure. He might be talking about a mosquito bite.

"I always rise at 6:00, Uncle. You know this."

"Indeed. I suppose you have always been a little lazy. Even as a child. I remarked upon it occasionally to your grandmother but she insisted you would grow out of it."

Concho swallowed a laugh. "Looks like you were both wrong."

Meskwaa only sighed.

"I wonder why you are here to see me this morning, Uncle?" Concho said. "Or is it only to decry my laziness?"

"I came to answer your question."

"What question?"

Meskwaa frowned as smoke wreathed his lined face. He pulled the cigarette out of his mouth. "How would I know what question you intend to ask me?"

Concho wanted to ask, "how would you know I had a question?" but it would do no good. He sighed and squeezed his way into the second chair which creaked ominously under his bulk. He realized that he indeed had a question.

"I dreamt of my naming ceremony last night," he said. "And there was something I did not remember before. A rattler struck at me."

Meskwaa nodded. "Yes, you were bitten."

"What?" Concho could hear the shock in his own voice.

"When we came to bring you to the council chamber, we saw the fang marks on your heel. A very large snake. A veritable Concho among rattlers."

"Why was I not told?"

"You would not have been ready to hear it. Besides, the wound had already started to mend."

"How did I not die?"

"A different question entirely."

"Huh?"

"People die when it is time for them to die. You know this."

"I know I've been told that. I'm not sure I believe it. Maybe... the snake's venom sacs were empty. If it had previously struck some other prey, the sacs might not have refilled before it bit me."

Meskwaa shook his head. "I pray one day you will stop being a white man."

"In case you haven't noticed, I'm a long way from a white man."

Meskwaa shrugged. "Such words are more proof that I speak true."

Concho felt a retort forming but both men heard the sound of the toilet flushing inside the trailer. Katy was awake and Concho found he wanted to get Meskwaa's input on the young woman, to see if his own judgment on her was sound.

"I have company," Concho said. "Her name is Katy Delchamp. A friend of sorts. I'd like you to meet her."

"I also came for that reason," Meskwaa said.

CHAPTER 36

Meskwaa sucked deeply on the butt of his cigarette and let the smoke trickle from his nostrils. "Katy is in trouble," he said. "And her family. But before she comes to find you this morning, I must speak to you of one more thing."

"I know. I've not remade my war shield yet. I will soon."

"About the shield."

"Oh?"

"The original was buffalo hide. I thought you might remake using deer. But…I see you must use another material."

"What?"

"The hide of a boar. Perhaps the one you saw last night on your way here."

Despite the surprise jolts Meskwaa had given him already this morning, Concho found himself startled anew. Meskwaa could have heard through the reservation grapevine about the white woman staying at Kickapoo tribal police headquarters. He probably had been told of Concho's involvement. But the fact that Concho and Katy had crossed paths with a sounder of wild hogs the night before?

"How did you know about that?"

Meskwaa grinned and pointed to his head. "I am crazy with

knowing things."

"Crazy, for sure," Concho said.

Meskwaa nodded. He took a fresh cigarette from his pocket and lit it from the first, then pinched out the one he had been smoking and tucked the butt into his shirt pocket. The bitter smell of bruised tobacco brushed Concho's nostrils.

The door to the trailer opened behind Concho, and he turned his head to see Katy come down the steps and start toward them. She wore the sundress she'd worn yesterday. It looked like she'd slept in it. He should arrange for her to get something fresh to wear. He'd try to do so today.

"Katy," Concho said. "This is Meskwaa. To hear him tell it, he is the wisest Kickapoo who ever lived. Meskwaa, this is Katy."

Meskwaa offered Katy a bow of his head. "Good morning, young lady. You look very thin. Did the great Ten-Wolves not offer you anything to eat from his tremendous store of foodstuffs?"

Katy giggled but said. "He was actually very generous with his bacon and eggs."

Meskwaa let his eyes widen in mock surprise. "It is indeed a momentous occasion. He usually leaves me to starve."

Concho snorted. Katy giggled again.

Meskwaa rose from his chair. He snuffed out his newest smoke and tucked it into his pocket. "I'm afraid I must leave you, Miss Katy. I have much to do this day. It is a pleasure to have met you." He turned toward Concho. "And you I'll see soon enough again. After you have made sure this deserving young woman is safe."

"Good day, Uncle," Concho said. "Thanks for answering my questions."

Meskwaa waved his hand and turned back into the brush beyond Concho's yard. Quickly, he was gone.

"I like him," Katy said.

"And he must like you as well. He didn't even insult you."

Katy grinned. She scratched her head. "Could I borrow your phone again? I'd like to try Vera one more time."

"This early?" Concho asked while pulling his phone out of his pocket and handing it over.

"She won't mind. I can't stand to wait."

Concho nodded and Katy took a few steps away and pressed the number to call her sister. The phone rang, and rang. No one answered. Finally, it went to voicemail.

Katy looked back at Concho. Her eyes swam with frightened thoughts. "Something's wrong!" she said. "She should have answered. She would if she could. Mason French has her. I know it!"

***

Mason French snapped awake. A diffuse gray dawn peered through the windows of his vehicle. He shook his head to clear away the snooze he'd just taken and checked his phone for the time. He'd dozed a couple of hours. Fine. He'd needed it.

Climbing out of the white 2015 Chevy Malibu he'd stolen from behind a bakery in Eagle Pass, he stretched and gazed around. A few doves winged their swift way across the morning in search of food. They passed above an abandoned farmhouse standing amid a small grove of oaks and other hardwoods. A rickety gray barn with a gaping double doorway was the only other building visible, though a small concrete shed surrounded the farm's wellhouse.

Apparently, the farm belonged to some subsidiary of one of Lucio Zapatero's companies. It couldn't be traced back to Zapatero, not without a lot of effort, at least. And Mason wasn't staying long himself, though that little bit of time was going to earn him a big payday—and maybe more. He'd have to thank Scout, who'd turned him onto the opportunity.

With a smile on his face, Mason French popped the trunk on the Malibu, which he'd needed to replace the Chevy Trailblazer the cops were surely looking for. A whimper came from the cargo area inside, where a young woman lay bound. Her hands were cuffed behind her and cuffed in turn to a rope tied around her ankles, drawing her body up in a bow.

Above a scarf-gagged mouth, brown eyes stared up at Mason with terror. At least part of the terror probably had to do with the dead, sour-smelling body sprawled against the girl's back. The driver of the Malibu hadn't wanted to give up his car, a stupid mistake that had earned him a broken neck.

The girl hadn't been stupid yet. She looked no more than fifteen. Skinny in a gray Texas Longhorns T-shirt and nearly new jeans. Short brown hair, damp with sweat, stuck out in every direction from her head.

A mumble of desperate words came from behind the gag. Mason couldn't make them out. Nor did he care. Reaching in his pocket, he pulled out a bright red iPhone and held it up for the girl to see. Her pupils dilated even further.

Mason chuckled. "I see you recognize it. Seemed like it wasn't going to be any use to me. It was locked. But once I learned your name, I was able to figure out the password. Easy enough then to send you a little text. Supposedly from your sister. I like how you fell for it. Came right out of the house into my hands."

Leaning over the trunk, Mason grabbed an arm and a leg and pulled the girl out to set her on the bumper. He untied her feet, though left her hands cuffed and the gag in her mouth. She shuddered. He thought it might be with relief from being away from the corpse.

"Just so you know," he said, "I've got no compunctions about hurting a kid. You keep quiet and do what I tell you and you might make it through this. You're already trouble for me. You cause any extra and I'll waste you rather than waste time on you. Understand?"

Vera Delchamp met Mason French's gaze and nodded.

"You and your sister, Katy, seem tight," Mason continued. "I had her right in my hands until that…Ranger came along. I'll get her back. And you're going to help."

***

Concho listened to Katy's sudden claim that Mason French had kidnapped her sister Vera. He wanted to deny it. They had no evidence such had happened. But French was around and capable of it. And, Concho's heart had kicked into high gear; his breathing came fast. He started a quick walk to the trailer.

"Get your things," he said to Katy.

"What?" Katy demanded as she ran to keep up with his strides. "What are you going to do?"

"See your parents first. Right now!"

"I'll go with you!"

"No, you won't. This is a police investigation. I'll drop you off at tribal headquarters."

"She's my sister!"

"And if you want her kept safe, you'll do what I tell you!" he snapped loudly.

Katy's eyes widened. For the first time, Concho had raised his voice to her. Her steps faltered but she recovered and caught up as Concho flung open the door to the trailer and rushed in. She said nothing else but ran for her room. Concho kicked off his moccasins and stomped on his boots, then pulled a blue work shirt on over his tee. He grabbed his billfold and buckled on his twin Colt Double Eagles.

Katy met him at the front door and they rushed to Concho's truck. Concho drove fast, his wheels churning up dust on the dirt roads of the reservation. Katy sat silently, only speaking as they approached the Kickapoo police station.

"Please take care of her. Please!"

Concho glanced over into the young woman's frightened brown eyes. He reached out a big hand and squeezed her shoulder. "I'll do everything I can. I'll let you know as soon as I find out anything. If French does have her, he won't harm her. He'll try to use her to get to you. We have time."

Katy nodded. They swung into the parking lot of the police station and slid to a stop. "Get inside!" he told Katy. "Tell Echabarri what we think's going on. I'll call him later."

Still looking scared, Katy slipped down from the truck and started trotting for the door to KTTT headquarters. Concho shoved the truck into reverse and wheeled back out of the parking lot. He slammed the vehicle into drive. Tires squealed and flung dirt as the Dodge barreled down the road leading to Eagle Pass and the home of William and Maureen Delchamp.

CHAPTER 37

As he raced through town, Concho thought for an instant he'd picked up a tail. A Lincoln Continental much like the one Lucio Zapatero had ridden in hung with him for a few blocks. He lost it weaving in and out of traffic.

Fifteen minutes brought him wheeling his Dodge into the Delchamp's driveway. It was a quarter till 8:00. Both family vehicles were home. Concho bailed out of his truck and rushed to the door, hammering on it in lieu of ringing the doorbell.

Moments passed. He kept banging, stopping only when footsteps approached from inside. The door opened a few inches on its chain. Maureen Delchamp peered out, her face weary and almost colorless.

"What…what do you want? It's so early."

"I need to speak to you and your husband."

"Come back later."

"No. Let me in. It's about Vera."

William Delchamp appeared at his wife's shoulder. "Leave," he said. "We have nothing to talk about."

"Let me in or I call a judge and get a search warrant. And I stay right here until it's delivered and we come inside and tear your house up to find Vera, who I'm quite sure isn't home."

"What makes you think so?" William Delchamp barked. "And why is it any of your business anyway? We've committed no crime. Vera's committed no crime."

"I'm making it my business. And it's what Katy wants too. Maybe you remember your other daughter?"

Delchamp opened his mouth, snapped it shut again.

His wife turned toward him. "William! Maybe…"

Delchamp shook his head but said as he turned away, "Let him in. But it's on your head."

Maureen unsnapped the chain lock and pulled the door back. Concho entered and followed William down the hall into the same room he'd been allowed in during his last visit. As her husband seated himself on the same white loveseat as before, Maureen headed toward the back of the house.

"You too, Mrs. Delchamp," Concho called.

The woman turned like a zombie and came into the room. She perched on the very edge of the loveseat, as far away from her husband as she could get, with her body held as rigid as a statue.

"Where's Vera?" Concho demanded of them both.

Maureen winced as if he'd struck her. But she answered. "She's…she's at a friend's house. She spent the night."

"You're lying!" Concho said. "She's missing. Have you gotten a call yet from the ones who took her?"

Maureen Delchamp took two quick breaths and burst into tears. She could say nothing. William stared at his wife with disgust on his face. Finally, he answered:

"Yes. Early this morning. 4:47. I won't forget it."

"Tell me about the person who called."

"A man," Delchamp said. "American, I think. Texas accent. I've never spoken to him before."

"How did they get her?"

"She must have slipped out of the house. We don't know when or why. We've got a security system but it looks like she deactivated it on her window. She's smart. And there's a rose arbor just outside her window. She could have climbed down that way."

"What did the man say who called?"

"He said, he'd kill her if we brought in the police."

Maureen Delchamp cried out as if knifed and jumped up to flee the room. Concho let her go this time.

"They won't," the Ranger said to William Delchamp. "At least not right away. And if I can get to them soon enough, they won't have a chance. They want something. What is it? What did they ask you for?"

"I wish I'd never set eyes on you!" Delchamp said.

"Just means you'd be going through all this alone. Let's be clear, I don't give a damn about you but I'll do everything I can to save your daughters. Why don't you try to do the same!"

Delchamp looked like he was chewing bark. He glanced toward the door through which his wife had fled, then focused again on Concho.

"Money, of course," he finally replied.

"But not just money."

Delchamp said nothing.

"Still protecting yourself!" Concho snapped. "Instead of trying to help your daughters. Tell me what was stolen in that bank robbery. What were you trying to keep hidden?"

Delchamp twitched on the loveseat. "How did you…" He shook his head. "Never mind. It was a video recording. And it's certainly missing."

"When did you find out?"

"Friday. After the robbery. I…checked."

"A recording of what?"

"You might as well know," he said slyly. "Of me and Emily Clarke."

"Now Emily Zapatero?"

"Yes. Of us having sex."

Concho nodded. "I'm beginning to see. And I'm guessing Emily didn't know about it at the time?"

"No."

"Did you record all the women you had affairs with?"

"No. Just her."

"Why?"

A tiny smirk curled up one corner of Delchamp's mouth and Concho wanted to punch him.

"Have you seen her?" the gym owner asked. "She's gorgeous. And, she was very…adventuresome, I think you'd say."

"So, it was blackmail?"

Delchamp shook his head. "How could I know she'd marry a rich man? I kept it for my own…interest."

"But it became blackmail?"

Delchamp looked away.

"Don't clam up now!" Concho said. "This is the part that got your youngest daughter kidnapped. And this is how we have a chance to get her back."

Delchamp sighed. He still wouldn't make eye contact with the lawman but he began to speak:

"A few years back, things started going bad for me. I needed money. I knew who Emily had married. Hell, she just lives down the street from me. I…approached her. Turns out she really didn't want her husband to find out anything about her past. Can't blame her. Zapatero is her money ticket and he's got a bad, bad temper. Or so I've heard."

"I was told your wife had money."

"Not anymore."

"How much did you get from Emily Zapatero?"

"Four hundred thousand. But not all at once." Delchamp smirked again. "She's on an installment plan."

"And that's the amount Vera's kidnappers asked for?"

Delchamp sobered. He nodded."

"And the video?" Concho asked but shook his head before Delchamp could reply. "No, they already got it through the robbery. What else did they want besides money?"

"Any copies of the video I might have."

"And do you?"

"No. But I guess they don't know that."

"The video was in your safety deposit box at the bank," Concho said. "What kind of format?"

"A data stick."

"How did they know it was there?"

Delchamp shrugged. "Process of elimination, maybe. I couldn't keep it at home. Or at work. But they must have figured it out fairly early. I found out Emily Zapatero has only been employed at IBC for a couple of years. She started right after I first contacted her about money. Her plan all along must have been to get the video. Probably had her husband pull some strings to get her hired there."

"You had no idea she worked there?"

"Not till after the robbery. I would have moved the data stick. I saw her picture on the news. Knew right away it couldn't be a coincidence."

"I happen to know Anne Reese searched your home office at one point. She was probably looking for the video but she might have made a copy of your safety deposit box key."

"That bitch!" Delchamp snapped.

"Shut it!" Concho snapped back. "You're not going to play the victim with me."

Delchamp looked like he was about to retort, then thought better of it as Concho stepped toward him. He leaned back on the couch instead and put his hands in his lap.

"I don't understand why they staged the robbery, anyway," Delchamp said. "Why didn't Emily smuggle the thing out in her purse? Was it just to hurt me more by involving Katy in a crime?"

Something Parkland had said recently while talking about the robbery flashed through Concho's head. Just weeks before the robbery, bank officials had caught an embezzler on the staff, someone smuggling out small bits of cash. That's why they'd put in the guard who ultimately got shot in the robbery. And they'd set up a scanner that all employees had to go through. Emily must have been afraid she'd be caught smuggling the stick out and the whole thing would burst wide open. So, they'd gone with the robbery angle. The Ranger had no intention of sharing such information with Delchamp, however.

"Katy was angry with you over the affairs," Concho said. "She had every right. But she was in the dark about the real purpose of the robbery. Anne Reese never told her most of it."

Delchamp took a deep breath and let it out. "I guess, I'm glad she didn't know."

"She'll find out eventually. News like that doesn't stay hidden. You better tell her yourself."

Delchamp had just enough decency to shudder a little. He looked down at his hands. "So what now?"

"First, you tell me exactly what the kidnapper said."

Delchamp nodded slightly. He took a moment to gather his memories.

"He started with, 'We have Vera. She's unharmed but if you want to keep her that way, you'll listen carefully. We want four hundred thousand dollars and every copy you have of a certain video recording. You know which one. If we get both, you and your daughter live. If not, or if anything gets released later, we kill everyone in your family.' I remember it word for word."

"You think Zapatero is behind it?"

"He's got to be. Everyone knows he's a criminal."

"How long did they give you?"

"Twenty-four hours. I begged 'em for forty-eight."

"And?"

"They gave me thirty."

"Can you raise the money?"

"Probably."

"What about the recording? What did you tell them about that?"

"I said I wasn't stupid enough to have more than one copy."

"Did they believe you?"

"I don't know."

"Did you notice anything else about the call? Background noise? Anything?"

Delchamp frowned. "It was quiet," he said finally. "I mean, I didn't hear any traffic noise or machinery running. Actually, I heard an owl in the background. I think it was an owl." He shook his head. "Can't think of anything else."

"All right," Concho said. "Get started on the money but don't take any other action without talking to me. If you hear from the kidnapper, just listen and keep your mouth shut. Don't mention me or anything about the police. I'm going over to see Emily and Lucio Zapatero. Maybe we can end this before it goes any further."

"Do you… Am I…going to be arrested?"

Concho felt disgust twist his mouth. "Right now, you're not my concern," he said.

CHAPTER 38

It took scarcely a moment for Concho to drive down the street to the Zapatero's. The gate was open, as it had been on his last visit, but now there were two guards instead of one. They stopped Concho; he showed them his badge but let them call ahead for permission for him to enter. It came.

The Hummer he'd parked behind last time wasn't here but the ivory-colored Lincoln he'd seen Lucio Zapatero being chauffeured around in was. He parked behind it and strode up the walkway to the door which opened as he approached.

The Hispanic serving woman had been replaced by one of Zapatero's shaved-headed bodyguards. He smelled of sweat and gun oil. The jacket was missing on his expensive suit and his shoulder holster was visible. It held a bronze FN FNX Tactical. 45, a very nice handgun that came with a fifteen-round double-stack magazine. Concho had considered buying a couple for himself.

The guard led Concho to the sunroom where previously he'd spoken to Emily Zapatero. The furniture had been rearranged and the couch pushed into a more central location. Emily and Lucio Zapatero were already seated on the couch, close together in a united front against the invader.

Interesting, he thought.

Knowing Lucio Zapatero's reputation, and having met the transportation mogul, Concho had expected to see a cowed and perhaps bruised Emily. Lucio didn't seem the type not to lash out at a wife who was being blackmailed over a sex tape, even if it had happened before their marriage.

However, Emily showed no signs of being cowed. A faint smile curved her lips. Her hand rested comfortably and naturally on her husband's knee. She wore a black and white striped silk dress, with stockings and dark heels. Her makeup was impeccable but not overly heavy. Concho could see no sign she'd tried to hide any bruises.

A low table sat in front of the couch and across from it rested a big chair suitable for someone of Concho's size. Emily gestured toward the chair with an open palm, a clear invitation for the Ranger to sit. It didn't matter how worried he was at the moment over Vera Delchamp. If he didn't play this carefully, he'd have little chance of getting her back. He sat as he was invited.

The bodyguard who'd ushered Concho in stepped up behind the lawman's chair. His shaved-headed partner from before stood at the other entrance to the room. Concho let his gaze rest on those of the Zapatero's and said: "What I have to say is not for every ear."

Lucio glanced in turn at the two men and gave them nods. Both withdrew. After the guards were gone, Concho leaned forward slightly and spoke in a low voice.

"I know about the video. I know about four hundred thousand dollars in blackmail money. I know the robbery was a clever con to get the data stick with the video on it out of William Delchamp's safety deposit box and out of the bank." He focused his gaze on Lucio. "I know it was your men who picked up the bag holding the data stick when I was busy trying to arrest Anne Reese."

Neither Lucio nor Emily acknowledged Concho's words. They just sat.

"I haven't contacted my superiors with any of this information," Concho continued. "Anne Reese is dead and I don't like it. But she wasn't an innocent. She knew the hazards of the game. I don't know for sure who is responsible for her death but I'm prepared to let the sheriff's office handle it without further involving myself."

Emily Zapatero offered him the faintest of nods. He continued.

"There's also the matter of some twenty-three thousand dollars stolen from the bank. That money belongs to people who are innocent in this situation. I care about that. But what I care about above everything else is Vera Delchamp. She's fifteen. She didn't pick her father. She had nothing to do with any of this.

"I don't know how you made contact with Mason French and I don't have to. I doubt he's a friend of the family. Maybe someone recommended him to you. They did you a disservice. French is a very bad man. Without honor.

"What you probably don't know is, he has another interest in this game. Before he took Vera, he took Katy, Delchamp's other daughter. He would have raped and murdered her if I hadn't intervened. He still wants her and, after he uses Vera to get what he's asking for from William Delchamp, he'll try to use her on me to give him Katy. If he succeeds, he'll kill them both when he's done. I doubt that's any part of your plan, but it won't matter what you might say to him. And Katy isn't to blame for her father either."

Emily's facial expression had tightened as Concho spoke but the real change came in Lucio Zapatero. The man gradually stiffened until his body went rigid. Zapatero was surely not above violence but he understood honor. And pride. Maybe he'd begun to see that involving Mason French had been a mistake. Concho hoped so as he leaned forward a little more and put his own pride and honor on the line.

"You both know me," he said. "Or of me. You know enough to understand that I believe in keeping my word. If I get the money from the robbery, and Vera, I'll be finished with this investigation. But if French hurts Vera, I'm going to blame you. And I'll bring the world down on top of you both. No number of bodyguards will be able to stop it."

Lucio's face twisted in anger. He opened his mouth to say something and Emily squeezed his leg gently with her hand. Lucio fell silent and, for once, Concho was glad he couldn't arch an eyebrow. Any sign of surprise would have given his thoughts away.

"If I leave here with French's whereabouts and with the money from the bank robbery," Concho added, "I won't see the need to involve my superiors. The four hundred thousand dollars in blackmail money is between you and William Delchamp. I know he's trying to raise it. He says he doesn't have any more copies of the video and I believe him. But your issue is with him. I understand your anger. With him! Not with his wife. Not his daughters. If they're left alone, I'm out of it as far as you're concerned."

Lucio and Emily looked at each other. Something passed between them. Not a smile or a nod but Lucio pushed up from the couch and walked out of the room without a word.

Concho gazed at Emily Zapatero. When he'd spoken to her before, he'd caught her by surprise and seen her discombobulated. All that was gone. He'd thought she had a few flaws in her classical beauty. He couldn't see them now. She might have been sitting for a portrait. Rather, she might have been a portrait, a stunning painting by a master artist.

"I didn't expect to find you so intact," Concho said. "I figured when I was driving over here, I'd have to take you to safety too. I imagined you might be in danger from your husband. Given what he's 'seen' of your past recently. I take it, such is not the case?"

A small smile caressed Emily's lips. "No. My husband is tremendously angry with William Delchamp. But he loves me very much."

Concho nodded. "So I see. Makes me wonder how a woman who can inspire such love could have been taken in by someone like Delchamp."

"No one is born wise, Officer Ten-Wolves. Knowledge and skills have to be acquired from somewhere. But I learn quickly."

"Of course."

"One way or another, people like William Delchamp always pay for their sins," Emily added. "Unfortunately, others pay right along with them. I don't care for the mother. But the daughters. As you say, they're not to blame. I hope you can protect them."

"I will," Concho said. He added, "Your husband didn't know about the bank robbery, did he?"

"Not at first. I told him everything after your visit the other day."

Concho snapped his fingers. "The men in the Escalade were working for you when they took the money!"

Emily smiled just as Lucio Zapatero returned. Concho rose to meet him. Zapatero offered the Ranger a small slip of folded, heavy stock card paper. He opened it, read the address inside. He knew the place. He nodded and tucked the card in his shirt pocket.

Next, Zapatero handed him a bundle the size of a shoebox, wrapped in brown butcher paper and tied with crimson string.

"For me?" Concho said. "It's not even my birthday."

Zapatero didn't smile or speak. It was Emily who explained, though Concho already knew just about what she was going to say. "Twenty-two thousand, six hundred and seventy-eight dollars," she pronounced. "Every bit of money taken in the bank robbery."

Concho glanced toward the woman, gave a brief nod. He looked back into Lucio Zapatero's eyes, which were calm but as cold as anthracite. The Ranger tipped an imaginary hat and walked out.

***

Concho backed quickly out of the Zapatero's driveway and tore off toward the destination written on the card in his shirt pocket. He knew he'd find Mason French there. And Vera Delchamp. He hoped she'd be unharmed. If not, someone would pay.

He wasn't quite ready to bring in backup yet. Not until he got a sense of how the situation might play out. French would hurt or kill Vera the moment he sensed cops around. This required a one-man operation. Any more would be too big and draw unwanted attention.

However, someone needed to know the outline if things went south. While driving, Concho called Roberto Echabarri and explained everything to him in case he wasn't able to handle French himself. The man was big. Bigger than Concho. And he was ruthless. He'd be well armed. He might have others with him. Probably did.

Blood would run before this was over.

CHAPTER 39

As Mason French jerked Vera Delchamp off the bumper of the Malibu and pushed her toward the farmhouse, a beat-up old blue Toyota pickup pulled in behind him. Two men got out. French acknowledged them.

Both were Hispanic, both meth skinny. One had hair and most of his teeth, the other no hair and only a few yellowed teeth jutting up like bombed-out buildings in a ruined landscape. Otherwise, they were interchangeable. They smelled the same.

The haired one was named Vicente. He carried an old 30-30 lever-action Mossberg rifle. The other man went by Pablocito. He lugged a worn sawed-off shotgun that looked like it had spent the last few years lying in Rio Grande mud. Mason wasn't sure he wanted to be around if Pablocito fired it.

Mason had found the pair at a bar called Armando's, from a hint given to him by Lucio Zapatero. These weren't Zapatero's men; they worked freelance. Clearly, Zapatero didn't want his name linked to the kidnapping. Mason understood and was being paid to make do, though he would have preferred more competent help.

Of course, he had other help coming. Better armed help, at least. He'd called his bartender at Hot, Blue and Righteous. Ex-bartender now, he guessed. Jack had been arrested but released for lack of evidence. He and his brother should be here soon.

"Pablo," Mason said. "You take up guard on the porch. Vicente, I'll want you inside with me."

"Si, Boss," Vicente said.

Vera was pulling against Mason's grip and he gave her a good shake. "Remember what I said about causing me trouble."

Vera stopped struggling and let Mason push her toward the farmhouse. He watched the girl as she strode along in front of him. Her limbs were long and coltish but she reminded him of Katy, her sister. Mason liked that. Nothing said he couldn't enjoy an appetizer before the main course.

The farmhouse windows were boarded up on the first floor but the door opened when Mason pushed it. The door had warped; it scraped across the floor and stayed open once he released it.

He found himself in a big empty room, which must have been the dining area when the place was occupied. Marks on the floor indicated where a large table had originally sat, and two broken wooden chairs had been kicked into a corner. A few leaves and stems of grass cluttered the floor along with the dusty paw prints of what looked like a cat. Overall, though, the place wasn't in bad shape. He guessed there must be a caretaker who came by semi-regularly.

"Check upstairs," Mason told Vicente. "Looks like those windows aren't boarded up. Keep an eye toward the highway and give me a shout if anyone turns in. We've got more help on the way."

Vicente nodded and trotted away. Mason picked up one of the wooden chairs and sat it on its legs. The back was broken off but he pushed it against the wall and ordered Vera to sit. He tied her wrists to the front legs on either side of the chair, then tugged the scarf gag out of her mouth to let it hang around her neck.

"Now," he said. "We're going to get to know each other a little better.

***

Concho headed for the Camino Real International Bridge but turned off on the Texas 480 loop before crossing the bridge itself into Mexico. For the first part of its length, 480 ran parallel to the Rio Grande. Eagle Pass had been the first American settlement along the Rio Grande but this area had been mostly rural until relatively recently. Rapid commercial and suburban growth over the last fifteen years had dramatically changed the nature of the landscape but there were still pockets of largely untouched country.

The address provided by Lucio Zapatero lay in one of those rural pockets. It marked an abandoned farm that had once been a prosperous horse ranch. Being close to the Rio Grande and well-watered, the place sat like a green rose against a backdrop of seared land. An abundance of trees marked the property. It had been "on the market" for several years but hadn't sold. The owners didn't really want it sold—they only wanted the illusion of it being available.

Concho had walked over nearly every inch of this territory as a teenager. He'd visited the farm then and had revisited it about a year ago when he found it was still for sale. Besides harboring a secret wish to buy the place for himself—without having the money—he'd begun to wonder about its continued availability. He'd had no idea until now that Zapatero had an interest in the site; neither he nor any of his companies were connected to it. Supposedly, a rich, out-of-state fellow named Frank Leslie owned it.

The turnoff to the farm came up on Concho's right but he drove past it and pulled off into a deep spot in the roadside ditch a couple of hundred yards farther along. If French was at the farm, he'd be keeping an eye on the entrance road, which could be seen clearly from the farmhouse's upstairs.

Climbing out, the Ranger opened the Dodge's extended cab. His non-regulation hair was a legacy from his Kickapoo mother—long and straight and black. He tied it back with a leather thong. Tossing his work shirt into the truck, he pulled body armor on over his black T-shirt.

Next, he took up the yellow tin holding his war paint and

streaked his broad cheeks with red. His final task was to choose his weapons. He wore his two Colt .45s, of course, and his Bowie knife, but, beyond that, he had a decision to make. Should he take his scoped Remington .30-06 hunting rifle, or maybe the camo-colored 12-gauge tactical shotgun?

He decided on neither. Instead, he pulled out a cloth-wrapped bundle and unwound it to reveal a weapon far more "non-regulation" than his hair. It was a hunting bow he'd constructed from Osage orange found growing on the reservation. Strengthened with hide and horn, it had been lovingly polished and engraved with symbols the tribe considered holy. With it came a homemade deer-hide quiver and twelve arrows.

Softly, in the Kickapoo tongue, Concho sang the symbols etched along the bow. A prayer to the spirits. For years, he'd lived as if there were no such spirits. He still wasn't sure he believed in them. But Meskwaa's recent words, and the dream in which Concho had relived his naming ceremony, had reminded him of when magic had been real to him. He could use some magic now, to bring Vera Delchamp safely home.

Slinging the bow and quiver over his back, he slipped through the barbed wire fence bordering the highway. A field of wildflowers and dried grass stood before him. Beyond lay his farmhouse target. He couldn't see it because of trees but he knew where it lay.

It wasn't even mid-morning yet. The sun burned warm above, though not yet grown hot. Birds sang. Night would have been better for what Concho had to do but Vera was in danger and must be terrified. She could not be left to the mercy of Mason French which was no kind of mercy at all. He broke into a lope.

***

Mason French cupped Vera's chin, forcing the young woman to look up at him from the chair where she was bound. "You're going to be as cute as your sister when you fill out some more," he said.

Vera's eyes blazed. "You better leave Katy alone!"

"Too late," French said, chuckling.

Vera jerked her chin free and tried to bite French's hand. He yanked his fingers away and was drawing back to slap the girl across the face when he heard the guttural growl of a high-performance vehicle pulling into the ranch's front yard.

Vera heard the car too. Her mouth opened to shout but French grabbed the scarf he'd been using for a gag and pushed it back between her lips. He flicked her cheek hard with his finger. The stinging bite of it brought water to Vera's eyes.

"Quiet!" French said.

Drawing the Smith & Wesson holstered at his belt, Mason moved quickly to the open front door and peered around it into the yard. A bright purple 1969 Plymouth Roadrunner pulled up behind Mason's stolen Malibu. Mason shook his head.

This would be Jack Weaver, his bartender from Hot, Blue and Righteous. The car belonged to Jack's younger brother, Jay. Jay was thinner and taller than Jack with the same prominent ears and inbred features, but clean-shaven, or relatively so. Mason had told them to be discreet but neither acted as if they had any idea what that meant.

Holstering his Model 29 .44 Magnum, his Dirty Harry gun as he often called it, Mason wrenched the front door open all the way and strode toward the Roadrunner. Jay had just locked the door when Mason shouted at him:

"Wait! I want that thing in the barn where no one can see it. It stands out like a bull in drag."

Jay hesitated, then glanced at his brother, who nodded and climbed back in the car. With a resigned shrug, Jay joined his brother and started the machine. The glasspack mufflers popped and rumbled as Jay pulled around Mason's Malibu and the beat-up Toyota, and drove through the wide-open front door of the weathered barn next to the house. A moment later, blessed silence descended again.

Mason waited as Jack and Jay came out of the garage to join him, each carrying various pieces of ordnance. Both men wore bullet-proof vests and were strapped with sidearms. Each had a long weapon slung over a shoulder. Jack had an AR-15 while Jay had a Winchester Model 12 shotgun. Jack carried an extra bullet-proof vest and another shotgun. Mason took them both.

"This is base for a while," he said. "Y'all bring food?"

Jack nodded. "Got a couple of ice chests full of sandwiches and such in the car. Got some jerky and Slim Jims. Some jugs of water." He grinned. "Brought some beer too. Just thinking ahead."

"No beer until this is over," Mason snapped.

"Sure, boss, sure," Jack said. "What's goin' on anyway?"

"The only thing you need to know is there's good money at the end of it."

"Twenty thousand between us," Jay said. "Nice!"

"If you do the jobs I tell you to do," Mason said.

He hadn't told them he was getting paid seventy-five thousand for kidnapping Vera Delchamp and handling the ransom negotiations with her father. Nor that the twenty thousand would be split between Jack, Jay, and the two Hispanics. Who knew if they'd all live through the next thirty hours or so anyway?

As they stepped up on the porch, Mason handed the shotgun to Pablocito to replace his old one, then followed the Weaver brothers inside.

"So," Jack was saying, as he eyed Vera up and down. "Do we get to amuse ourselves while we wait?"

"She needs to be kept in relatively good shape until we get our money," Mason said. "In the meantime, the Mexicans are supposed to have some tools in their pickup. Get something to take the boards off the windows down here so we can get a better view of anything that might be coming. Afterward, we'll see about amusing ourselves."

CHAPTER 40

A grove of hardwood trees curved around the southern and western walls of the abandoned two-story farmhouse, screening it off from any view of the Rio Grande, and screening Concho Ten-Wolves from the sight of anyone inside the building. In the farm's heyday, the trees would have been kept cut well back from the building to help with the danger of fire. No one had maintained that practice which worked to Concho's advantage.

Two vehicles were parked in the farmyard, a newish white Malibu and a rusted old small frame Toyota. On his way across the field to the trees, he'd heard the sound of a souped-up muscle car, though he couldn't see any such vehicle around. In the barn, he imagined.

Concho pegged Mason French for the Malibu which was surely stolen. But who owned the other two vehicles? The only outlaw Concho could see—a bored-looking Hispanic man—stood on the front porch with a shotgun. How many others were with French? And where? And where in that big pile of a house was Vera being held?

A partial answer to Concho's questions came when two men with hammers strode out of the farmhouse and began using their tools to pry the boards off the windows along the front porch. The glass was broken out behind the boards, but it wouldn't matter.

The days were still warm and no rain was expected.

Of the two men, Concho recognized Jack, the bartender he'd had a verbal confrontation with at Hot, Blue and Righteous. The other fellow looked enough like Jack to be his brother. No doubt, he shared the family charm.

So, at least four men held Vera, including French. But Concho was skeptical of having seen everyone yet. The upstairs. Surely at least one observer would be stationed there as a lookout. Moving carefully and making sure to stay out of view from any of the second-story windows, the lawman worked his way from the west side of the house around to the back, looking for any route of ingress.

He found it. But it was being watched.

At the back corner of the house stood a rectangular cement trough for catching rainwater. If Concho could get to that, he could reach up and grab the slanting roof over the back porch and use it to reach the second floor. Two windows opened over that roof. The closest one either had the glass broken out or the window was up. Somebody stood next to it; the smoke from their cigarette coiled through into the open air and drifted slowly toward the sun.

Concho needed a distraction. He quickly searched around on the ground near his feet. The tree against which he leaned was a Texas persimmon, and some of the fallen fruit lay around him. He scooped up a handful.

Slinging his bow and quiver over his shoulder, he tightened both down so they wouldn't impede him. He inched as close to the edge of the woods as he dared and hurled the persimmons toward one of the windows on the west side of the house, toward the front. They rattled against the glass and wood.

An oath in Spanish came from inside the house where the guard stood smoking. Concho listened intently. He couldn't hear clear footsteps moving away from the back window but he heard boards creaking. Praying the coast was clear, he launched into a sprint toward the cement trough.

The distance from the woods to the house was less than thirty feet. Concho covered it in seconds, though each tick of the clock marked an eternity as he waited for a shout of discovery. None came.

He reached the trough, swung one booted foot up on it, then lunged upward to grab hold of the porch roof. Even as he levered himself upward by brute strength, he heard off-key whistling coming around the house from the front.

Ducking flat on the roof, against the wall of the house, he peeked around and saw Jack the bartender come into view, wielding his hammer as he stopped by the first window of the bottom floor to pry at the boards covering it. Just above Jack, the window on the second floor was open now and a Hispanic man peered through.

Concho had gotten lucky. The upstairs guard would assume the noise made by the thrown persimmons had been made by Jack instead. But soon he'd start toward the back of the house again, to the window that Concho lay beneath. The Ranger had to get inside before then.

***

Vera Delchamp watched nervously as Mason French paced back and forth in front of her. Finally, he turned and went outside. Vera immediately started tugging at the ropes binding her arms to the broken chair. They were tied tightly, both at the wrists and to the chair. She barely had any slack to work with.

Despair made her bite her lip. She'd seen the looks on the faces of French and the last two men to arrive. She knew what those looks meant. Before long they'd come for her. She didn't want to think about what they'd do. But she knew.

Had the same thing happened to Katy? Had French done that to her sister?

No!

She'd spoken to her sister. She'd sounded OK. And Vera had

heard from Concho Ten-Wolves—Katy was safe. A sob escaped her lips and she closed them tightly around her gag to prevent any more from leaking out. She wouldn't give that to French. Not that or anything else.

If only the Ranger was here. If he could help her the way he'd helped Katy. She jerked again on her bonds, jerked until she felt the skin on her wrists start to abrade. The pain made her stop. No one was here except enemies. She had to save herself.

An idea came.

***

The window right above Concho stood open, the glass miraculously intact. Jack still whistled as he worked at the windows on the bottom floor. The noise he made would help cover the Ranger's actions.

Concho rose to a crouch. He peeked through the window, saw nothing but an empty bedroom with faded and tattered wallpaper. But he heard footsteps coming toward him. He swung into the room and unhooked his bow. By the time he'd nocked an arrow, a man stepped through the doorway of the room.

The smell of marijuana stabbed Concho's nostrils. The man smoked a long, hand-rolled joint. His rifle, a lever-action 30-30, dangled loosely from his left hand. He was caught completely by surprise. His mouth gaped open; smoke roiled out. He started to cough, which would lead to a shout.

Concho shot him in the throat with an arrow at fifteen paces. The flint head of the arrow tore a hole through the rifleman's jugular vein, then punched into the spine at the back of the neck and sheared through bone and nerve endings before lodging between two vertebrae.

The man dropped. His rifle clattered to the floor. Concho leaped toward him but the fellow was dead before the Ranger reached him. Listening closely, Concho heard only the sound of Jack working outside. The bartender had moved to the next window on the bottom floor. He apparently wasn't bright enough to wonder about the clattering noise he'd surely heard from inside.

Concho rolled the corpse out of the doorway so it wouldn't be seen. Blood had spilled on the dusty floor. It glistened, and there was no way to hide it. It didn't matter, Concho thought grimly. He'd clear the house as he went. No one would be left to care about someone else's blood.

CHAPTER 41

Leaving the front door open behind him, Mason French stepped outside to use a burner phone to call William Delchamp. The deadline to raise four hundred thousand dollars wasn't up yet but the businessman needed reminding of the importance of being on time, and of the need to keep the cops out of it.

Of course, Lucio Zapatero's people should be keeping an eye on Delchamp, making sure he didn't go to the police. But it never hurt to reinforce a certain amount of fear in one's victims. Besides, it was a small pleasure Mason didn't like to deny himself.

As soon as he finished the call and hung up, Mason snapped the phone in half, then dropped it and ground it into a pile of plastic beneath his boot. He stretched and sighed pleasantly. Everything was going smoothly.

He turned and looked toward the house. Jack and Jay were finishing their work on the boarded-up windows. Pablocito still lounged against the wall on the front porch. Mason glanced up toward the second floor, where Vicente would be keeping watch. A frown crossed his face; his sense of relaxation scuttled into hiding. Something felt wrong. He drew his .44 and started quickly toward the building.

Pablocito actually seemed to awaken from his stupor as Mason approached him with intensity; he lowered his shotgun into something close to shooting position. Mason grasped the meth-head's arm and pulled him inside the house. A glance took in the room. Vera remained tied in her chair against the wall. She wouldn't look at them. Everything was quiet but nothing felt right.

Looking up the stairs made Mason's hackles rise. Vicente was up there. But he wasn't making any sound. Before, he'd been constantly making sounds, walking, spitting, puffing, sighing…breathing.

"Upstairs," Mason said to Pablocito. "Check on your friend."

The shotgunner started dutifully up the steps. Mason followed, his pistol at the ready.

***

Concho slipped out of the empty bedroom he'd entered the house through and into a short hallway. A ragged carpet, as threadbare as a dog with mange, still covered the floor. Another bedroom lay to the right. It was empty but two more rooms loomed ahead and then the stairs to the first floor.

Concho started forward, his bow ready, and a second Hispanic man stepped into view at the top of the stairs. He was bald and carried a shotgun. His mouth opened and his eyes flashed wide as he saw Concho.

"Huy!" he said in Spanish.

As the man started to swing his shotgun toward Concho, the Ranger put an arrow into him. The tip punched him high in the chest on the left side, drove him backward. Crying out, he dropped his weapon. His hands grabbed for the newel post at the top of the stairs and it broke under his grip. He plummeted downward.

Concho heard a sickening thud as the falling man hit the floor but, now, another outlaw appeared at the top of the stairs. This was Mason French, swinging up a big revolver. Concho had no chance to nock another arrow. He threw himself back down the hall, racing for the momentary safety of the room he'd just left.

The boom, boom, boom of a heavy revolver punctuated Concho's lunge. The concussion hammered his ears. The walls took the impacts; wood splinters flew. Concho rolled into the relative safety of the back bedroom. He came into a crouch and nocked an arrow.

But now French had picked up the shotgun dropped by his crony. It was an even bigger weapon than his pistol, with a heavier punch. The doorframe of the bedroom dissolved as heavy pellets of lead tore through it. Concho ducked. The shotgun fired again. A hole exploded in the wall. A shotgun pellet pinged off Concho's vest.

With his haven being blown to bits around him, Concho had no choice. He dropped the arrow and slung the bow over his shoulder, then threw himself toward the window he'd entered by. Lead pellets chewed up the floor where he'd been crouching as he flung himself through the narrow window frame.

He landed belly down on the slanting roof of the back porch, grated across the worn shingles and crashed downward toward the earth. Cat quick, he got his hands and knees under him. He landed hard but ready to move.

From above came Mason French's cry: "It's the Ranger! Get the son of a bitch!"

Concho heard feet thudding on dirt. Jack and his brother were still outside the house. It sounded like they were coming for him from both flanks. Concho's darting gaze found the screen door to the back porch. It hung askew. Beyond stood the wooden main door into the house. Closed.

Concho leaped to his feet, charged through the open screen and threw himself against the closed door. It ripped apart like rotten poster board and Concho burst through into the house.

***

Vera Delchamp cried out as someone fell from the stairs and crashed hard on the floor a few feet from her. It wasn't Mason French, but the Hispanic guy French had sent up the stairs ahead of him.

Now she heard French's gun bellow. Again and again. She wanted to throw her hands over her ears but they were bound to the legs of the chair. More shots sounded. Who was French shooting at? Could it be the police?

It didn't matter. Vera couldn't wait for the police to save her either. It sounded like they were on the run anyway. She had to put the thin plan she'd conceived into action. Immediately. While French remained distracted.

The broken back of the chair rested a few inches from the back wall. Vera pushed her feet against the floor, using them to rock the chair back and forth. As she rocked forward, she managed to get her feet under her and stand. It was awkward but she'd spent a lot of time in the gym during down periods for her Junior High softball team. She was strong and used to maintaining her balance in awkward positions. And now she had the mobility she needed.

Knowing it would hurt but steeling herself against the impact, Vera hurled herself back into the wall. Pain hit her as the chair rammed into her legs and lower spine. But the chair was already rickety. The right side gave way; the leg snapped off the base of the seat and Vera's arm came free.

She twisted around, grabbed the chair, held it while she stomped her tennis shoe into the other wooden leg. This one broke and both her hands were free, though ropes still dangled from her wrists. She yanked the gag out of her mouth.

The front door gaped wide open. Vera took a step in that direction, then realized she'd need a weapon. She grabbed the sturdiest-looking chair leg she could get and hefted it. It was a lot shorter and lighter than her softball bats but was better than nothing.

The gunfire had stopped upstairs. Vera heard Mason French shout into the silence, and the words sent a chill down her. "It's the Ranger! Get the son of a bitch!"

The Ranger! Concho Ten-Wolves!

He was here. To help her. But he was outnumbered. She had to help him. How?

Running footsteps sounded upstairs. French! Coming back. He'd look downstairs, see her free. He might shoot her; he'd certainly recapture her. She couldn't help anyone if she were dead or back in bonds. She raced for the front door and through onto the porch.

A car and truck sat in the farmyard but she knew they wouldn't have the keys in them. And they didn't provide much shelter to hide behind. To her left loomed a big gray barn. She took off running toward it, was halfway there when she heard French bellow a foul curse at finding her gone.

French's voice rang out: "The girl's got free! Find her if you wanna get paid."

Now they'd be looking for her! And they wouldn't be gentle if they found her. She raced into the barn, threw herself into a crouch behind a purple car parked there. Her damp hands clenched on her makeshift club. It felt completely inadequate but was all she had.

Again, gunfire spoke from inside the house. She tucked her tongue over her upper teeth to keep from screaming.

CHAPTER 42

Concho found himself in the ranch house's kitchen, with the shattered back door behind him. Marks on the linoleum-covered floor showed where a stove and fridge had once stood. For some reason, a folding table had been left upright in the center of the room. To one side stood a bathroom, with the outer door gone and only bare and rusted steel pipes poking up through the linoleum.

Ahead of Concho stretched a short hallway floored in pine. Floral print wallpaper hung in shreds to either side. Concho drew his right-hand Colt and started forward. At the same instant, Mason French appeared at the other end of the hallway, only twenty paces away.

The two men saw each other at the same moment. French must have emptied the shotgun. Only the sinister bulk of a .44 magnum filled his hand. He swung the barrel up but Concho fired first—with no time to aim. The .45 slug caught French in the chest, punching into the bulletproof vest.

French staggered back, his own shot going wild. Concho shifted the barrel of his pistol, aiming for the head. His finger took up the slack on the trigger. A clattering noise came from behind him and he spun.

Jack pushed into the kitchen through the smashed back door. The AR-15 hung like a coiled cobra in his hands but before he had a chance to use it, Concho shot him in the face at close range.

Jack's head rocked back, then forward. A third eye opened in his forehead right above and between the other two. It was big and blue and began to weep blood. Most of the back part of the man's skull painted the wall behind him in gore.

Something like King Kong's fist struck Concho in the back, just below the shoulder. He stumbled into Jack, who was sliding toward the ground, and when he got turned around he realized Mason French had shot him. The pain gonged throughout his body. He couldn't catch his breath. But the bullet hadn't penetrated his vest.

French had given up temporarily on his pistol. Or maybe he hadn't reloaded and it was empty. He charged down the short hallway. Concho found that he wanted to face his enemy fist to fist. He stabbed his Colt back into its holster and threw himself forward.

French was taller than Concho and heavier. He had the momentum. The two slammed together near the doorway of the kitchen. Concho found himself driven back. They crashed into the table and it folded under their combined weight.

Concho went down, with French straddling him. He still couldn't quite get his breath. French tried to club the Ranger with his pistol and Concho caught the wrist, held it. He swung a hard fist at French's face only to have that blow caught too. Each strained to move the other, with muscles bunched and tendons stretched.

"Never met the man who could best me," French snarled. He twisted the barrel of his pistol down, tried to point it at Concho, to shoot him point-blank.

Concho held on to his opponent's wrist. The pistol barrel moved an inch, looming huge in the corner of his vision. French shifted his weight, leaned forward, pushing with all his strength. He had the advantage of gravity. The .44's barrel shifted another half inch. A triumphant smile split French's face.

But now Concho's breath came flooding back. He tightened his grip on the other man's wrist; he closed his fingers, let them dig. French's smile fled. He looked down at his arm. Surprise spread across his features.

Concho began forcing French's arm out to the side. His hand kept tightening around the wrist, constricting blood flow, cutting off nerve impulses. A grimace of pain flashed across French's lips. His fingers spasmed; the pistol dropped free to clunk on the floor.

"No!" French croaked.

"Afraid so," Concho said.

Concho jerked his right hand free of French's grip and slammed an open-palmed thrust into the chin. The head snapped back. The kidnapper was stunned. Concho twisted to the side, coming up into a crouch as he smashed French to the floor. French grunted and, suddenly, he was the one struggling for breath.

Concho rose. French tried to get up too. The Ranger smashed a knee into his face, sending him flailing back and down. Concho stepped toward the struggling man, grabbed an arm and the front of his shirt. He hauled French upright.

French clawed at Concho. The lawman slapped him brutally and slung him across the room. French slammed into the wall, twisted around, gasping for breath. Bloody drool dangled from the side of his mouth; the impulse to flee flared in his eyes. Concho saw it and stepped in the way.

"Never…met…the man…who could…" French mumbled.

"Now you have," Concho said. "And you're under arrest."

French stabbed fingers into the front pocket of his jeans and pulled out a knife. A click of the handle and it snapped open. Concho hadn't seen a switchblade in years but French had one. He lifted it; the blade caught a shaft of light and gleamed like a scalpel.

Concho snapped a standing kick into the kidnapper's chest. French cried out as he stumbled backward. He lost his balance, fell into the open bathroom. Concho winced at the sound of the outlaw's head slamming down on the rusted pipes sticking out of the floor.

***

Vera crouched behind the purple muscle car. She heard footsteps approaching the barn. A stolen glance showed her one of French's men, the one who'd been driving this very car when he arrived. He had a shotgun in his hands. His face was intent, listening.

"Saw you come in here, girl," the man drawled. "You cain't hide from old Jay. Might as well make it easy on yourself. Come out and I won't have to hurt you. Not too bad anyway."

Vera swallowed a whimper, tried to swallow her breath. She inched down the side of the car, reaching the front and sliding around it just as the man who called himself Jay, leaped forward to look down the passenger side of the vehicle.

"Gotcha!" Jay shouted.

But he didn't have her. She was on the other side of the car now. And still moving, toward Jay this time, rather than away. She could just glimpse his head over the hood of the car. He was looking up.

"Maybe you got up in the loft, huh?" he asked. "No place to go from there." He chuckled. "Maybe there's still even a bit of hay so's we can have some fun."

Vera stood up. "I'm not in the loft, asshole!"

Jay spun around and she clubbed him across the mouth with her chair leg. He screeched, his hands flying to his face. The shotgun dropped, hit the side of the car and bounced off into the dirt. Jay staggered backward.

Vera leaped forward, grabbing for the gun. She clutched it and straightened just as Jay dropped his hands from his face and started toward her. He froze as she swung the huge barrel of the shotgun around and pointed it at his chest.

"Don't move!" she shouted.

Jay's face was ghastly with blood and snot, his lips pulped and swelling. Two of his teeth had broken off in the front.

"You little—" he started to say and Vera hefted the shotgun to her shoulder and took aim.

"You watch what you call me," she snapped. "Or I'll shoot the rest of your teeth out."

Jay's eyes were as brown as beans. They glittered. He wiped his mouth and spat out blood and part of a tooth. "Oh I don't think you will, honeypot. I don't think you have the guts." He took a step toward her.

Vera backed up and knew immediately it was a mistake. The man took another step and another. He started to grin, a gap-toothed monstrosity of a grin.

Vera backed up again. The shotgun shook in her hands, partly out of fear, and partly out of tension as her mind screamed at her to pull the trigger.

"You don't wanna do that," Jay said, moving toward her. "It'll give you nightmares the rest of your natural life. Shooting a man down. It ain't easy. Takes it out of you. Give me the gun!"

Vera shook her head, but she kept backing up. She reached the rear of the car, then backed around the corner. Jay followed, his hands out, the tension dissipating in his brawny frame as he gained confidence. She wouldn't shoot him.

"Please!" Vera begged.

Jay smiled again as he straightened to his full height. "Sure thing, little girl," he said. "Jay'll take sweet care of you."

But Vera hadn't been speaking to Jay. Her gaze focused over his shoulder, behind him. Jay realized it too late. He spun around and a big black hand caught his throat and tightened.

Jay gasped, then choked. He swung a fist at Concho's face and the Ranger brushed it casually away with his free hand. He bent Jay back, over the trunk of the Roadrunner.

"Live or die. It's up to you," Concho said.

Jay's eyes gave up the fight. His body slumped. Concho let go of his throat and twisted him around face down over the trunk. He slapped handcuffs on and wrenched them tight.

Vera watched the whole thing, with her eyes damp and wild.

Concho had been in a hard fight. She could see it. His breath came harshly. Gouges streaked the side of his face, like raw, red drainage ditches against his dark skin. But when he looked at her, his eyes were calm and comforting.

Vera sagged in her shoes. She stepped toward Concho, offered him the shotgun. He took it, then pulled her into a one-armed hug.

"It's done," he said.

CHAPTER 43

Three hours after it was "done," Concho pulled his Dodge pickup into the parking lot of KTTT headquarters. It was only early afternoon. Vera sat in the passenger seat, leaning forward with an eagerness she couldn't conceal.

The Ranger had already called Katy to tell her Vera was safe but the two had not gotten to speak. By that time, the police had arrived at the farmhouse with many questions to answer. And, ambulances and the coroner had to be dealt with.

Sheriff Isaac Parkland had arrived and chastised Concho for going in alone. It was merely a formality. Both knew the words would have no effect and neither let it interfere with their friendship.

It would be a different story when Concho reported to Max Keller, his direct commander in the Texas Rangers. Keller would undoubtedly give him a blistering tongue lashing. Not that it would have any more effect than Parkland's words. It would be less pleasant though and Concho wasn't quite ready to deal with it yet. He had an excuse. All the case's i's had not yet been dotted nor all the t's crossed. In fact, there was still one major point to resolve and he thought he'd figured it out.

As Concho killed the Dodge's engine, the door to Kickapoo

police headquarters burst open, and Katy Delchamp came barreling outside. Vera threw open her door and leaped down. The sisters met in front of the truck and hugged furiously.

Both Nila Willow and Roberto Echabarri came outside to watch. Concho joined them. Vera was crying with Katy "shhh, shhhing" her younger sister. The Ranger wondered if he were intruding but decided he was enjoying the reunion of the sisters too much to deprive himself.

Nila and Roberto went back inside after a bit. Katy and Vera finally pulled a little way apart and walked toward Concho, each with an arm around the other. Both stopped to give him a hug. Katy mouthed "Thank you" to his ear.

"You two hang out for a while," Concho told them. "I've got an errand to run and then I'm going over to see your parents."

Vera bit her lip and looked down. Katy merely nodded and led her sister past him into the building without saying anything else. Concho dialed Maureen Delchamp and got her.

"Yes?" Maureen asked. Her voice shook.

"It's Ten-Wolves. Vera's safe."

"Oh, thank God! Where is she? Will you bring her home?"

"She's with Katy. I want them to spend some time together before I bring her home. Vera is OK physically but emotionally traumatized. She needs her sister's support. And her mom's."

"Of course. I…I love my daughter. Both my daughters."

"Good to hear. I'll be over in about an hour to talk to your husband. He better be there."

"I'll…tell him. Thank you…for everything."

Concho ended the call. He walked over to his truck, caught a glimpse of himself in the side-view mirror. His hair was tangled with sweat. The remnants of his war paint had smeared like dried blood down his face to mix with real blood from four gouges on his cheek. He didn't remember Mason French clawing him. But he remembered the dark rage of that fight. It all made him look mean. Perfect for the end of this case.

He climbed into the Dodge and headed out. He had one stop to make before he spoke to William Delchamp.

***

At a few minutes past the hour, Concho pulled into the driveway at the Delchamps'. The door opened quickly at his knock. Maureen looked like she'd been crying but was trying to suck it up. She let him in with nothing more than "He's upstairs. First door on the left."

Concho nodded and started up the stairs, his eyes noting everything about the house around him—what was there and what was missing. The room behind the "first door on the left" apparently served as a home office for William Delchamp.

Delchamp sat behind a broad cedar wood desk. A couple of open and empty suitcases lay on the floor next to him. Piles of papers were scattered around on the desk but the man's attention seemed focused on the computer monitor in front of him. He looked up when Concho entered, his face sour with irritation.

"What do you want?" Delchamp said. "Thanks for doing your job?"

"Going somewhere?" Concho asked, ignoring Delchamp's question while gesturing at the suitcases.

Delchamp frowned and snorted through his nostrils. "Maureen is insisting we have a period apart. I guess I'll be sleeping on the couch in my office at the gym."

"For the best," Concho said.

Delchamp chewed over a retort but apparently decided against it. "I asked you what you wanted?"

"A couple of things," Concho said. "What about the money? For the ransom?"

Delchamp tried to look surprised. It wasn't very convincing. "What ransom? You got Vera back didn't you?"

Concho chuckled without humor. "You aren't naïve. The money is owed. To Emily Zapatero. Though her husband will collect it. You don't want to cross him but you know that. How much did you raise?"

Delchamp released a long breath. "Three hundred and twelve thousand. That's all I could get together."

"Where?"

Delchamp glanced at a gym bag sitting on the edge of the desk. He didn't say anything or need to.

"To get the information I needed about Vera's kidnappers," Concho said, "I had to make clear to certain parties that the four hundred thousand dollars involved only you and them. Not your family. And that it would be returned. So, I'll take what you have and give it to them. Should be enough to make sure they won't come after Vera again. Or Katy. The rest of it, you'll have to deal with."

Delchamp frowned. He glanced at the gym bag again and shook his head. But all he said was, "Fine. Take it and go. Leave me alone."

"Just one more thing?"

"Who are you?" Delchamp asked. "Columbo?"

Concho smiled. "I'm flattered. But I'm not half the detective Columbo was. However, I did have a talk with Jade Harmony a little while ago."

"Who?"

"You know her. It's her real name, by the way. Just the way she signed it at your gyms when she worked out there."

Delchamp stiffened. His eyes focused intently on Concho. His hands twitched on his keyboard. "I don't have the faintest idea what you're talking about."

"Jade's not your type sexually," Concho continued. "But you had something going with her. Could be just a friendship between criminals. Maybe you supplied her steroids. Or, who knows how you swing. She was a prostitute. Part-time anyway. But what I'm sure of is that you paid her to kill Anne Reese in jail. Probably to keep Anne quiet about a lot of things. Possibly just as punishment for what she did to you. But you'll serve prison time for it."

"Jade's lying if she said I had anything to do with Anne Reese's death. She's a career criminal."

"So, you do know her."

"Big deal. I know her. She's been a customer at my gyms. And not a forgettable one. But I never had anything to do with her."

"Why lie when I first asked you about her?"

"I knew you'd make something out of it. You cops are all the same. But Jade Harmony is a congenital liar. You can't take her word for anything."

"Oh, she didn't actually give me any words about it. I just figured it out on my own. But I'm glad to have your confirmation on my thoughts."

Delchamp's hands slid off his computer, dropped into his lap. "You'll never make that stick!"

Concho rested one big palm on the butt of his right-hand Colt. "And you'll never reach the shotgun you've got under the desk before I shoot you in the face."

Delchamp froze. His brain fought a war with his body. Brain won. He lifted his hands into sight again and placed them on his keyboard.

"I noted your case of fancy shotguns underneath the stairs the last time I was here," Concho said. "Four of them then. Only three today."

"You're a son of a bitch!"

"Guilty," Concho said as he plucked a pair of handcuffs off his belt.

***

Concho pulled into another driveway, that of Lucio and Emily Zapatero. He waited, not getting out of the truck, not turning it off. Emily came out of the house and walked over to him. She looked nice in a yellow sundress with her hair down across her shoulders. Through the Dodge's window, Concho handed her the gym bag he'd gotten from William Delchamp. She took it with a little "oomph" at the weight.

"Three hundred and twelve thousand is what I'm told. I didn't count it," Concho said.

"We will."

"Right. But whatever amount it is… Katy and Vera Delchamp, and their mother, are out of it."

"We know."

Concho felt no need to tell her that William Delchamp might soon be serving a long stint in jail. He merely nodded, slipped the truck into reverse, and backed down the driveway. Emily Zapatero watched until he passed the guard gates, then turned back inside toward her loving husband.

CHAPTER 44

Concho took his leisure getting back to the reservation. Let Katy and Vera have their moments together. He also needed to decompress. He stopped by his house and took a shower, changed clothes, ate a sandwich, called Maria Morales, felt better.

The sun was dimming toward evening when he pulled up in front of KTTT headquarters. He found Katy and Vera in the officer's lounge. Vera was sound asleep on the couch, snoring in little peeps that made her seem younger than her fifteen years. Katy came to meet him at the door to the lounge, then smiled back at her sister before turning with Concho and walking outside.

"Thank you again, for everything," she said. "Vera was so exhausted. She just passed out."

"She needs the rest. She's a good kid," Concho said. "You both are."

Katy laughed in disbelief. "Not me."

Concho met her gaze. "You made a mistake," he said. "A bad one. But it doesn't have to define your life."

"Oh, how can it not? Pretty sure I'm going to jail for bank robbery."

"You will," Concho said. "But I doubt you'll serve much time. Especially if you cooperate with the police. And I'll testify on your behalf, to all the things you did to help me in the investigation."

Katy stared at him. She rubbed her eyes, then wrapped her arms around herself. "It's getting cold," she said.

Concho laughed. "Low seventies," he said. "You can tell you're a southerner."

Katy smiled too.

Concho sobered. "I do have something to tell you, though. I wish I didn't."

Katy stiffened. "What?"

You didn't tease people with bad news. Concho had learned that from his grandmother. You said it, got it out where it could be dealt with.

"Your father is the one who paid to have Anne Reese killed in jail."

Katy blinked. She looked like she'd been slapped. "My God! You… How do you know?"

"The woman who did it. Jade Harmony. She worked out at your dad's gyms. She got a phone call at the jail the same morning she killed Anne. No recording of it and the phone had to be a burner. No information on the number. But I stopped by to see Jade before I talked to your father. I asked her about the call and mentioned your father's name. She denied it. Claimed the call was from her lawyer. But we'll be able to check that. And the look she gave when I mentioned your father. The startle response. I think under further questioning, she'll give him up."

Katy looked like she was about to throw up. "I don't want Vera going back there!" she said vehemently. "I don't want her around him."

"She won't be. I confronted him. He said enough to indict himself so I arrested him. And when Jade talks, he'll go to jail for longer than you will. Besides, your mother was already throwing him out."

"My mother?"

"Yes."

Katy sighed. "About time she grew some spine."

Concho sighed. He had something else to say, something hurtful. But Katy needed to hear it.

"The same goes for you," he told her. "About the spine. French is gone. He's no threat to you anymore. Your father is going away. He's not worth rebelling against. And…Anne Reese is gone too. Maybe she was there when you needed her. Maybe she was your friend sometimes. She wasn't always. She was damaged herself and she had her own agenda. You can be stronger. If you will it."

Katy stared up at him. Her eyes brimmed with tears. She let them fall. Concho pulled her into his arms and hugged her tight while she cried.

***

Dark had arrived before Concho finally called it a day and returned home. He'd watched Katy and Vera talk more while they all ate fast food hamburgers together. Both young women were shaken but he thought they'd started along the river of recovery.

He phoned his boss, Max Keller, who was already gone for the day. After a brief and sanitized report for the recorder, he ended the call and built himself a small fire outside his home to stare into.

Not everything about the Delchamp case was cleared up. It was usually that way with crimes, he'd found. Someone had put Mason French in touch with the Zapateros and maybe planted a burr under Lucio to suggest kidnapping Vera. He didn't know who that someone was, though he had certain vague suspicions, in part because the someone seemed to have a particular grudge against Concho Ten-Wolves.

And, even though the reservation lay quiet tonight, there was still a mystery here he'd have to turn his attention to soon. What was the thing with purple eyes? Who was stealing animals on the Rez? And who had left Concho's own arrow broken on his doorstep?

None of those questions would get answered tonight. Concho dashed out his fire and went inside. Somewhere, in the distance, a lonely wolf howled—or something pretending to be a wolf. The Ranger ignored it and went to his bed where he slept the sleep of the righteous.

A LOOK AT: PATH OF EVIL (CONCHO BOOK THREE)

Concho Ten-Wolves left the army to join the Texas Rang-ers. He lives on the Kickapoo reservation just outside Eagle Pass, Texas, on the Rio Grande Border between Mexico and the USA. His mother was a full-blooded member of the tribe; his father was black…both of them disappeared soon after his birth.

Concho does his job and takes his hits. He's made plenty of enemies who want him dead and now even his past is coming back to taunt him. A knock on his door late one night sets a chain of mysterious events in motion. He uncovers two skeletons on the reservation, a woman and child – murdered.

It doesn't matter that his enemies are coming for him, or that he doesn't know who they are or how they'll strike. The innocent dead deserve justice, and he'll see they get it.

"One of the most entertaining writers in the business!" – James Reasoner, Author of Rattler's Law.

AVAILABLE AUGUST 2021

ABOUT THE AUTHOR

Charles Gramlich lives amid the piney woods of southern Louisiana and is the author of the Talera fantasy series, the SF novel Under the Ember Star, and the thriller Cold in the Light. His work has appeared in magazines such as Star*Line, Beat to a Pulp, Night to Dawn, Pedestal Magazine, and others. Many of his stories have been collected in the anthologies, Bitter Steel, (fantasy), Midnight in Rosary (Vampires/Werewolves), and In the Language of Scorpions (Horror). Charles also writes westerns under the name Tyler Boone. Although he writes in many different genres, all of his fiction work is known for its intense action and strong visuals.

Made in the USA
Las Vegas, NV
15 May 2022